A Matter of Attitude

A Matter of Attitude

A Matter of Attitude

Hayden

A MATTER OF ATTITUDE

ISBN-13: 978-0-373-83089-3
ISBN-10:   0-373-83089-0

© 2008 by Hayden

www.KimaniTRU.com

Printed in U.S.A.

Now faith is being sure of what we hope for and certain of what we do not see.
—Hebrews 11:1

Dedicated to those who never gave up their pursuit of a dream.

CHAPTER I

At seven o'clock the vibing beats of Marvin Gaye's song "What's Going On" drifted from the alarm clock and around my bedroom, waking me out of my sleep. One of my survival rules was if you knew the day was going to be a straight-up crazy one, at least wake up to some good old-school music. I was scheduled to work the morning-to-early-afternoon shift at my family's restaurant, the Island Shack, but did not want to spend the last Saturday before Labor Day weekend in that place. My summer vacation had gone by so quickly. It seemed like only yesterday I was wearing the burgundy graduation cap and gown that signaled my last day at Kressler Junior High. As family, friends and the graduating class sat in the air conditioned auditorium of Queens College, everyone's mood was jubilant. But I refused to believe anyone could be happier than I was. Squeezing the rolled-up diploma in my hand, relishing the coarse texture of the paper, I ticked off my plans to make the next two months the best ever.

All those dreams of vacation fun burned up like a campfire and turned into an ash pile. Mama kept me on the schedule at the restaurant. Every day. The only time off she gave was for the Fourth of July. Independence Day. At the time, I wanted to give her a smart remark about granting me freedom for that occasion, but I kept my mouth shut. Coney Island Amusement Park turned out to be the happening spot. I could smell the faint scent of shellfish captured in the Atlantic Ocean breeze, while I sat on a beach towel eating cold watermelon with my feet buried in the warm sand. I savored those precious hours. It would have been great to spend every day at the beach. Some kids got that luxury, but not me.

To help shake my negative mood, I had set the dial on my clock radio to a station that played songs from the seventies instead of rap. My friends thought I was strange because I liked listening to a lot of old jams while they were all strictly on the hip-hop tip. A lot of the other kids thought I was strange because I dressed a bit crazy—every day I wore striped stockings, tights or socks—but I didn't care. Lots of people would have loved to imitate me; they just didn't have the guts.

I reached out and hit the off button on my alarm, which was sitting on the nightstand next to my bed. My intention was just to close my eyes for a few minutes more, but I must have dozed off, because I woke up to my mother's voice calling out my name and the sweet smell of frying bacon in the air. I opened one eye to peek at the alarm and was surprised to see that I had fallen asleep for half an hour.

"Angela, get your lazy butt out of that bed," my mother yelled from the bottom of the staircase. "C'mon now, you're supposed to help out at the restaurant this morning."

The Island Shack was a business my mother had bought two years earlier with life insurance money her father, my grandfather Louis, had left her. Grandfather Louis's dream had always been to own his own autobody shop, but he could never get that vision fulfilled and had retired disappointed. After his funeral, my mother was really surprised to hear that the entire life insurance policy was left to her. I sometimes think she bought the restaurant out of guilt. Since Grandfather Louis hadn't been able to get a business off the ground, Mama was determined to see his dream realized.

Right after depositing the check, my mother found a real estate agent who specialized in commercial properties. It didn't take her too long to find a location. The agent took her to see exactly four places in one day. When Mama stepped out of the car and studied the last corner property at the intersection of two major boulevards, she knew it was the one. She was so impressed by the location and size of the place that she wrote a check on the spot to secure the deal, never mind the fact that the diner previously on the premises had gone belly-up.

Even though we weren't rolling in money, a lot of people assumed we were sitting on some major paper. Our restaurant was pretty spacious, which caused people to gossip. In the dining area, we had fifteen tables that could seat six people each without making anyone feel claustrophobic. So between the restaurant and my wardrobe, a lot of girls in the neighborhood threw jealous words my way. A wave of anxiety washed over me like a scary premonition. I seriously did not feel like facing the public today. I rolled over in bed, covered my ears with my pillow and pulled the blanket over my head.

"Angela, do you hear me?"

I peeked out from under the blanket and yelled back, "My stomach hurts. Can't somebody else take my place?" Deep in my heart, I knew some customer at the restaurant was going to try and work my nerves today. I could feel it. It seemed as if I was always getting into it with somebody.

My mother stayed on my back about the customer always being right, but when a customer got rude and started dissing you, it was best not to stay quiet. This was Springfield Heights. A small town in Queens, New York. Even though my neighborhood was a mixture of working-class people who worked office jobs in Manhattan, just a few blocks away were the Benson Hill Projects. And even though we used to live there, and some really cool people still lived there—like my best friend, Adrian—there were also some troublemakers who hung around and didn't mind testing you. So if somebody was dissing me, I usually gave it back to them on full blast; otherwise, people labeled you as soft and stupid and would constantly pick on you.

"Hard work will take your mind off your upset stomach, so you better get up out of that bed!" my mother screeched. Man, I hated when she started screaming, especially in the morning. You would never believe she was one of the soloists who got major play in the church choir on Sunday, because right then her voice sounded like nails on a chalkboard—major irritation. From his spot on the floor, my cat, Smoky, a black Persian with green eyes, shot me an evil look that told me to get up so he could get some peace.

Sitting up in bed, I yelled back, "Mama, I really don't feel like helping out at the restaurant today." Silence greeted my complaint, and I knew I was not going to get off the hook so easily. Mama didn't like long, drawn-out arguments, she liked to just get to the point.

Annoyed, I flung one of my pillows across the room, and it knocked over the plastic life-size mannequin that was held up by a metal stand in the corner of my bedroom. The cinnamon-colored figure, which I had named Ms. Understood, landed with a bang on the bare wooden floor, as if it had been hit with a bat. *Dang, I didn't think I threw the pillow that hard, I thought.*

Clump, thump. Clump, thump. Clump, thump.

Uh-oh. Mama was coming up the stairs to my attic bedroom, her bad knee making it difficult for her to hustle up the two flights quickly.

Minutes later, her scowling walnut-brown face loomed in

the doorway. She looked accusingly around my lavender-painted room, observing the four custom-made walk-in closets that my father and his friends had built for me. Then her gaze went to my clothes, shoes and sneakers that were organized by color and season; to the oversize plastic bins that were lined up against the opposite wall, in which I kept my sewing fabrics; to the desk where my sewing machine sat; to the large corkboard on the wall above, cluttered with pages torn from fashion magazines. Finally, her gaze rested on the mannequin, lying faceup on the floor. For a strange moment it almost looked like a lifeless human, and I was overcome with a sense of guilt.

"Are you trying to sass me this morning? Because I'm not in the mood for your nonsense!" Mama snapped.

"Sorry. That was an accident." Throwing my feet over the edge of the bed, I slipped them into my camel-colored shearling slippers. "Mama, why can't one of the boys help out instead of me?" I whined. I had two brothers: Omar was thirteen, and two years younger than I was, and Quincy was eighteen years old. I didn't get along with my younger brother; after a few minutes of conversation we were usually trading insults. On the other hand, I got along great with Quincy, who had a down-to-earth personality and was also a talented DJ and music producer. Quincy was all about making fast money with his musical skills and liked everybody to call him Quick Digits—including my parents. He was real easygoing most of the time, but he stubbornly refused to help out at the restaurant. Still, since he was able to pay Mama monthly rent from his gigs, she left him alone.

"Why don't you try and get Quick Digits to work today? He never puts in any time over there. He's slick, always hiding out in the studio. Mama, you always let him get over on you."

"He makes his money that way, and he doesn't have to ask me for anything—unlike you, the begging princess. You should be grateful to have a job where you can make a couple of dollars."

Eager to get her off my case, I tried another approach. "Why can't Omar help out? He could take his nose out the books for once and pull some kitchen duty."

"Your brother has to finish up his prep courses. You know how competitive his school is."

"But he's such a wizard," I snapped. "It wouldn't hurt him to miss a session." I crossed my arms, angry that I was losing this battle. My mother loved to toss around the fact that Omar was in a prestigious preparatory school. He used to be in public school like me, but he kept scoring so high on the standardized tests that his teachers alerted my parents to his brilliance. Then Mama bragged to her employers, the Levys, a wealthy, well-connected elderly couple. My mother used to work full-time as a home care attendant for Mr. Levy, who was bedridden from a stroke. The Levys insisted Mama bring Omar to meet them, and they adored my nerdy, glasses-wearing, well-mannered brother. They were the ones who got Omar hooked up with a scholarship at Norman James Tisch Preparatory last year, when he was in sixth grade.

Mama treated Omar like a prince and never really made him do household chores. Always claimed the little twerp had to study because he was going to be a scientist, and she didn't want to put any additional pressure on him. Even now, during summer break, Omar was enrolled in advanced math and science classes.

My mother leveled a searing look at me that seemed capable of producing smoke. "Jealousy doesn't look pretty on you. Get that pout off your face and get dressed." She turned around, pausing to rub her bad knee before heading down the stairs.

Throwing the blanket off as if it were covered with bees, I jumped out of the bed and walked over to the corner of the room where Ms. Understood was lying on the floor, her smiling face looking up at me. The mannequin was a gift my grandma Rachel had given to me, and I felt nervous that I had possibly caused some type of damage to it.

Grandma Rachel was Mama's mother, a seamstress who was so talented, everybody in her small town of Columbus, Mississippi, went to her to get their special-occasion outfits made. She loved that mannequin and had given it to me when her arthritis had gotten so bad that it disfigured her hands and made it difficult for her to hold scissors or a needle.

Back in the day, Grandma Rachel used to visit us in the summers. She taught me how to sew and play different card games like bid whist and spades. She was a hoot and loved to tell corny jokes that nobody got except her, but that didn't stop her from cracking up with laughter.

Everybody said I inherited her gift of working with fabric and her devil-may-care sense of style. Grandma Rachel was a petite woman, but she always wore four-inch heels and the most colorful hats with some type of enormous accessory pinned to the side, like plastic butterflies, flowers or feathers. A lot of people gossiped about her, saying she was a little off kilter, but their opinions didn't slow her down. One of her favorite sayings was "Live for the moment and never let anyone take away your essence." My grandma had been an old lady who was totally on point, and I really missed her. She died in a head-on car accident about six months after her husband, my grandfather Louis, passed away. Everybody said it was tragic how they died within a short time of each other, but at least they were together in heaven.

"So sorry," I mumbled guiltily, and gently picked Ms. Understood up. She was a serious member of my fashion team. Once again we stood at eye level, my golden-brown eyes looking into her charcoal-colored ones. Standing on tiptoe, I adjusted the Afro wig on her head, then carefully examined the half-sewn black-suede-and-purple-satin coat that hung off her. I was grateful the needles hadn't fallen out—trying to pin the stiff suede fabric had almost driven me nuts.

Noticing that one of my notepads of sketches had fallen off the scuffed wooden desk that doubled as my sewing table, I scooped it from the floor. As I flipped through the pages, I was happy to see that the colored-pencil sketches weren't smudged on the crinkly white tracing paper. I had drawn the sketches during a period when I was feeling down. Two girls I had known for years and thought were my friends had turned on me. They stole some jewelry off my dresser that had been given to me as a birthday gift. They denied it, and I might have believed them if I hadn't seen them the next week wearing the gold bangles. It hurt my feelings deeply. That pain of betrayal stayed with me for a while. Grandma Rachel had always encouraged me to sketch and put my emotions on paper, so when I was frustrated, I created—long black lace dresses with corset waists, black capris paired with billowy white blouses, long black leather cape coats with stiff high collars—the kind of stuff you would wear to a Transylvanian dinner party. Each of my notepads featured designs created for a certain time period, and if I felt especially rebellious and bold, I wasn't above bringing the outfit to life and wearing it. Strange, huh? Guess that was why my name was always on people's tongues, whether they were hating or praising. I wasn't afraid to take a fashion risk.

"Yo, Triple A," a familiar voice called from outside, followed by three sharp whistles. Triple A was the nickname my best friend Adrian and I called each other. The third A stood for attitude, because we had lots of it. I met Adrian when she was five and had just moved from the Dominican Republic with her mom. Our families used the same babysitter and we instantly became the best of friends.

Walking briskly across the room, I opened the window to see Adrian standing on the sidewalk. She was dressed in a pink T-shirt and tight denim cutoff shorts and held a can of Malta in her hand. The sun's rays bounced off her chestnut-brown hair that hung past her shoulders, causing the blond highlights to shimmer. She sipped the beverage through a straw, then impatiently pulled off her face a few ringlets of hair that had escaped her ponytail holder.

"What you doing up so early making noise?" I lifted the screen and leaned out the window.

"Going to the store. Carmen forgot to get milk yesterday so now I gotta get it. What you doing today?" Adrian asked.

"Mama's making me work at the stupid restaurant, what else?"

"Jeez, we only got two weekends left before we gotta go back to school," Adrian complained.

"Yeah, I know school's coming, but I really don't mind, 'cause this year we're in ninth grade. High school," I said proudly.

"Big deal. Ninth graders are bottom of the barrel." Adrian sniffed.

"Not at Kressler High. Everybody knows they have a serious fashion design department, and the freshman class rules because of their holiday fashion show." I had read in Kressler's brochure that past winners who captured the show's director title got a load of prizes and the chance to spend some time in a real designer studio, like Gucci, Baby Phat or Chanel. That was awesome, because they really gave you a behind-the-scenes look at what made their companies so successful. That knowledge could give me a head start when I opened my boutique after college. Winning the contest would really shut up all the kids who hated on me and talked about my style, and I would gain some major respect.

"Whatever. You still need to have fun until then. You sure you can't get off?" I shook my head. Adrian stared at me as she noisily drained the last of the Malta through the straw. She tossed the empty can in my neighbor's metal garbage can. "Everybody's going to be at the park today," Adrian argued, her hands fluttering like fireflies as she spoke.

I shrugged. "Me and my mother already had it out. She won't unlock my chains."

Adrian giggled. "Your mother keeps you on serious lockdown. I'm glad Carmen doesn't stay on my back like that, or we would be going at it. Catch you later." She trotted up the street, her mass of curls bouncing behind her. I shook my head. Adrian was the only girl I knew who called her mother by her first name. She was also the only girl I knew who treated her mother as if she were her sister. I guess it was because her mother had had her at sixteen, and it had just been the two of them for so long, until her baby brother, Kwan, came along. Those two could fuss for hours, flipping back and forth between English and Spanish, then giving each other the silent treatment, but the next day they would be ransacking each other's closet. Adrian and her mom were the same height, five foot two, but Ms. Gomez was chunkier and in denial that she couldn't wear every style. Still, they had the same taste in clothes: anything tight. Go figure.

Pulling myself from the window, I headed for the bathroom. Every morning, I examined my face for fresh pimple breakouts. Today I was instantly annoyed to see a new one starting to form on the tip of my nose. "Yikes!" I exclaimed. "I'm going to look like a witch with a wart if I don't get rid of this pimple."

After washing my face with my acne soap, I brushed my teeth before dashing into the shower. Quickly toweling dry, I dabbed on acne medicine, then raced back into the bedroom to get dressed. Since I was totally feeling the 1970s today, I combed my thick, shoulder-length, never-seen-a-perm dark brown hair up on top of my head and held it in place with a rubber band. Then I clipped on a huge purple-and-red-streaked Afro puff. I completed my look by outlining my eyes in black liquid eyeliner, putting on mascara and hitting my lips with cherry gloss.

Thank goodness I had laid out my outfit for the day on the twin guest bed the night before—a red T-shirt with purple denim trim on the sleeves; a short purple denim skirt with peace signs outlined in red glitter, and red fabric fringe down the sides; and some red Pro-Keds I had glued glitter designs on. My purple-and-red-striped stockings topped my look off. I stared at myself in the full-length mirror and grinned. None of the other girls would have this outfit, because I was totally original—kept my style fresh. Who cared about criticism? One day I was going to be a fashion designer, and I was building my reputation one outfit at a time.

As I walked into the kitchen, my nose wrinkled in distaste. Mama had recently painted the walls lime-green, and the citrus color, not my favorite, still took some getting used to. She had totally gone overboard with that color, buying lime-green curtains and place mats decorated with lime slices. She'd even redone the floor with ceramic lime-green titles, which she washed every week with Clorox to keep them gleaming. My mother was totally on the home makeover tip. Daddy and Omar were both at the table eating and reading the New York Times. My father, who was reading the sports section, was wearing a gray-and-yellow Nike tracksuit, with matching fresh-out-of-the-box gray-and-yellow Nike sneakers. Omar, predictably dressed in a plaid shirt and starched khakis, was reviewing the metro section.

My father raised his eyes from the paper and smiled. "Good morning, pumpkin," he said as I planted a kiss on his cheek.

Peeking over his newspaper, Omar looked at me and screwed up his face. "Yuck. You look wack!"

"Go crawl back to your hole, you troll," I shot back,

and plopped down in one of the newly upholstered chairs. The plastic-covered green-and-white-checkered cushion let out a slow hiss. Another one of Mama's annoying remodeling projects.

My mother turned around from frying bacon and gave us both an irritated look before she sighed and said, "Can't you two give all this bickering a break for at least one day?"

"Mama, he started it!" I screamed. My mother knew that it was part of Omar's daily ritual to make a remark that would rile me up. It seemed his day couldn't end on a satisfactory note without his hurling at least one snide comment my way.

"Angela, you're older than Omar. Sometimes you've got to be more mature. Learn to walk away and let it be. Turn the other cheek." She spun around, went back to frying bacon and started humming a hymn.

All I could do was roll my eyes. It seemed that my mother always chose Omar over me. When I complained, she denied it—said she loved all her children the same.

Yeah, right. Maybe because he was smart and could get all *A*s without breaking a sweat. I couldn't wait to do something that would make Mama real proud. Like winning that fashion contest. That would prove to everybody that I had talent.

"Cora, did you put sugar in my oatmeal?" Daddy asked, his forehead wrinkled in concern.

"Just a little. I like for my food to have a little taste," Mama said as she put a plate of crispy bacon, scrambled eggs and wheat toast in front of me.

"Woman, why are you trying to sabotage my diet? You know I'm staying away from white flour and sugar. How else am I going drop this weight?" Daddy questioned as he studied his bowl of oats.

"Mannie, don't you start with me this morning. You and I both know that the little bit of sugar I put in this food won't make you fat," Mama replied, then bowed her head in a quick, silent prayer before eating her oatmeal and eggs.

Poor Daddy was always on some new diet in a useless attempt to get rid of his huge stomach. Even though he was tall—six foot two—and stocky, his big belly almost made him look kinda fat. My father used to be a boxer when we were much younger, and he was always dropping hints that he was going back into the ring. We kept an old photo album of his boxing pictures on the living room bookcase. Back in the day, he was all chiseled and muscular. He resembled a warrior. I don't know why Daddy had this crazy dream to get back in the ring. He really was too old. We'd just celebrated his forty-third birthday in March. It was true that some boxers won major matches after they turned forty, but those cases were rare. What really scared me was that all my father's sparring partners at his gym were in their twenties. My jaw always hurt after watching those matches. Yes, Daddy had endurance and a good right hook, but he was also wearing protective headgear. It frightened me to think what might happen to him in a match with men hungry to make a name for themselves. But I was proud of my father's determination and would never reveal my doubts. And even though he wasn't in top condition right now, he always looked fly. He had skin the color of butterscotch, and kept his curly, thinning hair cut real low in a fade. He worked as a garbageman for a private trash removal company, and when he wasn't on the clock, he dressed real sharp.

"Mannie Jenkins, you need to put in some extra hours at the restaurant instead of the gym," my mother stated, and forcefully scooped up a mound of oatmeal with her spoon.

Daddy cocked one eyebrow and put his spoon down. "You and your brother Clyde aren't going to run me into the ground like a Georgia mule working on a plantation. I got other things to do besides sweating over pots of collard greens." Daddy refused to work at the restaurant. Well, when Mama first bought the place he'd worked there, but Uncle Clyde got on his nerves so bad that he quit. Daddy said that Uncle Clyde spent too much money on unnecessary stuff and was going to bankrupt the place. He also claimed that Mama wouldn't listen to him and always took my uncle's word as the gospel truth.

Siding with Daddy and hoping to gain sympathy, I said, "It was better around here before Mama bought that place. Daddy, you used to give me an allowance. Now I gotta work like a slave for a few dollars." And that was no lie. Because I was the only girl, my father looked out for me. I used to get the princess treatment and got everything I wanted—within reason. No, we weren't wealthy, but Daddy used to pull a lot of overtime hours to keep the household going. Suddenly everything fell out of balance.

Management changed at his job, and the extra hours dried up. Then Mama bought the restaurant, which further depleted our funds.

Omar laughed. "What do you need money for? All you gonna do is get more clothes for your creep collection." He folded the newspaper and placed it on the table.

"Doesn't matter what you wear, nobody will ever notice you, you four-eyed midget," I replied nastily.

Omar got real quiet and self-consciously touched the frames of his glasses. He was several inches shorter than me and hated when I cracked on his height.

"All right, now," Mama said, cutting us off before more insults flew.

It was silent for a few moments before Daddy said, "Cora, I'm sorry, but I just can't help out. I told you and Clyde two years ago how hard it was going to be to run a profitable restaurant. Did anybody listen to me? No. Now we're struggling with this mortgage and the monthly bills for that restaurant."

It still seemed hard to believe that we'd left the Benson Hills projects two years ago. Although we lived on a nice block where everybody's house looked the same—three-story red brick with a porch and a manicured green front lawn—we were still only a couple of blocks from the housing development, where trouble was always ready to jump off.

"I'm always telling you, Cora, you got to pace yourself. You wanted to live in a nice place, so we moved, but who buys two properties at the same time?"

My stomach started to knot up. Whenever my father started fussing about the bills, it scared me. As if one day it was actually going to come true: we were going to lose everything. My parents had rarely disagreed about the bills before Mama inherited that money. Plus, her not taking Daddy's advice on where to invest her inheritance had put a strain on their relationship.

"Forget it. I don't need a lecture, just an open heart and some willing hands," my mother said, her mouth set in a tight line.

Daddy reached for the milk in the center of the table, then poured some into his coffee. After he took a sip, he gazed at the empty chair. "Where's Quick Digits? Doesn't he have the sense to join us for breakfast?"

"Is he in his room?" Mama asked.

"No, he spent last night at his boy Marlon's house. Quick said they were working on some new music tracks," I answered.

"Humph. Somebody better tell Quick Digits that just because he just turned eighteen last month, it doesn't mean he can come and go as he pleases. He needs to let me or your mother know what's going on. Otherwise, he can find his own place," Daddy said.

The room got uncomfortably quiet for a few moments after Daddy's threat.

"Daddy, I like your tracksuit. Are you going to start running today?" I asked in an attempt to break the tension.

"Sugarplum, your father is sure enough going to head out to the track. Maybe I'll run ten miles. I'm going to get back in fighting shape. If I get my stamina up, you can bet on me getting back in the ring."

Daddy had been a major contender for a title years ago and always said he could have won a championship belt, but something happened that had stopped him. He never said what—just said he could've been a champ.

Omar snorted and said, "You'd be lucky to do one mile without us hearing from the paramedics. On the Science Channel last night they said once you hit the big four-oh, you lose your metabolism and speed. In some boxing divisions, the judges won't let the older guys get back in the ring. They feel their skills are too diminished."

"Don't believe everything you hear. Those rules don't apply to everybody," Daddy countered with a defensive glint in his eyes.

"But you're totally out of shape with all that fat around your stomach. It'll be a miracle if you don't have a heart attack." Omar snickered before dabbing the corners of his mouth with a lime-green napkin.

It took my father a minute to really digest Omar's nasty comment. He didn't say anything for what seemed like a long time, just kept giving Omar a bug-eyed stare.

Mama always said that Daddy was really counting numbers in his head, trying to keep his blood pressure down and not lose his temper, when he did that look. "Boy, you should learn to have more respect for the man who's putting food on the table," Daddy answered in a restrained tone. "Back in the day, they didn't call me Lightning Fists for nothing, and I'd hate to give you a demonstration."

"But that was a long time ago," Omar replied with a sly grin.

"Don't make me prove you wrong," my father threatened. Omar didn't respond, just lowered his eyes to his plate.

I didn't know why Omar was always giving my father and me a hard time. Maybe he couldn't stand the fact that he was so smart and was my mother's trophy child. The fact that he always seemed to be a few steps ahead of me and easily earned her praises filled me with envy. And even though Daddy never said it, I always felt that Quick Digits' musical talent made him number one in my father's book. My third-place rank in the family always left me feeling insecure. How I wished that one day my fashion talent would make me shine. That it would change people's attitudes and they would give me respect. Treat me special. If I couldn't accomplish that at my new high school, then I had no chance at all.

CHAPTER 2

After we finished eating breakfast, Mama went outside so she could start our old Chevy van. Each morning she had to warm the van up for at least ten minutes because it was twenty years old and had a tendency to cut off in traffic if we didn't. My brothers had nicknamed our family ride the Cappuccino Blast because it was chocolate-brown on the sides and creamy white on top, and on some days it would drive real slow, just chugging along.

When I joined Mama outside minutes later in our driveway, she had the hood up and was adjusting some wires. "What's wrong with it this time?" I asked. It always amazed me that she could understand all those strange wires and engine parts.

"The battery cable came loose," she said, pulling yellow plastic gloves off her hands and rolling them in a ball, "but it was simple enough to fix."

My mother would have made a great mechanic. She always kept a pair of gloves in the van so she wouldn't dirty her hands when she had to change a flat tire or get under the hood to figure out why the van was acting up again. She had learned a lot about cars from growing up on a farm down south. Her father never got rid of his old cars when he bought a new one. He loved to pull them apart and tinker around on them, and my mother loved hanging out in the garage with him.

"Why don't you buy a flossed-out ride, like a Mercedes-Benz or a BMW SUV? This old van breaks down all the time, and we should be styling in something better than this. Everybody says so." I studied our old clunker in dismay. There were rust spots all along the bottom of the vehicle. It was definitely time for an upgrade.

Mama ignored my comment as she opened the driver's-side door and climbed in. My guess was she was tired of repeating her "Don't be so materialistic" chant to me. She put the key in the ignition and the motor sputtered a few times before it roared to life. When the muffler began rattling like a bag of tin cans and the engine started making familiar knocking noises, she stretched her arms out and looked upward. I know she was sending a grateful prayer to heaven that the van was still running. Mama was raised religious and believed in constantly thanking God for small miracles.

Placing my palms over my ears, I yelled, "This is embarrassing! Mama, you just bought that truck for the restaurant. You could've bought us a new car first."

An exasperated look swept over my mother's face. "I don't need you to question my decisions. Every successful person has to invest in their business if they want to prosper. The noise will die down soon." I let out a huff, yanked open the passenger-side door and got in the van.

Our cranky neighbor across the street, Mr. Keith, stuck his head out of his screen door and stared at us real hard. He looked about a hundred years old, stayed in a bad mood and always had a pair of binoculars hanging around his neck. "Y'all need to get that racket fixed. All that noise don't make no sense," he boomed at us.

"So sorry." Mama smiled and waved at him. "I'm taking it to the shop later today."

I sucked my teeth. "That old man needs to mind his business. Daddy would have put him in check."

"You can't go around arguing with everybody who says something negative to you. Then you'd be fighting every day. Besides, Mr. Keith doesn't have any family who comes to see about him, so he tries to look after the block." Mama hit the gas pedal, and we turned onto the street and headed toward the restaurant.

We drove off the block and rode in silence for a few minutes. Bored, I stared out the passenger window as we turned onto Elm Boulevard, which was a mixture of store-front churches, check-cashing places, grocery stores and homes. There was a lot of new construction happening lately, and every other block or so there was a skeleton of a new house going up. "Everybody's hanging out at the park today, but I gotta work at the restaurant," I grumbled.

My mother glanced at me, then replied, "You don't know how lucky you are. God has blessed us with a business. We have the chance to be self-sufficient and independent. Many people never get that chance."

"What good is it if you have to work all the time? You work two jobs. I don't wanna be like that. You never have any time for fun." I turned to face my mother and noticed she looked tired and a little sad. She was wearing a short-sleeved black linen shirt and sensible black slacks. Back in the day, my mother used to wear beautiful, colorful dresses all the time. Now it seemed all she wore were neutral color schemes. Suddenly, I regretted my words and had the urge to make her happy. I searched through my imitation Louis Vuitton pocketbook and found some lip glosses. "I just bought these in watermelon and mango flavors. Wanna try one?" I held up the small plastic tubes.

She smiled and shook her head no. "Girl, why are you always trying to get me to wear makeup? The good Lord made my face just fine, and I'm not trying to cover it up."

My mother used to wear makeup—eye shadow, mascara and false eyelashes. She was totally on the glamour tip, and when she stepped out to dinner with my father, she put everybody on notice. Now it seemed that she couldn't concentrate on herself anymore. All her energy went into the restaurant, from decorating to planning the menus to doing the payroll. Mama said all that dress-up stuff was frivolous and she didn't have time for any of that foolishness anymore.

Sighing in defeat, I leaned against the headrest. Ever since my grandfather had died and left my mom that money from the life insurance policy, she'd been on a mission to be queen of the food biz. She was always buying magazines with articles about quitting your day job and building your own empire, tips that promise to help get your bank account as fat as Oprah's. Shoot, I loved money, too, but jeez, Mama needed to learn how to hit the pause button and have some fun.

It took us about fifteen minutes to reach the Island Shack, and I noticed the parking lot was full. We always had a good breakfast crowd on Saturday mornings, and everybody thought my family was making mad money. The truth was we were just about breaking even after expenses each month.

Mama pulled the van into the spot marked Reserved and shut off the engine. "Now don't give me no sass," she threatened as she climbed out. "Let's get to work."

Peeling myself off the seat, I slowly got out of the van and slammed the door shut. The morning sun was beaming on my back, and I knew it was going to be a nice day. Too nice to be working. Better for chilling. Mama must have been reading my thoughts, because her face was balled up as if she'd just eaten a sour grapefruit. There was no use arguing, so I just followed her through the glass door with the hand-painted sign that read *Welcome To The Island Shack*.

My mother had done a good job creating a cheery tropical atmosphere inside. The walls were painted lemon-yellow, and pale yellow tablecloths and fresh vases of flowers were on each of the fifteen tables in the dining area. There were potted palm trees tucked in every corner by the floor-to-ceiling windows, and the four bamboo ceiling fans circulated a light breeze.

The aroma of hot biscuits wafted in the air. "Mmm, it smells good in here. Marvin must be on the grill," Mama stated, vocalizing my thoughts. Marvin was the new chef, hired to cook Southern dishes like hot buttered grits and biscuits with sausages and gravy and Caribbean dishes like ackee and codfish. Since Mama was from Mississippi and Daddy's family was from Belize, they wanted to serve dishes from both their countries.

"Yeah, he cooks better than Rolanda did," I said appreciatively. Rolanda had been the head chef for the restaurant for about a year until she met a new man and couldn't get to work on time anymore. Uncle Clyde, who worked as the manager, gave Rolanda a three-strike warning before he fired her. Everybody said that was real cold because Rolanda had two kids at home, but Uncle Clyde didn't play when it came to somebody messing up his money.

"Good morning, Miss Cora, Angela," said Armani, the assistant manager.

"Morning, Armani," my mother replied. "I'll be doing the books if you need me." She headed past the counter and down the hall to the manager's office.

Armani studied my mother's retreating back, then settled her full focus on me, which made me nervous.

"Hey, Armani," I squeaked out.

"You're helping out in the basement cleaning fish, right?"

"Uhh…" I really wanted to say no but was afraid of making her angry. "Yeah, but I'd like to work the register today." Everybody on staff knew I hated to clean fish. Armani knew it, too. She was on a power trip and wanted to keep me in check with crappy tasks.

"Maybe later. Right now they need you downstairs," Armani said, and walked away. Armani was scary. She had come from Africa about ten years ago but had a serious New York attitude. She was taller than Daddy—about six foot three, with big, broad shoulders. She seemed to be all muscle, and I bet if Daddy had to go toe-to-toe against her in the ring she'd probably have been able to go all twelve rounds and would still have been standing at the end.

Filled with frustration, I headed through the door marked Employees Only, which led to the basement. As I walked down metal stairs painted yellow for safety reasons, my footsteps echoed loudly as if I were the only one down there, but I knew that probably wasn't the case. The restaurant basement was huge and divided into sections. People were always amazed at how much space we had down here, and the employees had nicknamed it the Cave. Besides the men's and ladies' locker rooms, which each had a shower, we had a large room for storing stuff like rice, potatoes and pasta, and another room where the freezers and refrigerators were kept.

When I reached the bottom of the stairs, I heard somebody walking behind me, and I turned to see Marcy Turner grinning at me. "Angela, what they got you doing today?"

"Cleaning fish," I said, and sighed, then pushed open the door to the women's locker room.

"Me, too!" she shrieked as if it were the greatest thing in the world, and followed me through the door. I'd known Marcy for a long time, since we were in the same second-grade class and Sunday school together. She was a really nice person but a bit of an oddball, with no sense of style. Mama really loved Marcy because she was a church kid, always there at least four times a week for Bible study, choir practice or youth leader meetings. She had two older brothers and one sister, but she lived with her eighty-year-old aunt, Ginny. Nobody knew why Marcy didn't live with her parents; it was something she refused to talk about. It had to be hard for her to live with her aunt, because Ginny was a retired schoolteacher who believed in throwing down some strict rules. So in spite of Marcy's nonexistent fashion sense, I didn't really mind her hanging around me.

"Why you so happy about cleaning some smelly fish?" I grumbled and placed my pocketbook on the bench.

"Because I get to make some extra money. Mr. Clyde usually doesn't let me work over twelve hours a week, but since he's shorthanded, I get to make some rainy day cash."

We walked to the far side of the room where all the orange jumpsuits were hanging. I grabbed a medium one, and Marcy took an extra-large. It was Uncle Clyde's idea to have the folks who cleaned the seafood dress in the jumpsuits and then put long plastic aprons over them. He thought the idea was brilliant, but I always felt ready for lockdown at the Rikers Island correctional facility when I put it on. "When my fashion designing career jumps off, I'll never clean fish again."

"Cleaning fish ain't no big deal. It's just good to be making money." Marcy sang out the word *money* as she opened the door to her locker. I stared at the back of her head and fought the urge to pop her. She sounded just like her old-ass penny-pinching aunt.

"So, you going to C-Ice's party tonight at Rochdale Center?" Marcy asked as she strained to button her orange jumpsuit. Marcy seriously needed to lose some pounds. She was too short to be so heavy. I looked down at her size-six feet encased in white Keds. It was amazing she didn't have ankle or foot problems from hauling all that weight around.

"Nah-uh, I ain't heard about it," I said, trying to sound nonchalant as I refocused on my locker. My ears were all open for that bit of sizzling information. C-Ice was a DJ who used to live in the projects; then he was featured on a mix tape that went platinum. So now C-Ice had major cash and Hollywood connections. "Who told you?"

"You know me, I got my sources," Marcy replied smugly as she put her street clothes in her locker and slammed it shut.

Marcy was one strange chick. She always knew the latest gossip and party news, but she never went anywhere except church. I always wondered if it was because of her weight. It had to be. Marcy was four inches shorter than me—five foot three—but weighed close to a hundred and ninety pounds. When we had height and weight measurements in gym class, I was in line behind her and heard the teacher give her the information. She was real self-conscious about that. But her size should not have stopped her from having fun. There were some heavyset girls in my neighborhood who thought they were the most fabulous creatures ever. Once those girls got to a party, they were not leaving until they saw sunlight. In spite of her weight, Marcy was a pretty girl with high cheekbones and skin like a Hershey's dark chocolate candy bar. Her petite, upturned nose and close-cropped curly hair actually made her look like a doll. It was a shame she kept herself on the sidelines.

I finished buttoning my jumpsuit and whipped around to face her. "How do you know all the details?"

"Just do," she said, and shook her head slowly from side to side. She seemed overjoyed about having the inside scoop. "Heard JaRoli Price gonna be there, too."

"What!" I squealed. "He is so cute! Are you sure JaRoli will be at the party?"

JaRoli was the finest guy at our old junior high school. Athletic and smart, he had smooth chocolate brown skin and the cutest set of dimples when he smiled. My eyes had been on JaRoli since sixth grade, when he'd first moved to New York from Maryland, but he barely knew I existed. When he became a major player on both the school's football and soccer teams, all the girls took notice because he was tall, gorgeous and talented. Somebody was always gossiping about him at lunchtime in the cafeteria. I never had the courage to take part in those conversations, just wished I could claim him as mine. JaRoli and I shared a lot of classes, and I really wanted to talk to him but could never catch him solo. Also, part of the reason I never approached him was because I didn't feel pretty enough. Only the most popular girls were ever seen walking around school with him. Another fact that caused me doubt, I never knew what he thought about me or my clothes.

Marcy held up her right hand. "Gossip's honor."

I started bouncing up and down in excitement, then pulled my neon pink, rhinestone-studded cell phone out my pocketbook, which was still on the bench.

"Don't take a long time on the phone. We're supposed to start our shift now," Marcy said with a worried look on her face.

Scrolling through the directory, I quickly dialed Adrian's number, then put my other hand up to stop Marcy from saying anything else. Adrian's voice mail clicked on after four rings, and I rolled my eyes because she always had some long song playing. Finally the beep sounded, and I left a message telling her about the party and to come by the restaurant at two, which was when I would take lunch. I clicked off, then speed-dialed Quick Digits, letting him know that I desperately wanted to attend the Rochdale party. My parents had a rule: if I wanted to go to a party, my older brother had to be there. Satisfied, I shut off my phone and pulled a tube of lip gloss and a compact mirror out of my bag. I touched up my lips and patted some loose strands of hair back into place.

Just then the door of the locker room swung open and Armani took a step in. The frown on her face was so deep, her thick eyebrows merged to form a unibrow that resembled a caterpillar. She held a clipboard in one hand and balled her fist at us with the other one. "Marcy and Angela, you both know the rules. No lounging in the locker room when you're on the clock. I'm about to start docking pay if you're not in the cleaning area in the next two minutes."

Marcy gulped like a goldfish that had just been dumped out the bowl and looked as if she were about to have a heart attack at the possibility of losing some money. She jumped and raced out the door. Man, she was shaken up.

I was angry about getting bossed around and took my time putting my cell phone, lip gloss and mirror back in my pocketbook. I slowly zipped it shut, then placed it in my locker and slammed the door. Then I clicked the lock in place, giving the dial a few extra spins for good measure. When I walked out the door, I swore I could feel the back of my jumpsuit heating up from the evil stare Armani was giving me. Damn, it just wasn't right. My mother owned the restaurant, and the assistant manager was acting as if the mortgage papers were in *her* name, as if this were her joint. Armani was not going to punk me out. I wished my mother would gain a backbone and remind her employees that she owned this place and I should be treated as if I was special. Shoot, I knew I wasn't an heiress like Paris Hilton, but I should have been given preferred treatment. Instead, when Mama first opened the restaurant, she had advised the staff to treat me like everybody else. Said she didn't want me to get an inflated ego. I still couldn't believe she'd done that. What kind of ridiculous message was that to send?

The room that we used to clean fish and other meats was located at the end of a long hallway. As I opened the metal door to the cleaning room, I noticed that Marcy had already slipped on her plastic apron and gloves. Wow, she moved really fast for a fat girl, and she wasn't even breathing hard, I thought. Joseph Carter, who everybody called Mr. Cee, was in charge of the cleaning room for the day. He was gutting a fish and looked up at me. "C'mon, pick your spot and get to work."

Eyeing what seemed like a mountain of fish sitting on ice in the cooler, I blurted out, "This ain't no way to spend the last days of summer."

"Gal, you better grab some plastic and help out. If your mother got you here, then you better work on getting this catfish ready for the lunch crowd," Mr. Cee admonished.

I rolled my eyes. It seemed all of Mama's workers were getting on my case. Even Mr. Cee with his old-ass self. He was lucky to be working here. Everybody knew he was always walking around the neighborhood begging for some type of job. Last week I'd seen him pushing around a shopping cart and filling it with cans and bottles, trying to make some money from returns. He'd looked straight-up homeless, and I'd pretended not to see him because I didn't want to be caught talking to him.

I walked over to the far side of the room, grabbed an apron off the rack and put it on. Then I put on a plastic bonnet and gloves.

"What you want to do? Gut or scale?" Mr. Cee drawled in his thick Southern accent.

"Scale," I said, and took my spot next to Marcy at the long wooden table.

Maria Ramos, a short Mexican woman whose twin sons had been in my class last year, was the other person in the room. *"Hola, mami,"* she said, smiling brightly while splitting open a fish.

"Hello, Ms. Ramos," I said, forcing my lips to form a smile.

Our little line worked real quietly for the first few minutes. Mr. Cee would keep bringing over buckets of ice and fish, then grab a couple of fish and chop off their heads and slice them open. Maria would remove all the guts and dump them in a gray metal garbage can; then Marcy and I would take our scrapers and remove the scales from the fish. Once we got a huge pile of cleaned fish, I would put them in a large plastic bowl, take the bowl over to the sink and let them soak in cold water until one of the cooks came for them.

"What you gonna do with your paycheck?" Marcy asked. Her eyes were bright, and I bet she was counting dollars bills in her head.

"Buy some material so I can create a pantsuit for the first day of school."

"Oh yeah? What color?"

"Something bright. Maybe fuchsia or red."

"I don't like wearing bright colors like you. I hate it when people stare at me," Marcy confessed.

"That's how I like to wear my gear," I replied.

Marcy smiled. "You are so lucky that you can sew good. A lot of your stuff is so out there, models on the runway should be wearing it."

"True," I said. I loved funky, offbeat clothes like the kind of stuff Betsey Johnson and Gwen Stefani created. I also loved the way André 3000 from Outkast put together his gear. Anything that was bold and colorful and made heads turn, that was what I liked. Plus, I admired people who had the courage to walk to the beat of their own drum and be different.

By 11:30 a.m. we had been going strong for three hours, and the smell of fish was seriously getting to me. "My hands are getting cramped!" I exclaimed, and put the scraper on the table, flexing my fingers. "I am so tired of doing this." Marcy and everybody else stayed quiet and kept working as if everything was fine. Dang, they reminded me of robots.

Just then, Armani came through the door to check on us. "Mr. Cee, is everything okay in here?"

I saw my opportunity to escape fish duty, so I called out before he had a chance to reply. "Armani, you told me I didn't have to work in the cleaning room all day. You know I wanted to work the register, and I can't take the smell of this fish much longer."

Armani put that caterpillar frown on her face again and looked as if she was going to say no, but Mr. Cee spoke up. "The rest of the team can handle this. You can let her work upstairs."

I flashed him a grateful smile. "Thanks, Mr. Cee."

"Besides, I can't take too much whining. Young folks ought to be glad they can work a few hours for some honest pay. Back in my day it wasn't that easy," Mr. Cee continued, a look of disdain on his face.

Armani nodded. "Okay. Go change and get on the register in ten minutes."

"But I gotta shower," I protested.

"Fifteen minutes. That's all I'm giving you."

I silently cursed her in my mind. That was not enough time to shower, change and get my hair ready for the customers. Forget her, I was going to take my time.

"You kids need to pull your share of the weight and stop acting so spoiled," Mr. Cee chastised as I tossed my plastic apron into the garbage pail. It took a lot of self-control for me to keep from turning around and telling him off, but I forced myself to keep putting one foot in front of the other and stay focused on getting to the ladies' locker room to shower and change clothes. I really wanted this to be a peaceful day, so I was going to try my best to keep my attitude in check.

CHAPTER 3

Man, was I happy to be upstairs and out of the basement, I thought as I plopped down on the stool behind the glass counter where the register sat. I liked being on the register because it felt like the most important job in the place—handling the money. Customers would also place takeout orders at my station, and the waitstaff would bring all transactions to my machine as well. Messing up was something I never worried about since we had a top-of-the-line computerized system; all I had to do was hit a few buttons and voilà, I hardly had to think.

"What? They got you up here on the money machine today?" Rose declared, walking over to me with a stack of menus in one arm, her high heels clicking loudly. Rose was seventeen, two years older than I was, but we were in the same grade because she'd gotten left back twice. Uncle Clyde had hired her to work part-time as a waitress until Labor Day. She really wanted to work year-round, but Uncle Clyde said he was not going to play a role in her getting left back for a third time. He was concerned that she was never going to graduate from high school.

"After I started getting loud down in the basement. I

can't take too much of that fish cleaning. Armani knows I hate doing that crap."

"Armani can't stand you. That's why she's always sticking you in the Cave," Rose said to me, then looked around suspiciously as if Armani were about to come out of nowhere to give her a sucker punch.

"I know she don't like me. She's jealous that my family owns this place and she's just a foreigner who works for us," I said, feeling smug.

"Hard to tell that you the owner's daughter, the way you get ordered around. Hell, if my family owned this place you wouldn't never catch me busting fish guts."

"Whatever," I said dismissively, unable to come back with a good response because she was telling the truth.

"You stupid for letting people tell you what to do," Rose said, and flashed a crooked smile that lifted only one side of her mouth.

Sometimes I really couldn't stand Rose. She thought she was all that, and she wasn't. The girl had a banana-yellow complexion, a pinched nose and a dark mole that sat on her left nostril, right above her extra-thin lips. And to top it all off, she was always wearing way too much makeup and some cheap high-heeled shoes that made her pretzel-rod legs look like they were about to snap off at the ankles. "Rose, stay out of my business. You don't know what my paycheck looks like, you hater," I shot back.

"Hah, you ain't seeing no Donald Trump money up in here," she spat, and walked off toward a group of people who had just entered, her shoes clicking loudly.

Peeved, I looked down and noticed that the rubber taps and fabric were gone from around the heels and she was walking around on metal rods. "Tacky heifer needs to get those shoes fixed," I muttered.

I was so busy beaming Rose an evil look that I didn't hear

Mama approach me. She stood in front of me with a worried look on her face.

"Everything okay?" I asked.

Mama ran both her hands through her short curls and let out a breath filled with anxiety. "Angela, make me a cup of coffee—two sugars, a little cream."

Sliding off my stool, I walked over to the food service area where the large stacks of foam cups and coffeepots were kept. Grabbing a cup, I filled it with the steaming black liquid, poured in some sugar, added a swig of cream and put a stirrer in the cup.

"Hope you like my specialty," I joked as I placed the cup in front of her.

Mama picked up the stirrer and starting chewing on it while staring at the items in the display under the register. Our restaurant sold items like baseball caps, T-shirts, cups, big plastic mugs and pens, all with the Island Shack logo on them. "Did we sell any of these today?"

"I dunno. Armani had me downstairs for the longest."

"You gotta remember to push this merchandise when people pay their bill. These items could help us to pull our profit margin way up." Mama picked up her cup and took a sip.

It was weird to me that she was stressing. Everybody who sat behind the register knew that. My eyes shifted to the large index card on the wall next to my counter. Written in heavy black marker was: *Rules for cashiers 1) Make sure to check for counterfeit bills. 2) Double-check to give back correct change. 3) Did you push the Island Shack merchandise? 4) Always be courteous to the customer. A good attitude equals success.*

"From now on I need every nickel to count. There's going to be new ground rules around here," Mama stated.

"More rules!" I was seriously getting cranky with the way Mama was running the establishment. She was taking whatever perks I had left and smashing them to smithereens.

"Yes. Until I can get the books figured out, nobody's

getting any more freebies unless they are on the clock that day. No more free sodas, desserts or meals."

That ridiculous new rule didn't sit too well with me because when my friends came by I always gave them stuff. What was the point of having a restaurant if you couldn't give somebody a slice of cake? "Why don't you have Uncle Clyde help you figure out the books?"

"He's going to have to. The numbers aren't adding up," Mama concluded, then sipped more coffee and headed back around the corner to the manager's office.

That concerned me quite a bit. What did that mean, the numbers didn't add up? I wished I were stronger in my math skills so I could lend a hand on the books, but that was out of the question. The algebra and calculus classes I would have to take in high school were going to kick my butt because simple fractions sometimes threw me for a loop.

It was quiet in the restaurant, with a majority of the breakfast crowd gone and the staff getting prepared for the lunch hour. Grateful for the break, I pulled out a napkin from the holder on the counter and started drawing some flowers and diamonds. Sometimes when I was just messing around and doodling, I came up with some really cool designs. Then I would redraw them on some fabric and use my glue gun to attach rhinestones or sequins.

"Yo, I wanna order some breakfast to go," a voice said loudly. Startled, I looked up from my artwork and was surprised to see a tall, light-skinned girl with a wild, spiked Afro standing in front of me. Her hair was the weirdest shade of orange, like she'd meant to go for another color but left the dye in too long and ended up with that look—a Halloween surprise.

Pasting on my most professional smile, I said, "I'm sorry, we stop serving breakfast at eleven-thirty." I pointed to a large sign next to the silver-plated clock on the wall across from my register. It stated breakfast was served from 6:00 a.m.

to 11:30 a.m., lunch from 11:30 a.m. to 5:00 p.m., and dinner from 5:00 p.m. until 11:30 p.m.

The girl looked at the sign and squinted, like she needed glasses or something to help her read. I noticed she had a spray of freckles across her nose, and her eyes were deep green, like grass. She would have been pretty if she weren't so mean-looking. Plus, the faint scar across her right cheek didn't help her win any points. "So what? I'm just a few minutes late. Y'all should still have eggs and grits back there. Give me the sunrise platter to go," she demanded.

Out of the corner of my eye, I saw several customers walk through the door and head toward my register to place takeout orders. It was just my luck that Tyrone "The Jerk" Davidson was one of them. I couldn't stand him. He was the biggest instigator around. He had a mouthful of pink gums, always had a bad haircut, as if he cut his hair himself, and loved talking bad about people. Worst of all, he loved to see a good fight. "Our policy is to stop serving lunch at eleven-thirty. You're fifteen minutes late. We've got jerk chicken, stewed chicken and fried whiting platter as our lunch specials," I said patiently, and pointed to the photographs of lunch dishes that were posted above my register, near the ceiling and wrapped across the food area.

All of a sudden she exploded. "You dumb idiot, if I wanted lunch, I would have said it."

Her words hit me as if somebody had thrown a shovelful of snow in my face. I hadn't expected her fury, because I was trying to be polite. I felt embarrassed—there were four people in line behind her who witnessed the verbal assault, including Tyrone.

"Day-um!" Tyrone yelled. "Boo-ya! Angela just got dissed *hard*."

I glanced over at Tyrone and rolled my eyes. "We're not serving breakfast anymore, so either order lunch or leave," I said through clenched teeth.

"No, you need to get your ass to the back and find me a sunrise platter," the girl snapped.

Who in the hell did she think she was talking to? I didn't deserve this humiliation.

"Damn, Angela, you taking that? I know you ain't letting that slide," Tyrone said gleefully.

It was hard to tell what made me angrier, her insults or Tyrone's big mouth, but I couldn't take it anymore. "You dummy, can't you read? I told you we're not serving breakfast anymore, so either order lunch or step." I knew it was wrong to lose my temper, and that Tyrone was being a meddlesome devil, but once the words slipped past my lips, I didn't care.

Tyrone started egging us on with his loud, cackling laughter. His voice started getting higher, until he sounded like a barnyard hen. "Ooh, Angela just gave it back. Round two. Ding."

Somebody on the line said, "I thought the customer is always supposed to be right."

"Apparently nobody told her that, because she's laying down rules, ghetto style," somebody else added; then a wave of laughter drifted through the takeout line.

The tall girl with the wild hair got mad, and her face started turning cranberry-red. She picked up a cardboard box of straws lying on the counter next to the register and threw it at me. I started to scream at her, but my mother came running from the back office. "What's going on?" she demanded.

The girl just beamed an angry look at me and started walking toward the door. She took a few steps before she turned around and yelled, "This ain't over!"

What ain't over? I thought. It was just a stupid argument over a breakfast platter. That crazy girl still wanted to beef about something so minor? I felt as if I were in the twilight zone. Shaking my head, I desperately wished I were back home in bed and could start the entire day over.

"Yo, A, you better watch your back," Tyrone taunted, and started his wild, cackling laughter again. "That's a whacked-out chick you just rumbled with. She's gonna beat the crap outta you."

Embarrassed, I started to walk off, but my mother grabbed my upper arm and whispered, "Ignore him. We've got customers to take care of. We'll discuss your behavior later."

"My behavior? That hood rat started with me," I exclaimed in disbelief.

"Angela, you better tuck that temper away. I said we'll talk later," my mother said through gritted teeth. A second later she plastered a warm smile on her face as she took an order. It was all so unfair. No matter what happened in the restaurant, everybody else was always right and I was always wrong. Man, I was so sick of Mama taking up for everybody and always coming down on me.

CHAPTER 4

Around two o'clock, Adrian came bopping through the door of the restaurant. She had headphones on and was listening to her iPod. Halfway to my register she paused and broke into a dance. "Aw, this is my song," she said loudly, and started singing to Keyshia Cole's hit, "Let It Go." Adrian's singing voice was okay, but she would be no threat to an American Idol finalist. I shot her a look that said shut up, but she ignored me. Sometimes she acted as if she were getting paid to be an entertainer, the way she would break off and start performing. She knew I hated when she did that, especially in the restaurant. Some of the customers eating lunch at the tables turned around to stare at her. Adrian was a real good dancer, and the attention she received just boosted her up. She broke out doing a dance that had just hit the street, motioning with her hands and twisting her hips for a few seconds more. Finally she ran out of energy, or the song was over, and she walked up to the counter. "What's up, Angela?" she said loudly.

"Why you got to be so hype all the time?" Adrian was my girl and all, but sometimes she got on my nerves with all her noise. She loved being the center of attention, and a lot of the girls from around the way didn't like her because she was such a show-off.

Adrian banged her hand down on the counter. "So, what's good on the menu today?"

"Stewed chicken with red beans and rice, crispy fried chicken with French fries, jerk pork, smothered chicken, red snapper—" I droned as if I were on autopilot.

"Forget the rundown," Adrian interrupted. "The crispy chicken wings here are the hot diggity. Lemme have that with the French fries." Just then Armani emerged from the basement to take over the register from me so I could take lunch. "Okay, now hook a sister up."

Suppressing the words I wanted to say, I simply came from behind the counter and walked over to the area where steaming trays of food were kept behind a glass display a few feet away. Grabbing two aluminum plates off a shelf, I heaped one full of stewed chicken and rice and beans and the other with four crispy chicken wings and fries for Adrian. After I put each plate on a plastic eat-in tray, Adrian took one and was headed to the seating area when Armani called out, "Angela, is your friend paying for that now, or do you want it docked out of your wages?"

Shocked at the thought of losing some money from my already tiny paycheck, I was temporarily speechless. Suddenly I recalled Mama telling me everything was going to change and there would be no more freebies. I didn't know how to tell Adrian that she could no longer get a free meal.

"Who's going to pay for that food?" Armani repeated in a firm tone.

"Oh please," Adrian said, and walked back to the counter in a huff. "I never pay for stuff here. Angela's like my sister. We're homegirls."

"Oh no." Armani waved her hand from side to side, then pointed a long, red-polished acrylic nail at Adrian. "No more free food for visitors."

"That's crazy," Adrian protested. "I'm not a visitor. Me and Angela been tight since I was five. I'm practically family."

"Unless you can show me a birth certificate proving that you're blood kin, then you can't have any more free food. You don't want to pay, go to the church up the street and get in line. They're giving out free canned food today," Armani said with a stern look on her face, her accent getting thicker, a sure sign her tolerance was getting low.

I tugged Adrian's sleeve. "She's right. Rules changed around here. You got money to pay for your lunch?" I asked, embarrassed by the new restrictions and praying that she had some cash.

Adrian narrowed her almond-shaped hazel eyes, then opened her Gucci purse and pulled out a crumpled ten-dollar bill. "Here," she said, pushing the money to Armani. "And I want a Pepsi, too!" Armani took the money and immediately hit the buttons on the register to record the sale. I went to get two cans of Pepsi from the refrigerator, one for me and the other for Adrian.

"What's happening, everybody? Everything good?" Uncle Clyde's deep bass voice boomed out as he came strutting into the restaurant wearing a sharp navy pin-striped three-piece suit. Many of the customers looked up from their plates and called out hellos. A warm smile was on my uncle's mahogany-complexioned face, and his grin was so broad that it revealed his gold teeth. A lot of people liked Uncle Clyde because he was ice-cube cool, didn't take anybody's mess. He had a personality that was larger than life and instantly likeable, and his six-foot-five stature commanded attention. Plus, he was always on point with his designer suits. He had a whole closet full of them and wore one every day to the restaurant.

A lot of people referred to Uncle Clyde as an old-school playa, and they were right. Years ago, Clyde had run the streets, hustling drugs and hooking people up with stolen automobiles and any kind of identification papers they needed. All that illegal activity eventually landed him in a state facility for ten years. Grandfather Louis never forgave him for his notorious lifestyle and purposely cut him out of the will. Truth was, Uncle Clyde never fully gave up his street lifestyle—he enjoyed it too much—but now he was just involved in gambling. When Mama gave Uncle Clyde the management job out of sympathy, Daddy advised her not to do it. But Mama insisted blood relatives should come first and gave him the job even though he had zero experience.

Armani put a big Kool-Aid smile on her face as Uncle Clyde approached. "Hello, Mr. Clyde. How are you?"

"Fine, just fine. Is everything going well around here?"

"Everything's in order," Armani responded, still smiling.

"Hi, Uncle Clyde," I called out.

"Hey, Angela," Uncle Clyde boomed, and walked over to pull me into a hug, his whiskers tickling my cheek. He smelled like sweet cigars and Perry Ellis cologne. "How's my favorite niece?"

"Better than I was this morning," I said, and glanced over at Armani, who still had a fake smile pasted on her face. My uncle chatted for a few minutes more with me before asking Armani to send a plate of catfish, sweet potatoes, collard greens and biscuits to the office. He intended to work on next week's schedule and couldn't work on an empty stomach.

I walked to the back of the restaurant, where Adrian was sitting. "Jeez! What's going on around here? Armani has got a major attitude," Adrian complained while pouring ketchup all over her French fries, then splashing hot sauce on her crispy wings.

"That's a mean woman. I just try and stay out of her way," I said and shrugged.

"Yeah, but the way she came at me was foul. This place has got to be making a ton of money." Adrian looked around at the tables full of customers. She bit into her crispy wing and munched while complaining, "It's not gonna break y'all to give me a free plate every once in a while."

"Something crazy is going on," I confided, digging into my stewed chicken. "My mama was having a hard time trying to figure out the books today."

"Humph. If there's a money leak, I can tell you where it's going," Adrian said in an accusatory tone while shoving French fries into her mouth. She chewed and swallowed. "From the cash register to your uncle Clyde's pockets. That old man be wearing some fly suits."

"Nah," I replied, defending my favorite uncle. I could never believe that he would skim money from the register. "He's just real lucky with gambling and hitting numbers." And that was true. My uncle Clyde was a die-hard gambler. Every weekend he went to visit this brownstone up in Harlem. The building was on a residential street, but on the first floor and in the basement they had slot machines and poker games; they even had craps tables. It was like an illegal miniversion of a casino in Atlantic City. One night as I headed to the kitchen for a snack, I overheard Daddy telling Mama about the spot. Daddy mentioned that Uncle Clyde had won ten thousand dollars on the poker table. That was back when Daddy was on good terms with Uncle Clyde. Now they didn't hang out at all. Daddy claimed Uncle Clyde bragged too much.

"Yeah, that's right. He does that numbers-running business on the side."

"Who are y'all talking about? Mr. Clyde?" Marcy appeared at our table holding a tray full of food. Adrian and I stared at her plate. She had two cheeseburgers, four crispy wings, fries and two orange sodas. "Can I sit with y'all?" Marcy said, then slid into an empty chair without waiting for a reply.

"Why are you assuming we're talking about my uncle?" I questioned

"Half this town knows Mr. Clyde runs numbers. He's always taking bets from men in the barbershops all up and down the boulevard." And that was true. Uncle Clyde's

2008 mint-condition cherry-red Cadillac CTS-V was a familiar sight in certain parts of town.

"Marcy, I hope the restaurant made you pay for your food. Because you've got enough stuff on your plate for three people," Adrian said, then popped a French fry in her mouth. That was one thing about Adrian. She didn't mind telling the truth, even if it was a painful one.

Marcy didn't reply; she just popped the tab on one of her sodas and inserted a straw.

"Angela, you should let your mother know that I should not have had to pay for my meal. Marcy's eating more than her share—she's probably the reason this place is losing money," Adrian stated rudely.

Marcy noisily slurped her soda, never taking her eyes off Adrian. Finally, she took her lips off the straw. "I'm not the reason this place is leaking cash. Angela's mom is spending too much. That brand-new catering van has just been sitting in the parking lot. It hasn't moved for not one party."

"Don't worry about it. We're working on that," I snapped, wishing the conversation would stop. But Marcy was right. The brand-new white Dodge Sprinter van with the Island Shack logo painted on both sides had remained stationary since it arrived in early May. I had accompanied Mama to the auto dealership thinking we were getting a new family vehicle. It wasn't until they brought out the customized commercial van that I realized I had been tricked. It was the most backward thing she could have done, but she was smug about her decision. She gave me a jumbled-up story about successful people gravitating toward us, and the van helping us to project a lucrative image. She also stated that soon we would increase our wealth tenfold if we believed it could happen. I wanted to ask her what Cracker Jack box she pulled that fortune from. But I kept my mouth closed because my protests weren't getting me anywhere and she was starting to get heated up over my questions. My mother definitely needed to find a way to get the catering business off the ground since she was making hefty payments to the finance company each month.

"Marcy, you said you were on a diet," I said, abruptly changing the subject.

"Nah, not anymore."

"Obviously," Adrian blurted out.

"Didn't your aunt take you to a diet center?" I asked.

"Yeah, but the food at that place was nasty. Everything tasted like chalk and grass," Marcy said, and began to take huge bites of her food. Boy, she could eat really fast. It seemed as soon as the food went into her mouth, all she did was chew twice, swallow, then poof, it was gone. Watching Marcy eat was like being in the first row of a magic show. Her act could have been called "Where Did the Food Go?"

"Check it, I need to go up on Jamaica Avenue to get me an outfit for tonight. That Rochdale party's going to be banging," Adrian stated gleefully.

"You going?" Marcy asked, pointing her pinky finger at me while the rest of her fingers were wrapped around a crispy wing.

"If Quick Digits is gonna come with me. My mother and father won't let me go to a party if he's not there."

"So ask him," Adrian said. "Triple A needs to be there to represent."

"I left him a message, but I don't know if he'll go. He's been in a real grumpy mood for a little while."

"He been deejaying lately?" Adrian asked.

"Not since that block party on One Forty-fifth Street," I said.

"Hate to say it, because you know Quick is my boy and all, but he needs to put in some serious practice time on the turntables," Adrian quipped.

"I been hearing the same thing," Marcy chipped in.

"What y'all talking about?" I screeched. "Quick Digits always turns a party out."

"Not every time," Marcy said, and raised her eyebrows.

"Yeah, sometimes he can be straight-up Jekyll and Hyde. Half the time he's fierce, the other half whack-o-matic." Adrian giggled.

"Well, sometimes he gets nervous in front of crowds," I said defensively.

"He didn't just get nervous at that last gig. He straight-up choked," Adrian said, and burst out laughing. A second later Marcy joined her.

I was ready to tell them both off, but my mother appeared at the table. She had changed into a crisp white long-sleeved shirt and a pair of white slacks, her black tote bag on her shoulder. That was the outfit she usually wore for her home-care-attendant job, so I assumed that was where she was headed.

The mood at our table turned syrupy sweet as Adrian greeted my mother. Adrian admired my mother and was always trying to get on her good side. The real truth was, my mother didn't care for her. She always told me Adrian was too fast and wasn't a good influence on me. My mother coolly greeted Adrian and Marcy, then informed me that she was going to work an overnight shift for the Levys. She advised me to go straight home after I finished, then gave me a look that pierced right through me, as if she knew I was planning something. Or maybe that was just my conscience playing tricks on me.

Adrian's hazel eyes flashed, and she grinned really wide once my mother stepped out the door. It was crazy, but at that moment she reminded me of my cat, Smoky. "This is great. Your mom won't be home tonight, so you can go to the party!" she squealed.

"Why you always trying to get Angela in trouble?" Marcy complained.

"Am not," Adrian said with an irritated expression.

"Isn't your father home tonight?" Marcy asked.

Even though she had told me about the party, it seemed as if she was trying to block me from going.

"Actually, his hours got changed. He's working tonight, too," I said, feeling reckless and excited about the party.

"Shoot, I'm surprised you feel like going out tonight after that argument you had with LaQuita Mercer's cousin," Marcy said. Her comment hit our table like a hammer.

"LaQuita?" Adrian shrieked. A look of disdain clouded her face. "The chick from building D?"

Marcy nodded as she grabbed a cheeseburger and took a bite.

"Wait a minute," I said, suddenly feeling a chill racing through my body. LaQuita Mercer was a mean chick who ran the Benson Hill projects. She was always fighting girls and guys, and rumor was that she'd beaten one guy up so bad he'd had to go to the hospital. In fact, the whole family was plain old bad news. A lot of people avoided building D because someone related to the Mercers resided on every floor. That building stayed hot with undercover police officers making frequent busts. Most of the family members had seen the inside of a prison cell due to various crimes like vandalism, robbery, credit card theft and assault with a deadly weapon. "Who we talking about? That girl with the orange Afro who was in here before? She's LaQuita's cousin?" I refused to believe my luck could be that bad.

"Yeah. Her name is Shayla Mercer. Heard she just moved here from North Carolina. She only got out of juvie jail a few months ago," Marcy informed us.

"How do you know so much about her? You never hang out on the streets," I said, my voice rising several octaves. "You just go to school, church and work."

"I know people who tell me things," Marcy replied smugly as she polished off the rest of her cheeseburger.

"Angela, don't worry about nothing. If anybody tries to

start any beef with you, I got yo' back," Adrian said confidently. I was grateful that Adrian was extremely loyal to me and would be down for a street brawl in a minute, but going up against those Mercers would be suicidal.

"Y'all better watch out for those girls. They're big trouble," Marcy warned.

"Ain't nobody scared," I lied. Meanwhile, I was shaking on the inside. How could I have gotten into it with the cousin of the roughest girl in the projects?

"I'm ready to bounce," Adrian announced. "Angela, you coming with me to the avenue?"

"Uh-huh," I answered, trying to calm down my racing heart.

Marcy looked from Adrian to me and shook her head. "Angela, you crazy. I hope you don't get into trouble over that party." In the bottom of my soul, I felt Marcy was the wisest one at the table. For an instant, I tried to convince myself that her boring, safe, stay-at-home life was the better choice. Then I zapped those thoughts out of my head.

"You starting to act more and more like a stale old lady," I snapped at Marcy to cover my frightened feelings. I picked up my tray and headed to the garbage container. All the while, I prayed that Shayla would forget our argument so I could enjoy what was left of summer vacation.

CHAPTER 5

Adrian and I boarded the MTA bus to downtown Jamaica, a major shopping area where lots of restaurants, discount stores and clothing shops were located, as well as the train and subway stations to connect you to the other boroughs. We got off at the last stop, and I was surprised at how gray and overcast the skies had become. It had been so sunny earlier, but it seemed that after I got the news about the Mercers, the atmosphere seemed to mirror my mood. The streets were filled with pedestrians: I usually did not prefer crowds, but I drew comfort from being among so many people. I felt a tiny bit protected, because if one of the Mercers were to attack me, I figured there would be at least one Good Samaritan in the crowd to rush to my aid.

As we maneuvered toward the mall area, we found ourselves walking in the street alongside the automobiles to quicken our pace and to avoid the shoulder-to-shoulder congestion. It struck me as funny that there seemed to be an intensity in the air and that everybody and their mother was there to either buy clothes for next week's Labor Day barbecues and parties, the new school year, or to just walk the streets and hope somebody would pay them some attention.

"Damn, now, she know she wrong for wearing that,"

Adrian said, nodding at a hefty woman wearing a short white T-shirt, fire-engine-red spandex bike shorts, and sky-blue sneakers. There were bulges squeezing out from under her T-shirt, and when she turned around, it looked as if she were hiding bags of marshmallows in her pants.

I giggled in agreement as we rounded the corner to our favorite spot—the Coliseum mini-mall. We loved going to the Coliseum, because the building was set up like a huge flea market: some merchants had booths and others had actual stores. It had two levels, and there were all kinds of businesses, like barbershops, beauty salons, nail shops, sneaker and shoe stands, jewelry booths and my favorite fabric store, Khan's House of Fabrics. That store was fascinating and I could actually roam the aisles for hours, touching each fabric and visualizing new concepts.

"Yo, these are pretty." Adrian pointed at a pair of pink high-top Converse sneakers in the display window for the Sneaker Explosion booth, which was on the upper level.

"Ooh, those are cool. Let's go inside," I said, "but first let's stop by Khan's."

"You can't get enough of that place. Every time we come here it's the first spot you gotta hit."

We took the escalator down to the lower level where Khan's and a lot of the other sneaker stores and jewelry booths were located. There had to be more than twenty jewelry stands packed next to one another in the same common area. Shopping for expensive jewelry was not my thing. Gold was too expensive for my budget, but I loved costume jewelry. Adrian was fortunate enough to have a whole collection of gold rings and necklaces—gifts from various guys she'd dated. Lucky her.

The sound of Indian rap music filled the air, and I knew it was originating from the two huge speakers in front of Khan's House of Fabrics. The store was the largest on the floor, and the owners kept the sliding doors open as a welcome policy. Once you crossed the threshold, it was like fabric heaven. They had huge rolls of material in every color and texture imaginable located on horizontal metal racks or propped against the walls. There were also tables of assorted precut fabrics that were on sale.

"Hello, how's my favorite young customer?" Mr. Khan called to me as I walked through the door.

"Hey, Mr. Khan," I called back.

"How are you two young ladies today?" Mr. Khan walked over to us wearing a wide, toothy smile. He really was a nice Indian man, and he sometimes gave me discounts because I was a frequent customer. I'd started shopping at Khan's five years ago, when I'd tagged along with Grandma Rachel. "Angela, is there anything special you are looking for today?"

"Not really. I just wanted to see if you had anything new in the store."

Mr. Khan pointed at a wall behind the counter where fur pelts hung from hooks. "We just got these pieces in…that's rabbit, fox, beaver and mink. They can really accessorize any garment."

"Ooo, you could really make an outfit pop with that mink," Adrian cooed as she gazed wistfully at the fur piece.

"Yeah, I know," I replied, and started walking toward the counter.

"Let me know if you need anything," Mr. Khan offered, and hurried off to a customer who was impatiently gesturing for his help.

"Adrian, I have to figure out a way to get a mink piece," I said after staring at the pelts for a few minutes. "There was this crazy cool suede jacket in last month's Italian *Vogue* that was trimmed in fur. It would be so easy for me to make. You know I'm so good I can cut fabric without a pattern."

"Girl, I know your skills are dope," Adrian agreed.

"I'm supposed to get paid next week for my time at the restaurant, but I need to use that check for something else."

"Can't you just ask your father for the money?"

"Naw. He just gave me money two weeks ago for some silk I bought here. He's not going to give me any more money for a while."

Adrian looked around. "You know, I'm surprised Mr. Khan doesn't have a security guard posted at the door. This place is huge, and them fur pieces are tempting."

"Don't I know it?" I said, feeling frustrated at my lack of funds. "Let's get out of here before I get depressed."

"Man, those silver high-tops are off the meter!" I screamed as we walked into Sneaker Explosion. I walked over to the display table and held one of the sneakers up to the light. The color resembled shiny aluminum foil, and rays of light seemed to bounce off it.

The Korean storekeeper came up to me grinning and nodding. "What size you want to see that?"

I glanced at the price tag: one hundred and eighty dollars. "Damn, why is this so high?"

"Latest model. Everybody wants it." The storekeeper shrugged.

"Lemme see this in six and a half," Adrian demanded, and showed the storekeeper a pair of baby pink Converse sneakers. The same ones we had seen in the window. He never stopped grinning and seemed to fly to the back of the store where he disappeared behind a curtain.

"You not getting those?" Adrian pointed at the sneaker in my hand.

"Nah. My money's kinda funny right now."

"Huh, if my parents owned a restaurant, I'd get new kicks every week. You ain't playing the game right."

"I do all right. Just gotta wait until I get a few other things out the way."

The shopkeeper reappeared with Adrian's sneakers. She tried them on and started squealing; then she walked around the store making goofy faces and posing. The storekeeper never grew annoyed with her, just kept smiling broadly and repeatedly asked if she was going to buy them. Adrian was smitten with the pink sneakers and assured him that he was going to have a sale. I felt so jealous. Adrian was right. All I did in my free time was work at the restaurant, but I should have had a lot more to show for it. She didn't have to work. Her boyfriends kept her hooked up. All my sweating at the restaurant for a few measly bucks just wasn't cutting it. But my parents would have been outraged if they knew I'd asked a boy for stuff like clothes or jewelry. They urged me to be independent and strong, to never rely on someone else for my own happiness.

Adrian, on the other hand, had a lot of boyfriends, and she wasn't ashamed to ask them for anything. She was really pretty, and if she simply walked down the street, guys' heads would swivel. Plus, in the last year her body had blossomed, and she wasn't shy about showing off her curves. Since it was hard for me to speak to cute guys, Adrian was constantly trying to give me tips in that department, but I always felt stupid, stuttering and stumbling over my words, coming off like a complete geekazoid when I tried to get my game on. People could never understand how we were best friends. It was hard to explain, but sometimes two friends didn't have to be exactly alike to have a strong bond. Did it bother me that she was with a lot of guys? Yeah. I really wished she would slow down. She hadn't always been that fast, but in the last year or so, Adrian had discovered her appeal. Now she was unstoppable.

Adrian finished buckling her sandals, sat up and smiled. "Angela, you my girl, and I can't let you come to that party tonight without some new kicks." She walked to the shopkeeper, who had already taken her sneakers to the register. "Before you ring me up, pull those silver sneakers in size seven."

"But those sneakers are one hundred and eighty dollars!" I shrieked.

"Don't worry. I got it. We need to keep up our Triple A rep."

Thrilled, I raised my hand and gave her a high five. "That's right, Adrian and Angela have got major fashion attitude," I said gleefully as we smacked palms. It didn't really matter to me what people said about Adrian. She had a good heart and would never leave me hanging.

We stepped out of the Sneaker Explosion store with our bags and headed over to the Jeans Boutique. I stopped dead in my tracks. "Oh my gosh, that's JaRoli." I grabbed Adrian's arm in excitement.

"Uhm, looks like summer did a brother good," Adrian quipped.

And he did look good. JaRoli was coming out of the Style Makers Barbershop, and I could tell he just had his braids hooked up. His skin looked sun-kissed, and he was wearing a blue Izod polo shirt, Sean John jeans and tan Timberlands. Man, he looked fine.

JaRoli stood in front of the shop, and a moment later his friend Tyrell came out.

"Whew, it just got hotter up in here. Tyrell is sooo cute." Adrian started blushing and giggling. "I bet he's coming to that party tonight."

"Well, if his boy JaRoli is coming, he's going to be there."

"I want to dance with that cutie." Adrian began staring intently at Tyrell. "We need to be at that party."

At that moment, Karen Frasier and her girlfriends Candace and Inez walked by us. For some stupid reason, I automatically smiled and waved at them, and Karen looked at me as if I had two heads.

Karen could be such a snot, I thought as I watched her stroll away, enviously noting her emerald green Gucci dress and gold patent leather gladiator sandals. From first grade to fifth we'd been friends because we both loved to design clothes and sew. We had a lot of fun messing up material back then as we developed our designs. We even had plans to open a boutique after college where we would sell our garments. The name of our store would be KaLa, which was the first two initials of her name and the last two initials of mine.

Everything changed when we entered junior high school. One afternoon I had seen a program on television about this actress who always wore headbands. It was what she called her signature look, and it made her memorable. I thought that was a brilliant idea and came up with graphic legwear for my signature look. Karen took one look at my striped tights and hated them. Flatly told me not to dress like that anymore. We got into a huge argument. She cut me off cold when I didn't listen to her commands—wouldn't return my phone calls or even come to the door when I dropped by her house. Depression consumed me for a few weeks after that until Daddy broke it down for me. He said some people were intimidated by strong personalities and didn't want others to shine. Daddy also said if she or anybody else couldn't accept me and my style, she wasn't really my friend and I was better off without her. After that conversation, the cloud of funk I was under finally went away. It was only recently that Karen had finally started speaking to me again, but our friendship could never be the way it was.

As they walked farther away, I heard Candace say loudly, "That chick dresses so freakin' colorful. She always looks like she came out of a clown parade."

"Yo' momma," Adrian yelled, and put her hand on her hip, her stance daring them to challenge her.

Candace glanced back but didn't say anything more. She turned to her friends and whispered something, and they all giggled.

"Why you even try to be friends with them?" Adrian huffed.

Karen was so two-faced. On Sundays at church she always said hello, but during the week when she was with her crew, she acted as if her memory had been erased. Hypocrite! Fuming, I watched the group of girls. Sometimes it was easy to hate Karen. Everything came so easy for her. Everybody liked her. She was real pretty and wore genuine designer clothes all the time. She was an only child, and her parents owned several businesses in Queens and Brooklyn. And to top it all off, she had clear, flawless skin the color of caramel pudding, and her hair was always silky straight and smooth and hung down her back like a black silk curtain. I watched them walk away; then, to my horror, they stopped to talk with JaRoli and Tyrell.

"Let's go over there. Those skanks are getting all up in their faces," Adrian said, angrily swinging the plastic bag containing her sneaker box like a weapon. One of Adrian's problems was her temper. She liked to settle scores by fighting. That was one of the things I truly hated about her. Over the years, she'd gotten into so many fights with girls she thought were bad-mouthing her that she'd earned the nickname Crazy Adrian. After a while, everybody kind of shied away from her. She became sort of an outcast, and I guess that was why we clicked—because I felt I was on the outside, too.

"That's all right, they just talking," I assured her, eyeing the security guard patrolling the floor. The last thing I wanted was for us to start fighting in the mall and get arrested. "Let's get out of here."

After we left the Coliseum, we walked down the street and passed rows of Chinese shops. Adrian stopped suddenly. "Look at this cool jewelry." She pointed to a row of charm bracelets in a store window.

She was right. The bracelets in the window were pretty cool. They were made of clear and colored plastic beads that had tiny charms inside them. All of a sudden I realized what store we were in front of. "Hey, this is Karen Frasier's parents' store."

"So? C'mon, let's go inside."

"I don't feel like making her pockets fatter."

"Ah, c'mon, we can just look." Adrian stepped through the door. Dragging my feet, I reluctantly followed her across the threshold. Every inch of the store was packed with trinkets, hats, scarves, socks and unique items, like hand-made parasols. The store smelled slightly musty, like gym socks that needed washing. A generous spraying of Febreze and an open door would have worked wonders.

An old Jamaican lady looked up from her newspaper when the bell chimed as we walked in. "Can I help you?" She peered at us suspiciously over her cat's-eye glasses.

"Yeah. I want to see some charm bracelets like the ones in the window," Adrian explained.

"We have those displayed in the back. Follow me." The woman hopped off her stool and motioned to Adrian.

Reluctantly I glanced around and noticed a pretty light blue bracelet on top of the counter on a stand. The color would set off some of my outfits. I pulled it off the stand and held it up. "How much for this?" I called out.

"That's one of our most popular. We usually sell it for fifteen, but I'll give it to you for ten."

I started looking through my purse, knowing there wasn't enough money in there. *Why shouldn't I just take it?* I thought. Karen was nothing but a snot-nosed snob. Her folks didn't need the extra money. "That's okay," I yelled back. I pretended to slip the bracelet back onto the stand, but I kept it hidden in my hand.

"Angela, I'm getting these." Adrian walked up to me and held her arm out, jingling four plastic bracelets.

The clerk headed toward the cash register, and I decided to make my getaway. My heart was doing an African dance in my chest. "I'll meet you outside. Gotta make a phone call."

"Give me a minute," Adrian said, but I walked out the door.

Adrian bugged me all the way to her apartment with questions about why I'd left her in the store. She wanted to know if I'd boosted something, but I refused to tell her. For some reason I just needed a little time to think about what I had done. That was the first time I had ever stolen anything, and I was feeling a little weird, even though I was trying to justify my actions in my mind. I kept telling her that the place smelled like an old basement and I felt nauseated, but I didn't think she really bought that excuse.

As we reached the walkway to Adrian's home, building B in the Benson Hills projects, there was a group of boys standing in a circle, watching another boy breakdance in front of the building. "Hey, make sure you don't kick me," Adrian yelled. Sometimes I detested coming back because there was always a bunch of people hanging out in front, cursing, playing loud music and making noise. The boy was spinning upside down on his head. His long legs resembled a helicopter propeller as he defied gravity and whirled in a clockwise direction. A large piece of brown cardboard served as a cushion against the cement.

"Don't worry, little shorty, he ain't gonna kick you," one of the boys in the crowd assured. He shot Adrian a wide smile that displayed his gold-capped upper and lower teeth. "Besides, you too cute."

"Whatever." Adrian shrugged off his compliment and threw a long curly ringlet over her shoulder. Guys were always admiring Adrian, but most of the time they ignored me, if they weren't cracking on what I was wearing.

It was funny that we were best friends, because sometimes I felt we were complete opposites. Adrian was five foot two and kinda thick and curvy with major booty. She made me feel like a stringbean 'cause I was about five inches taller, and slimmer, and I had a small but round butt. But I could always count on Adrian to have my back, whether it was for the right or not, and we vowed to stay tight like blood sisters.

When we got inside the building, we walked to the elevator and punched the up button. A short woman wearing an auburn wig entered after us. "It's still broken," she informed us and headed to the stairs.

"Dang. The last time I was here this piece of crap was broken," I complained.

"You know the deal." Adrian waved toward the staircase.

"Aw, man, I hate walking all the way up to the fifth floor."

"We ain't got a choice. What you want me to do? Get a plane?" Adrian said as she opened the stairwell door.

When we finally opened the door on the fifth floor, the smell of fried pork and yucca filled the hallway.

"Wow, that smells good. Is that your mom's cooking?" I asked. Adrian's mother cooked a lot of Dominican dishes and could throw down on some food. Even though I was not the least bit hungry, I could always sample her mom's tasty meals.

"You wish. That's Ms. Cruz next door."

Adrian opened the apartment door with her key. Her mom and baby brother, Kwan, were sitting on the white plastic-covered living room couch watching television. Adrian's mom had her feet propped up on the white oak center table.

"Hello, Ms. Gomez," I called out.

"Girl, I told you before to call me Carmen," Ms. Gomez stated. "I'm not an old lady. You can call me by my first name." I always pretended to forget her rules. The truth was, I felt more comfortable keeping things formal. She was old enough to be my mother, and I needed that buffer.

Ms. Gomez really looked like she could pass for Adrian's older sister. And she was always trying really hard to act as though she were part of our crew. She wore tight, tight clothes that threatened to cut off her circulation, and all kinds of blond wigs. She swore up and down that she looked like Beyoncé, but she had too much blubber hanging out all over the place, so she wasn't fooling anybody. Her shape had been better before Kwan had come along, but now she could forget about it.

Noticing the bags, Ms. Gomez swung her feet off the table and rose off the couch. She glided into the dining room in a few brisk steps. "Where you two been?"

"The mall. We needed some stuff for tonight's party," Adrian said matter-of-factly.

"I got some really cool silver sneakers," I added.

Ignoring me, Adrian's mother said, "You can't go out tonight."

"But you said I could earlier," Adrian said, her voice rising.

"I changed my mind. You need to stay here and babysit Kwan. I got a date."

Oh boy, here comes the argument of the century, I thought as I watched Adrian's complexion slowly turn strawberry-red. Just then Kwan started bawling at the top of his lungs. His screams were like a starting bell, 'cause those two started going at it, arguing back and forth, their loud words peppered with Spanish. Their relationship always amazed me. My mother would never go for me talking back to her like that. She always said if I even thought about mouthing off to her, her fist would send me back to last year.

Kwan screamed and crawled off the couch. Scooping him up, I walked into the living room. He really was a beautiful baby, with skin like a new copper penny, and a headful of wheat-colored curls. Kwan stopped crying and gazed at me curiously with bright hazel eyes, the same color as Adrian's and Ms. Gomez's.

Suddenly I heard loud knocking at the front door, and I was so glad they had to stop arguing. Ms. Gomez put an extra swing in her hips as she ran to the front door with Adrian right on her heels. She peered through the peephole. "Pietro, baby!" An angry look swept across Adrian's face, and she ran in the back to her bedroom. Ms. Gomez flung the door open and put the man in a bear hug and started kissing him before he could get one foot into the apartment. I knew she was showing off and acting phony, because that man was *ugh-lee*. He looked like a short, bloated frog with funny-looking bumps all over his cheeks and neck.

Disgusted, I got off the couch with Kwan cradled in my arms and headed into Adrian's bedroom. "So, what you gonna do about tonight?" I asked, and sat on the bed.

Adrian had slipped on her new sneakers. "Nothing. I'm still going." She walked to her mirrored closet, admiring her footwear from several angles.

"Damn, Adrian, you bold. If I yelled back at my parents like that, I'd be homeless or dead."

"That's y'all, this us. I told her earlier I wanted to go out to the party," Adrian stated coolly.

"Yeah, but still that's your mother. You gotta go by her rules."

"Whatever," Adrian said, waving her hand in the air. "You have to come to the party with me. I need somebody to hang with." She bounced as she sat on the edge of the bed.

"I'll call and let you know when I get home. Quick Digits should be in by then."

"You better come. I got you those sneakers for tonight." Adrian put a serious look on her face; then she broke into a smile. "Let's get some cherry Kool-Aid out the fridge. I'm thirsty." As we walked into the chocolate-and-beige-colored kitchen, I could hear Ms. Gomez and her boyfriend arguing. *What is it about this place?* I thought.

There was something crazy in the air at the Gomez house, and it was time for me to skip out of there and get home. I drank my glass of cherry Kool-Aid quickly and promised to call Adrian on her cell as I put Kwan in a chair and left.

My house was quiet when I opened the door, the smell of Pine-Sol greeting me. It didn't seem as if anybody was home, because all the lights were out on the first level. I walked through the living room and dining room to the kitchen, where I noticed there was a sinkful of dishes left from break-fast, then I heard the whizzing and chirping sounds of a video game and knew it was coming from the basement. Then I yelled out my older brother's name as I walked down the steps.

Our basement was divided into three parts. Quick Digits had a big bedroom on the left side; on the right was the music room, where my father kept all his old albums in crates and his old record players. We also had a futon in there that was covered by a zebra-print throw. Quick Digits kept his turntables, speakers and other musical equipment in there as well. The middle of the basement was like a chill-out spot where we had an old color television and a couch. Quick used that space a lot for his company. I knocked on the partially open bedroom door. "Quick, you in there?" No one responded, but I could tell by the exploding rocket fire from the game system that someone was in the room.

Impatient, I gently opened the door, eager to speak with Quick Digits. I was annoyed to see that it was Omar handling the controls. "What are you doing in Quick's room?"

"I got tired of my Xbox 360 and wanted to use the Play-Station3 for a while." Whenever Omar took his head out of his books, he loved the challenge of a video game. He was an avid gamer since he didn't have much of a social life.

Sometimes I felt sympathy for him, but Omar assured us his real friends were at school. He was playing some type of war game and had placed a new high score on the board.

"You been home all day. How come those dishes are still in the sink?"

"Waiting for you to bust some suds and clean 'em."

"That ain't right. You should have washed them already." All the warm, fuzzy feelings I had for Omar evaporated like ice cubes on a New York City sidewalk in August.

"You'd better do them before Mom and Dad get home. You know they like you to keep the house clean."

"Ain't nothing wrong with your hands. They may be the perfect size for a midget, but they can still wash a plate."

Omar blinked rapidly behind his thick glasses. "All I got to say is I've been studying all day for school. You know the rules—my studies come first—and I'll get you in trouble for not doing them. Everyone knows I'm the shining hope for this family. Nobody can depend on your rag-making business to become a Fortune Five Hundred company."

"Screw you, Omar."

"Yeah, that's what we'll be—screwed—if we put all our hopes on your raggedy fashion line."

Angrily, I turned around and slammed the door. Omar knew how to hurt my feelings. I also felt that what he said was true. Mama would probably yell at me for not doing the dishes and make up excuses for Omar.

My spirits were down, so I went into the music room, closed the door and sat on the futon for a moment. We had crates of old albums in that room, and I spied an old Otis Redding album lying on top and decided to listen to it. Daddy liked to keep a lot of old stuff, including the record player he'd bought back in the 1970s. Even though most people would have called it an ancient piece of junk, Daddy and I loved it. It was a floor model that looked similar to a wooden box on four legs. You had to lift the lid to reveal the turntable inside. I placed the vinyl record on the rubber surface, flipped the on switch and placed the needle on the recording. Soon the sounds of "Sittin' on The Dock of the Bay" were floating around the room. That was how I felt a lot. Kind of lonely, kind of hopeless, like sometimes nothing was going to turn out right.

I must have browsed through Daddy's record collection for two hours or so, listening to albums by the Temptations, Ike and Tina Turner and Aretha Franklin. Both Daddy and I liked listening to the classics when we were feeling bummed. Daddy told me I had an old soul, because I appreciated the lyrics and wisdom from those recordings. I was also the only kid who could go through his music collection without asking permission first, and that made me feel special.

Bill Withers was crooning "Lean on Me" when the door suddenly flew open and Quick Digits stuck his head in. "What's up, Angela?"

"Hey, I'm glad you're home." I jumped up and lifted the needle off the record. "Did you hear about that party in Rochdale tonight?"

"Yeah. C-Ice is going to give me a chance to rock the turntables."

"Oh good. You're going to be there already. I want to go with Adrian."

"Naw. I'm not babysitting tonight." Quick Digits shook his head.

"Babysitting! I'm almost grown, I don't need you to hold my hand. You know Mama and Daddy won't let me go to any party without you being there," I reasoned.

"This party is my big shot. C-Ice said the same dudes who gave him a distribution deal are going to be there. I gotta keep my head in the game, not worry about you."

"Quick, why you acting like that? You know it's always been cool whenever we hang out." I tried to keep my voice calm in an effort to win him over.

"Not when you got man-crazy Adrian in the mix. She's always up in some dude's face, ready to start fights with other girls."

"Aw, that," I said, recalling the fight that took place at last year's block party. Adrian had felt that a group of girls were disrespecting her by giving her a stare-down. She stepped to the ringleader to ask what her beef was. The girl said Adrian's skirt was too short and she looked like a ho. The slap Adrian delivered was heard over the music. After that, all hell broke loose, the cops were called, and the situation got way out of control. Needless to say, the party abruptly ended, and the organizers told Adrian she was not welcome back to next year's event.

"Yeah, that. I'm not looking for a remix version of that madness."

"Everything's gonna be different this time. I swear." I crossed my first two fingers, kissed them and lifted my hand skyward. This was a childhood ritual my brothers and I had always done. It meant that you had given your word, and it would be a sin to break it.

"I know. Because you're not going with me." Quick Digits smirked and walked away, cutting off further conversation.

Stunned, I just sat down on the futon, looking at the doorway for a few moments, not believing what had just happened. Usually I got along great with Quick Digits and was shocked that he had dissed me like that. I was totally angry and fed up with being disregarded. The stupid rules around the house and restaurant were just too much. I felt used and abused, and it was time I went and had some fun. Forget everybody. Time for me to look out for me. I was going to that party. No matter what.

CHAPTER 6

After I washed the dishes, I marched up to my room and got my outfit together for the party. Feeling totally rebellious, I pulled one of my creations out the closet—a long black taffeta skirt with white-and-silver ruffled layers—and laid it on the bed. The skirt would definitely make some noise, because it was scoop cut to my thighs in front and got longer to my ankles as it went to the back. My silver-and-black striped stockings with my new silver sneakers would hit off my look. "Aw, sukie, sukie," I sang as I danced around the room. "I'm going to turn that party out." I hoped I would catch somebody's eye this evening—mainly JaRoli's. It was time for me to get a boyfriend, especially since I was officially a high school student.

The last time I'd tried to talk to a guy was in eighth grade. His name was Billy Martin. He was lean and tall, with mocha skin, a sandy Afro and hypnotic green eyes. He always wore a black motorcycle jacket and was like a bad-boy rebel. Billy was the only boy I ever met who knew he wanted to be an actor. He had done some extra parts in movies and had even had a line or two in some commercials. Even though I'd attended grammar school with him, once he announced in junior high that he was going to pursue acting, he became ten times more desirable to me and my female classmates. Foolishly, I told a group of girls who I thought were my friends that I wanted him for my boyfriend. They turned their noses up and hinted that I couldn't catch him. I ignored my inner voice, which agreed with them. One day during lunch period, I boldly approached Billy as he sat on a wooden bench in the courtyard. As soon as I got within speaking distance, I got hit with a major case of nerves and began to stutter when I introduced myself. Billy looked bored as I rambled on, and to add to my humiliation, he pulled a cigarette out of his jacket pocket, lit it up and purposely blew smoke in my face. A sure hint that he wanted me gone. The cackling from my supposed friends engulfed me as I slinked back into the school building in defeat. Billy's family moved to California shortly after that incident, and I never heard anything about him again. But I promised myself that the next time I stepped to a boy, things would turn out differently.

Pausing in front of my closet, I decided to complete my outfit with a white satin baby tee that showed my belly button and a black satin hooded jacket. I was feeling really nervous about my plans to sneak out of the house and felt sewing would help me calm down. I threw the hip-hop version of "Ladies Night" into the Sony stereo mounted on my wall. Soon I was rapping along with Missy Elliott and Lil' Kim as I stitched the words *So Fabulous* on the baby tee.

"Where you going?" Quick Digits appeared in my room, his gaze fixed on the dress lying across my bed. His lanky six-foot frame filled the doorway. He was wearing a yellow T-shirt with the image of Bob Marley on the front. I also noticed he was wearing some old Levi's and scuffed-up black construction boots.

Shooting him a brief glance, I tried to ignore him as I continued my sewing.

Quick looked at me suspiciously, then said, "Where's Mom and Dad?"

"Why you looking for 'em?" I asked in a cold tone.

"I hate when people answer my questions with a question."

Rolling my eyes, I said, "Mom's working for the Levys tonight, and Daddy's working an extra shift. If you stuck around more, you'd know."

"I'm a grown man. I don't have to be here." Quick Digits stared at my silver sneakers, which I had taken out of the box and put in front of my bed. "Who gave you those? Those kicks just hit the streets for almost two C-notes."

"I don't know why you're so worried about my money. All you do is hoard yours. You need to buy yourself some new gear," I said, glancing distastefully at his clothes. And that was true. My brother hated spending money on clothes. He claimed black folks were too concerned with what they wore on their backs and not what they had in the bank. Quick Digits mostly wore no-name T-shirts and jeans, defiantly stating he didn't want to get sucked into being materialistic.

Quick Digits blew out a sigh, and I hoped he wasn't going to launch into his save-your-money speech. "Listen, how many times do I have to tell you, true musicians don't roll like that. We wear jeans and casual gear. It's what the public expects from us. Plus, I'm so good-looking that the girls are gonna holla at me regardless." My brother had a smug smile on his face, and I knew it wouldn't be worth it to start arguing. It was true. Girls were constantly running after him. He had the same butterscotch complexion as Daddy. He also had a head full of shiny, curly, jet-black hair. Women were constantly giving him compliments and touching his locks, which he took painfully good care of. Quick might not have spent money on clothes, but he sure spent it on deep-conditioning shampoos and conditioners. He was afraid of going prematurely bald and wanted to hold on to his hair as long as possible. The thinning-hair streak hit all the men on Daddy's side of the family with a vengeance before their twenty-fifth birthdays, and Quick was terrified of inheriting the curse.

"Don't worry about me, I'm going to be all right," Quick Digits bragged and cracked a smile.

His overconfidence made me think back on my earlier conversation with Adrian and Marcy about how he'd choked at his last party. I was really concerned about him and figured he might feel more comfortable with me there, but I also knew Quick hated admitting to weakness. "If you let me come along tonight, then you won't get so nervous when you're on the stage," I blurted out.

"What you talking about? The Quick Kid is never nervous on the mic." Quick Digits laughed and sat on the edge of my bed.

Solemnly I recounted what I heard had happened at his last performance. Quick Digits' face turned serious, then angry. He had an arrogant side to his personality, because he knew he was the only DJ among the local talent who could spin records and rap with the best of them.

"What haters you been talking to?"

"I ain't naming names...I'm no snitch."

"Bet it was your nosy-ass friend Adrian. That's why I don't want y'all hanging with me no more. Too much negativity," Quick snapped, and rose from the bed.

"Nah, come on, I didn't mean nothing by it. Just thought it was good for you to know. Lots of people in show business get nervous onstage, so it helps to have a friendly face in the audience," I reasoned.

"How you gonna drop some mess like that on me when I'm about to do a show? Damn, your timing stinks!" He stormed out.

A cloud of gloom descended on me for a moment, and I

became disgusted that my opportunity to go to the Rochdale party was about to evaporate. My intentions were to get Quick Digits to agree to let me tag along; then I was going to let my mother know. But that plan totally went out the window. *Why shouldn't I just go?* I thought. *Everybody else does what they want to do.* These disturbing thoughts filled my mind as I pressed the on button and my sewing machine whirred to life again.

An hour later I was ready. I had flat ironed my hair, glued some bright candy-apple-red weave tracks throughout the front and sprinkled in some sparkles. My party outfit was packed in my Tommy Hilfiger duffel bag since I was changing at Adrian's. No need to let anyone know what I planned.

Racing down to the second floor, I knocked on Omar's door. Even though it was wide open, Omar insisted that everybody knock before entering. That was one of the weird things the little twerp had picked up when he went away to prep school. I banged on the door twice and walked in. "O, I'm going to spend the night at Marcy's house, and Quick is going to deejay a party."

Omar was playing a video game on his Xbox 360 and wouldn't answer me until he finished the board. "Can't you put that on pause?" I grumbled, but he blatantly ignored me. Boy, he could be such a jerk at times that I could hardly stand to look at him. I gazed from his neatly made twin bed to the numerous plaques and awards on his wall he'd gotten for academic excellence. He had also hung astronomy posters and had old science fair projects with the first- and second-place badges still attached to them sitting on his shelves. Omar was really smart, but his head was seriously swollen.

The beeping sounds of the game finally stopped, and Omar said, "So I get the house to myself tonight?"

"Yeah. Marcy invited me to spend the night at her place, so I'm going over there to watch some movies and hang out."

"Right," Omar commented with a smirk. "Sell that weak story somewhere else."

"I am so going there," I said defensively, all the while wondering how he could know I was lying.

Omar started laughing. "You hate spending any time over there at the mothball house. The only time you did sleep over is because Mom made you."

My mouth opened because I was ready to scream at him, but my brain said I was busted, and the words froze in my throat. He was right. Last year the church youth group had scheduled a trip to Spring Valley, and Marcy's aunt had insisted it would be better if I stayed over so we could all get up early and travel to the event together. My mother loved Marcy's aunt because she was president of the women's club at church. I really didn't like spending too much time at Marcy's place, even though she lived in a nice area of Queens, Stanford Park, which was nicknamed Old Money Park because in the 1950s and 60s a lot of wealthy R&B musicians had lived there. Marcy's aunt had inherited the house years ago from her only brother. He had been a composer and songwriter who worked with some big-name acts. He had married young, but his wife and baby had died during childbirth. He'd never remarried, and died ten years later in a tragic plane accident. Miss Ginny had inherited the property, which was fully paid for, but I heard the real estate taxes were a burden. The house was large: six bedrooms, a living room, a dining room with a working fireplace and a den. But the entire place reeked of mothballs. Marcy's aunt had a phobia that moths were going to damage her antique furniture, so she tucked mothballs in every single corner of the house. Five minutes after I'd stepped over the threshold, the smell had been overwhelming. Marcy and her aunt had played the gracious host part well, offering me a nice baked chicken dinner, mashed potatoes and gravy, macaroni and cheese, corn bread and string bean casserole. But as I lay in the guest bed later that night, I found it hard to fall asleep. Creaking sounds coming from the attic and the long shadows cast on the wall by the moonlight kept my nerves rattled. I remember getting home and complaining loudly that I would never spend the night over there again.

"Things change. I don't have to explain myself to you," I said huffily.

"So if Mama or Daddy calls, that's what you want me to tell 'em?" Omar said, then turned back to the game.

"You better," I warned, and walked out.

It was starting to get dark by the time I got out of the house. The streetlights were just coming on when I finally made it over to the Benson Hill projects. My parents would have had a fit if they knew what I was doing. After we'd left our apartment there, my parents really didn't want me hanging at Adrian's. It seemed there was always some confusion going on—kids fighting, boyfriends and girlfriends arguing or somebody selling stolen goods or drugs—but it didn't bother me that much to go over there. I reminded myself to call Marcy once I got upstairs so my cover wouldn't be blown.

As usual, there was a group of people hanging out in front of the building, smoking and playing loud music on a boom box. My heart started beating fast, and I hoped that neither LaQuita nor Shayla was in that group. Even though they lived a couple of blocks away, you never knew when a relative of the Mercers would spring up. I rang Adrian's bell a few times but didn't get a buzz that released the door. After a few minutes, I was about to pull out my cell phone when a boy who looked about nine years old walked up to me. "What's up, baby? You trying to get in?"

I really wanted to say something smart back to this kid, who only reached up to my chest, but since I spied a key in his hand, I said, "Yeah. You going in?"

"Nah. I'm just helping out." He opened the door, and I

walked in. "So, shorty, can I get your digits? I'm into older females. You a little skinny, but we could still hang."

One of my eyebrows shot up, and I really wanted to slam him down with an insult, but I held back. "Sorry. I got a boyfriend," I said, and walked to the elevator.

"Oh well, your loss." He threw me a wink and closed the door.

After I hit the elevator button a couple of times, I realized it was probably still broken. Ugh, I hated having to walk up four floors to Adrian's place, but what could I do? Praying that the lights were on at each landing and hoping I didn't bump into any drunks on my way up, I ran as fast as I could.

When I reached apartment 5J, Adrian answered the door after my first ring. "Why you breathing so hard?" she questioned, wrinkling her brow.

"Just ran up the stairs."

"Girl, I don't know why you tripping like that. It ain't that bad here." Adrian sucked her teeth and walked toward her bedroom.

Adrian's mother was in the kitchen on the phone. Her back was to me, and she had changed into some tight peach pants and a floral peach halter top. Her triple row of back fat was seriously messing up what could have been a nice outfit. Pietro was sitting on the couch watching a karate movie and waved as I passed.

As I walked into Adrian's bedroom, I prayed she didn't have a stank attitude. She was never any fun when she was in one of her funky moods. "Everything okay?" I asked as I took a seat on her frilly pink bedspread. Adrian's favorite color was pink; she was really a girly girl at heart. Her curtains were the same cotton-candy-pink as the bed linens, and she even had a furry pink rug on the floor. I got up and walked to her white oak dresser, fingering the various perfume bottles, trying to decide which fragrance to wear. Adrian was obsessed with perfume and must have had at least fifty bottles of expensive scents in her collection. The Britney Spears Curious wasn't too overwhelming and I generously spritzed myself.

"Oh yeah. Since Pietro doesn't want to go out, she's not mad at me anymore. Now she's mad at him."

"Well, at least the heat's off you."

"Yo, I told my mother before to drop that sucker if he's gonna play the cheap role. There's way too many other men out there she could get with who'll spend money. Why waste your time and stick with somebody's who broke and cheap?"

All I could do was look at her in amazement. Adrian was only sixteen, a year older than me, but sometimes she acted so grown. She seemed to know so much about guys, and sometimes I wished I had an ounce of her confidence. We were in the same grade because she got left back in the fifth grade. That was another reason Mama didn't want me to hang with Adrian: she felt Adrian was too mature. Mama insisted that all of my friends be studious and well mannered, not boy crazy. The year Adrian got left back was the time Karen and I became tight, much to Mama's delight. It was also the time I learned that a true friend stuck by your side and didn't try to dictate their rules to you, or drop you because of the way you dressed.

"What're you wearing?" Adrian asked, and flopped on the bed.

"My black-and-silver ruffled skirt with a tee and a hoodie," I said, pulling them out of the duffel bag.

"Cool. I'm going to wear a black skirt, too, except mine is mini, leather and tight."

"Triple A ready to represent?" I asked.

"And you know that!" Adrian grinned. "Let's get dressed and get out of here."

We could hear the bass booming from a block away as we walked up to the building in the Rochdale complex where the party was being held. There were about thirty apartment buildings that made up the complex, which was actually a little community to itself. In the complex's center were a post office, grocery stores, banks and variety stores. It was an unusually warm summer night, and something about the air and the head-nodding music made it feel as if you had to be at this party. There was a large crowd standing outside on the sidewalk behind a black velvet rope, patiently waiting to get in. A huge man dressed in a black windbreaker with the word *Bouncer* written across the back was standing at the door blocking people from going in. He informed the crowd that they needed passes to gain access.

"Yo, this ain't no exclusive Manhattan party. Why you trying to front like that?" asked a skinny guy who was wearing low-slung jeans and a dirty white T-shirt. His clothes looked as if he had been sweating and playing basketball in them all day.

"Private party. Step aside if you don't have a pass," the bouncer snarled.

"Shoot, this ain't nothing but a community center. You shouldn't need a pass," the skinny guy said angrily, and walked off.

I tugged Adrian's arm. "We're not going to be able to get in. We don't have passes."

"Please. I'ma talk to him," Adrian stated confidently. "Follow me." She smoothed her short black shirt with her hands and swayed her hips as she cut the line and walked up to the bouncer. "Excuse me. We need to go in."

The big man crossed his arms and looked down at us. Boy, he looked scary huge. His arms were so big that he looked as if he could lift cars as easily as he lifted hamburgers. "You got a pass?"

Adrian crossed her arms as well and shifted her weight to one leg. "We don't need one. C-Ice is my cousin, and he told us to come on down."

"I'll bet everybody is going to claim they're his cousin tonight."

"Don't make me prove it. I'm not in a good mood," Adrian said as she raised an eyebrow.

"That makes two of us, so why don't you two kids run along and aggravate somebody else?" the bouncer growled.

"Mister, I'm not trying to make you lose your job, but you are working my last nerve," Adrian retorted nastily, not intimated at all by his gruff attitude.

Oh boy, Adrian's gonna make this man mad enough to hit us, I thought. I needed to say something quick before the whole night ended in ruin. "Excuse me, sir, but her cousin C-Ice said he was putting us on a guest list," I blurted out.

"I don't have a guest list," the bouncer said evenly through clenched teeth.

"Listen, I got my cousin's number in my cell. If I use it, he's going to have to get off the turntables and come all the way out here just to get us in."

"Yeah," I piped in, "and he'll probably be mad enough to fire you for blocking us." Adrian made me nervous with her bald-faced lying, but I was determined to get into that party.

The big man flinched at my statement and seemed to weigh the pros and cons in his head. He let out a sigh of defeat, unable to decipher whether our threats were genuine. "It ain't worth it getting into it with y'all. Go on in."

Adrian and I looked at each other, grinned and strutted to the door as if we were top models.

A woman was standing in the lobby holding a handful of neon-yellow plastic bracelets. She gave one to each of us. "You can keep entering and exiting the party as long as you keep your bracelet on," she said. "It works like a pass."

The party was in a large hall that the complex rented out for birthday parties, showers, christenings and stuff like that. When we walked in, the lighting was kind of low, but beams of colors bounced off the revolving disco ball that hung from the center of the ceiling, right above the wooden dance floor. Although I had been in that hall for a party before, C-Ice had decked it out. Sheer red and black curtains were draped over the walls, and streamers and balloons hung from the ceiling. On the beverage table sat a two-foot ice sculpture shaped like a guitar. There was a bar set up at the end of the room, opposite the stage. The bartender was a beefy man who wore a serious expression on his face. A card on top of his counter read If You're Not Twenty-One, Don't Step My Way. This Is Not a Joke. C-Ice was standing on a platform that overlooked the crowd. He was rapping and rocking the turntables. Everyone was getting hyped from his performance, and the crowd was giving him shout-outs and mad love.

Our friend Tia Anderson emerged from the crowd. "Hey, you guys. How ya doing?" Adrian and I screamed and hugged her. Tia looked real cute in her soft lilac sundress. She had cut her hair into an asymmetrical chin-length bob. The new hairstyle brought attention to the square-cut diamonds in her ears. We hadn't seen her all summer because she'd been away in Virginia with her aunt and uncle. Ever since her mother had died five years ago, Tia's father would send her to Virginia for the summers. It must have been really hard on all of them to lose Mrs. Anderson to breast cancer, but Tia and her two older sisters seemed to have a strong relationship with their father.

"How'd you get in?" I screamed.

"My cousin Monica used to go with C-Ice. They still tight," Tia said.

"Oh," I said. Monica was a chick I really didn't like. She was seventeen but acted twenty-five, always up in some-body's face, as if she knew so much more than everybody else.

We asked Tia if she'd enjoyed her summer vacation, and

she stated that she couldn't wait for school. Adrian labeled her as wack and we all had a good laugh. Tia was smart and usually aced all her classes. Unfortunately, I had to study hard just to bring home a B average. About the only class I could ace was sewing, but my parents were not impressed about my superior grades in a home economics class. They always told me that the glamour careers were not a sure bet and I needed a good education to fall back on.

"I'm going to check out the food table. You guys coming?" Tia ran a hand through her feathery tresses. I noticed her nails were painted the same soft shade as her dress.

Adrian glanced around the party. "Nah. We'll catch up with you later."

As Tia walked off, Adrian grabbed my arm. "Check out my cutie, Tyrell, straight ahead, six o'clock."

"Oh, he made it," I said. Tyrell looked exactly like Sean Paul, the reggae rapper. He was tall and light-skinned with shoulder-length cornrows. The only difference was Tyrell had lots of brown freckles across his nose and cheeks.

"He's going to be mine," Adrian declared, and began to openly stare at him so hard I started to feel embarrassed. I shoved her shoulder, but she continued to stare. We really needed to have a conversation about her being so outrageous. Hopefully, Tyrell had not come to the party with a girl, because something would have jumped off. To my relief, C-Ice put on a popular reggaeton record, and the sounds of Spanish rapping and hip-hop beats boomed around the room. "Ooh, that's my song!" Adrian screamed. "I'ma go holla at my boy," she exclaimed, and raced off.

"Dang," I said aloud. A feeling of anxiety came over me. There was no way I could ask a boy to join me on the dance floor. If I were a good dancer like Adrian, then maybe I could have, but my dancing stank, so I always stayed on the sidelines. Feeling abandoned, I walked over to the food station, hoping to spot Tia. There were two women in charge of the table, and they were getting frazzled trying to keep up with the fast-paced demand. Eventually, I was handed a plate of fried chicken, potato salad and a cup of fruit punch. There were tables and chairs lined against the wall, and I pushed through the crowd and managed to find a seat.

"Whoa, whoa" came the screams from the dance floor while I sat munching my food and I tried to figure out why everybody was getting so hyped; then the crowd parted and I spied Adrian dancing with Tyrell. She would dance with her back to him, shake her hips and throw her butt out to him; then he would dance all close up on her. Adrian looked exactly like one of those girls in videos.

"Damn, that girl can move," a guy standing near me said. "I need to find a partner like her."

His statement really made me feel pathetic and lonely and I wished somebody would notice me. As I looked around trying to catch somebody's eye, I saw JaRoli walk into the hall and hover near the doorway. He was wearing a New York Knicks jersey over a white T-shirt and had on matching blue jersey pants. He looked so fine with his cornrows and a diamond stud in his ear. A wave of boldness washed over me, giving me courage. This was the first time I'd seen him by himself. "It's now or never," I whispered as I got up, threw my plate in the garbage and headed over to him.

Since nobody was near him, I felt a little braver. "Hi, JaRoli, I'm Angela," I said in one breath. There must have been something in the fruit punch, because I suddenly felt warm all over and couldn't get myself to stop grinning.

JaRoli looked me up and down as if he didn't quite know how to take me or my outfit. "Hi," he said, and cut his eyes off to the side. In my nervousness, I couldn't determine if he was looking for an escape route or just observing the dance floor. My mind went blank from a wave of panic, and I grasped for something clever to say.

"We both went to the same school, Kressler Junior High. I used to see you in the hallways," I said loudly, bringing his full attention back to me and hoping this would not unfold like my failed attempt at romance with Billy Martin.

My comment must have jogged his memory, because his eyes lit up in recognition. "Yeah, I think I saw you around, too. We were in the same math class." His full lips formed a smile.

"Yup. So, who got you the hookup to get into this party?" I asked, trying to sound nonchalant but determined to get his full attention.

He settled his gaze on me. "Karen Frasier got me some tickets."

"Oh," I said, feeling a bad vibe at the mention of her name. My mind reeled and my confidence was shaken. I wondered if Karen was his girlfriend. There were rumors that she liked him, but no one knew if they were dating. How was I going to pull him from her side? It was painful to know that I had never beaten her out in anything before. She always had the advantage over me in clothes, hairstyle, looks, grades. How could I possibly win? It seemed as if a witch's spell were cast, because suddenly Karen and her crew, Inez and Candace, popped up. Karen was wearing an orange A-line dress with a gold link belt. Instantly I recognized that it was from the Prada collection because I had seen the dress in my *InStyle* magazine.

"JaRoli!" Karen screamed as she walked over and rudely stepped in front of me. "You made it." She dramatically balanced on her tiptoes in her five-inch orange patent leather Prada pumps as she threw her arms around him. I loudly cleared my throat and took one step to the side as I restrained myself from giving her a hard shove.

"I said I was coming." JaRoli laughed.

Karen looked at me, then rudely wrinkled her nose as if she smelled something. "Ja, let's go get something to drink."

She looped her arms around his and practically dragged him away.

"It was cool meeting you. I'll catch you later," JaRoli said to me over his shoulder, and tossed me a sympathetic smile. His body language conveyed that he would rather stay and talk to me but didn't want to cause a scene. His words lightened my spirits for a moment, until I realized I was left standing with Karen's two evil sidekicks.

Inez had a disgusted scowl on her face. "Hope you don't think you can step to JaRoli. You too weird with all your crazy-ass clothes."

"Yeah, 'cause he ain't into chicks like you," Candace added.

"Why y'all all up in my business? I ain't said nothing to y'all," I snapped, and sucked my teeth.

"Because you think you all that, but you're not, ragamuffin heifer," Inez said, snapping her fingers near my face.

"That's a good one." Candace giggled.

"Forget both of you losers," I snapped and walked away feeling hot and angry. I headed to the bathroom because I knew they had a lounge area with chairs, and I wanted a few moments to myself.

Pushing the ladies' room door harder than I should have, I nearly hit a woman trying to exit the lounge area. After apologizing, I flopped down on the tan leather chair and rested my chin in my hand. Adrian walked in a moment later, catching me sulking in misery. She gave me a disgusted look before turning to the mirror to reapply lip gloss. I wasn't sure whether she'd seen the spat between Karen and me, but reasoned she probably hadn't because she was acting relatively calm.

"Karen brought JaRoli here," I whined.

Adrian pulled a brush out of her bag and vigorously attempted to revive her limp curls. "You'd better learn to use what you got to get what you want. Shoot, you don't ever see me stressing about some chick moving in on my turf. You need to get out there and claim what's yours," Adrian stated matter-of-factly.

Forcing myself to stand up, I joined Adrian in the mirror. My downcast eyes told me that I needed some time before I approached JaRoli again. Maybe what Adrian said was true. Maybe I could claim JaRoli as my own. I fluffed my hair, which was beginning to lose its straightness, and wiped the moisture off my face. "It's hot in here. Let's go outside and get some air, 'cause I can't stop sweating."

CHAPTER 7

the cool breeze of the night air felt great on my face as soon as we stepped out into the courtyard. It was so refreshing to get away from the hot, packed community center. The brass-plated wall clock in the hallway read midnight, and I couldn't believe how the time was flying by. There were still loads people hanging out in front of the building. Many of them wore sour expressions or scowls on their faces. I guess they were mad that they hadn't gotten in but felt that if they hung around long enough they'd make the cut. But I knew it was more than likely that they would spend the night on the sidewalk, because people were not going to leave a C-Ice party anytime soon.

"Shoot, C-Ice knows how to mix it up," Adrian said while bopping her head to the heavy bass beat of Soulja Boy's "Crank That." "Yeah, boy, that's my song," she yelled out, and started swaying from side to side.

"Quick Digits is going to get on the turntables tonight," I said proudly.

Adrian gave me a funny look. "Word? He's going to be here tonight and didn't get mad that you came by yourself?"

"He's not my daddy. I don't have to ask his permission to go places," I stated, and twisted my lips to the side.

"Uh-huh," Adrian threw back sarcastically, her eyebrows arched high. Then we both started laughing at my obvious lie. I hoped my laughter hid the anxiety that was starting to form in the pit of my stomach. This was the first time I had ever pulled a stunt like sneaking out of the house. Most girls my age were seasoned pros at it, but not me. I was obedient and had always listened to my parents before, but I could feel myself changing. A rebellious streak had risen inside of me, giving me courage. But I hadn't totally lost my mind. My parents' reaction would not be a positive one if they knew I had snuck out of the house and was at a party.

The roaring sound of a motor caught our attention as it grew louder and louder. The crowd parted, and there atop a bright yellow miniscooter was our friend Kenny.

"Kenny!" Adrian and I shouted at the same time. Kenny had been our friend since we were in preschool and had gone to the same babysitter.

"What's up?" Kenny pulled off his matching bright yellow helmet and hung it off the handlebar. He looked great, dressed in a black G-Unit T-shirt and Rocawear jeans, a pair of Air Force Ones on his feet. He opened his arms wide, then gave me a big hug. When he turned around and hugged Adrian, they locked lips and kissed as if they were the only ones around.

"Excuse me," I said, slightly peeved as I tapped Kenny on the shoulder. "You guys are being rude." Waves of jealousy rose in me toward Adrian that had never appeared before. Why did every guy like her and not me? It just wasn't fair. Was it my wardrobe that stopped me from getting play, or the way I looked? There was nothing about my features that was overtly sexy or pretty. In fact, most of the time I felt average. Plain. Like vanilla ice cream in the middle of all the exciting flavors at Baskin-Robbins. I liked the fact that my graphic legwear made me stand out. But when would I have a boyfriend of my own? My lack of romance was becoming a serious source of irritation.

"Oh, my bad," Kenny said, and broke into a wide, toothy smile. No one could ever stay mad at him for too long. Everybody liked Kenny—he had a magnetic personality and was really good-looking. He had dark, smooth black skin and a sleek, confident walk, like a panther's. The short dreadlocks he wore stuck straight up on top of his head and added points to his coolness factor.

Adrian and Kenny gave each other sly sideways looks, and I wondered if something had gone down between them that she hadn't told me about. It was painful for me to dwell on. Had she really gotten with Kenny? My frustration was beginning to boil over from Adrian being able to pull every man and my not being able to pull anyone. JaRoli was still a mystery, and I knew Karen would not let him out of her clutches for the rest of the night.

A few moments of uncomfortable silence hung in the air, and I decided to change the subject. I asked Kenny about his summer in South Carolina. It was public knowledge that Kenny's family had enrolled him in a basketball camp to help him get ready for the NBA. There was no denying his talent. He was amazing on the hardwood courts and could rack up points from the free-throw line with his eyes closed. Kenny had even made the local news, and all the media attention was swelling his head. He constantly bragged about becoming the next Kobe Bryant. Adrian and I had heard through the grapevine that the camp was expensive, but that meant nothing to his dad. Kenny's father held a management job with the city's buildings department. That man believed in investing in anything his son wanted to do. It must have been nice to be the only kid at home. I would have loved it if my parents gave me anything I wanted. A lot of people told me I was spoiled, but I didn't believe it. If I were, I wouldn't have to work and I'd be rocking expensive stuff like a nameplate with my initials spelled out in diamonds or a closet full of genuine designer handbags.

"You better not forget me when it's time to sign that big fat contract," Adrian said, and wrapped her arms around Kenny's waist.

"I'm ready to go back inside," I stated, tired of watching Adrian throw herself at Kenny.

"Wait for me. My aunt lives in the next building, and I'm going to lock my bike up and leave it in her parking space."

"Okay," I said. "We'll wait." Kenny jumped on the bike, strapped his helmet on and zoomed off.

The heavy glass doors of the building opened, and more people came streaming out, some of them fanning themselves with their hands. Some people were so sweaty that their shirts were damp, and their deodorant had probably lost its power. "Angela and Adrian," a girl's voice called out. Adrian and I turned around and saw our friend Tia and her cousin Monica walking toward us.

"Hey," we both called.

"What's up, chickadees?" Monica said to us. She had a slight smile on her face, as if she was enjoying a private joke. Not wanting to open my mouth, I just nodded. Monica thought she was so grown and sexy, but being around her was irritating, and she could mess up my mood in a minute, the way a cloud of mosquitoes could ruin a picnic.

"So is this a down party or what?" Adrian asked, looking directly at Tia.

"This is so much nicer than I expected," Tia replied, grinning.

"It could be better. Too many youngsters here," Monica said smugly. "I can't stand being around all these kids under eighteen." She pulled a paper accordion fan out of the small silver pocketbook hanging from her shoulder. A bored expression clouded her vanilla-complexioned face as she waved the fan back and forth.

"What you talking 'bout? You only seventeen," Adrian said nastily.

"Yeah, not much older than us," I added.

"But I'm a lot more mature," Monica said snootily, and patted the sides of the short, spiked wig she was wearing. Monica had a huge collection of wigs, and no one had seen her real hair in years.

"Monica, why you have to act like you so much growner than us?" Tia complained.

"Because I am, that's why," Monica said, and started eyeing a group of guys smoking blunts in the far corner of the courtyard.

Rolling my eyes, I scanned the area for Kenny, praying he would come back soon. In answer to my prayers, I could suddenly make out his six-foot-four silhouette in the distance, his loopy gait easily recognizable. "Monica, you don't have to hang with us. We're just waiting for our friend Kenny." I hoped she would take my not-so-subtle hint and leave.

Monica locked her eagle eye toward where I had been looking. "Oh, Kenny Levert is y'all's friend? Well, a lot of girls are getting on his jock since they heard about him going away to basketball camp."

"A lot of girls are sweating JaRoli Spencer, too," Tia chimed in.

"What?" I said a little too loudly, and I noticed Adrian smirking.

"JaRoli was voted MVP of the junior high football team. I also heard the scouts were keeping an eye out for him," Tia said.

"Yeah, and he's been featured in the local newspapers as being an outstanding player on both the football and soccer teams, which means chickenheads are going to be sweating him big-time," Monica informed me.

"Yeah, big-time," Tia repeated.

"These girls start chasing ballers early. You trying to get next to him?" Monica looked me dead in the eye.

"Umm, not really, but it would be nice to have him as a friend," I replied a little nervously. I really felt like kicking myself for not being bold enough to come out and say yes. It made me wonder if she had seen me trying to talk to JaRoli earlier and was waiting to snap on me. But I was afraid to say I really liked him, because I didn't want to be teased and compared to Karen.

Monica gave me a long, disapproving look, as if she knew my confidence was weak. "Girl, you better step up your game if you gonna pull him. Otherwise those other chicks will put footprints all over your back." Then she sashayed away without saying goodbye, her silver dress and heels shimmering in the moonlight. Tia, who seemed to know the rules, gave a wave and followed Monica as if her ass were made of gold.

"Ooh, that woman knows how to work my nerves," Adrian huffed as she watched Monica saunter away.

"Y'all ready to get this party started?" Kenny yelled as he approached us.

"And you know that," Adrian yelled back. Adrian and I put our arms around Kenny's waist as we walked to the entrance. Kenny pulled the handle on the glass door, and we trotted through. The bouncer was in the lobby area. He cut his eyes our way and took a step forward, I guess to question Kenny, but then must have decided it was best just to leave us alone, because he held his spot and let us walk by.

C-Ice was still spinning Caribbean music on the turntables when we got into the party room. There were so many people dancing that it was elbow to elbow on the floor. The bar area was packed with folks taking advantage of the free alcohol. The Hpnotiq was flowing, and the blue liquor seemed to be glowing in everyone's clear plastic cups. Kenny and Adrian caught the rhythm of the latest dance hall record at the same time and started moving their bodies to the beat. I loved dance hall music, and I started bopping, too.

"Come on, let's get on the floor," Kenny said excitedly, and grabbed my arm without letting me respond.

Panic consumed me. Dancing in public had always proved embarrassing for me, so I dug in my heels. At that same moment, I saw JaRoli and Karen on the floor, effortlessly duplicating each other's moves. They looked like professional dancers. Great.

Kenny mouthed, "What's wrong?" and an impatient look painted his face. Not wanting everybody to start staring, I waved my hand, then pointed for him to keep going.

Kenny was a real smooth dancer, and I tried my best to imitate his moves. We were on the floor for a couple of songs, and I was beginning to feel nice and relaxed. Then I noticed Adrian on the floor with Tyrone "The Jerk," whom I couldn't stand. What the hell was she doing dancing with him? She knew that boy was at the top of my idiot list. Hoping Tyrone wouldn't notice me, I tried to do a sidestep move that would take me farther into the crowd. No such luck.

"Angela, what you doing? The funky chicken?" Tyrone's voice boomed out, and he stopped dancing and bent over and hit his knee, howling with laughter. Then Adrian, who was supposed to be my girl, started laughing, too. Showing Tyrone my open palm, which meant get lost, I hoped he would get the message. But he kept on howling, then started imitating my dance moves.

People threw curious looks in our direction, and some even starting chuckling at the clown show Tyrone was putting on. I waved my hand under my neck, signaling to Kenny that I was out. He had his eyes partially closed and was so caught up in the music that I didn't know if he saw my signal. It didn't matter; I was mortified and couldn't stay any longer. As I turned to leave, a girl wearing ripped jeans with a brunette weave down to her waist raced over to claim my spot.

Feeling despondent, I walked over to the table where the fruit punch fountain was located to get a cup of juice. Someone tapped me on the shoulder, and I turned around to see Adrian. Rolling my eyes, I ignored her, grabbed a cup from the woman pouring the drinks and walked toward the food line. "What's wrong with you?" Adrian yelled.

"Like you don't know," I snapped. "You supposed to be my girl, and you were laughing at me."

"If you saw what I saw, you would have laughed, too. You looked like a dancing turkey," Adrian said, and burst into a fit of giggles.

"Oh, shut up," I retorted, but then couldn't help laughing along with her.

"Yo, I got to seriously teach you some moves," Adrian commented. "I don't know where you learned them tired steps."

"I can't dance, but at least I can sew." My truthful comment instantly calmed the anxiety that had built inside me.

"Thank God for that."

"You getting some dessert?" I asked as we neared the buffet area.

"Nah. Not yet. I see somebody that I seriously need to holler at." Adrian scanned the crowd, then dashed off. Suddenly, I felt fed up with her. She was always running after some guy, then getting mad when everybody started talking about her. We were girls; she should have hung with me at least a bit more. Everybody was right. Adrian was seriously boy crazy. And that was really beginning to irk me.

C-Ice's voice floated over the music, announcing the names of up-and-coming DJs who were going to get some recognition on the turntables that night. He stated that Quick Digits was going to rock the system first. I was thrilled that it was actually going to happen for my brother and was happy for him in spite of our disagreement earlier that evening.

The dessert table drew my attention, and I walked over to see all the delicious treats. The tables were covered with white tablecloths and laid out in a classy way, with long-stemmed roses in crystal vases placed among the goodies. There was a card in front of each dish that told you the names: red velvet cake, sweet potato pie, strawberry short-cake, chocolate pudding and an assortment of cookies. There were also decorative Chinet serving plates and matching plastic utensils laid out.

Noticing that there was a long line for the food and dessert, I decided to wait on it even though I'm a real impatient person. I stood behind a man wearing a blue-and-white-striped linen suit. He was holding an empty plate and swaying to the beat. After a few long minutes, it seemed that I was still standing in the same spot.

"Hurry up. Y'all taking too long to get food," somebody shouted from the back of the long line.

"Yeah, a sister's getting real hungry back here," a husky-voiced woman yelled.

It puzzled me as to why it was taking so long to serve everyone, but I hoped they would quicken the pace. A negative vibe had snaked through the line; I figured everybody had worked up an appetite and was grumpy and hungry after all that dancing.

Just then, out of nowhere, a crowd of kids rushed the line, rudely jumping people in the front and middle sections. In the confusion, I felt myself getting jostled. Somebody stepped in front of me, and at the same time I got shoved from behind. The sudden movement caused me to lose my balance and spill my entire cup of fruit punch. To my horror, the girl with the light yellow blouse who had jumped in front of me now had a big red stain in the middle of her back. My hand flew to my mouth in shock. I knew the girl would probably be angry, because clothes were prized possessions, almost as valuable as gold to some people.

The girl turned around angrily, the back of her shirt wet from my beverage. In the midst of babbling apologies, it clicked that she looked a little familiar. Scanning my memory trying to place her face, the answer slammed home like a car crash. It was that mean girl Shayla. The one I'd had the argument with at the Island Shack. She recognized me at the same time because she squinted hard, then without a word balled her hand into a fist and hit me in the face. She struck me with such force that I felt my feet leave the ground as I went flying into the table where the strawberry shortcake, chocolate pudding, cookies, napkins and plastic forks and spoons were stacked. The one bizarre thought that crossed my mind as I was airborne was that I was going to ruin the dessert table and people were going to be mad.

"Girl fight!" somebody yelled as Shayla landed on top of me, swinging her fists. It was hard to get in a good punch because I was on my back and she was sitting on me. I couldn't toss her off. She felt solid and heavy, like a well-fed buffalo. All I could do was put my arms out in defense and wave them around, hoping to knock her off me.

"Get off my sister!" I heard a familiar voice yell as somebody pulled Shayla to her feet. It was Quick Digits.

Somebody grabbed my wrist and pulled me up. It was the man from the front door, the bouncer.

Shayla cursed at my brother, who had one of her arms twisted behind her back. Quick Digits released his grip on her arm, and she swung at him. Instinctively, he ducked, and she almost fell from the power in her swing.

"Okay, there's not going to be any more fighting up in here tonight." A second man dressed in black appeared. He was shorter than me, with big muscular arms like Popeye's, and a long beard that he'd made into a ponytail with three rubber bands. The man was wearing black jeans and a black T-shirt with the word *Security* across his chest.

"I'm gonna finish kicking your ass!" Shayla screamed,

and lunged at me, but the security guard grabbed her by her upper arm. A huge crowd had formed a semicircle around us, and a lot of people were smiling and grinning in delight, as if they were watching a professional wrestling bout.

Adrian came racing over, looked at me and started screaming at Shayla, "Why you starting trouble with my best friend?"

"This beeyatch threw juice on me, and I'm going to whip her ass!" Shayla howled in rage. I thought, *This girl is crazy*. The accident would not have happened if she hadn't jumped in front of me. She was filled with animosity and acted as if I was her worst enemy. How could she have so much hostility in her heart toward me? What had I done that was so horrible? I had tangled with bullies before, but this was madness. It made me wonder whether I was dealing with a lunatic who needed to be medicated to control her anger. That would just be my luck.

"I'm not playing with you people. There's not going to be any more fighting, because you're all leaving," the man with the *Security* T-shirt stated.

"But she started it!" I screamed, becoming more upset because I spied JaRoli and Karen standing on the edge of the crowd, staring at me.

"Every single one of you is leaving," the bouncer boomed, then pointed at Quick Digits. "Including you." A look of utter satisfaction crossed the man's face, and my heart sank. He was thrilled to get even with me and Adrian.

"Now, wait a minute. I'm innocent! All I did was break up a fight," Quick Digits howled at the injustice.

"Yeah, but you're related to her," the bouncer said, pointing at me, a smug look on his face, "and she and her friend have been nothing but trouble since they arrived, so you got to go."

"But I'm about to get up on the turntables. Didn't you hear the announcement earlier? I'm DJ Quick Digits. Some important people are here tonight to see me. They want to offer me a record deal," Quick Digits pleaded. "Please don't kick me out. This is my big chance."

A look of doubt came over the security guard's face. "Well, that's too bad, but those are the rules. You fight, then you lose the right to party."

"That's not fair. Y'all need to speak to C-Ice. You can't kick DJ Quick Digits out. He's about to turn this party out!" I screamed.

"Well, that's not my problem. Now, we're giving you all a head start to leave before we kick her out," the security guy stated, totally unmoved by my brother's speech.

"Y'all better run before I get my crew," Shayla snarled, her voice filled with venom.

The crowd started to laugh and throw taunts at me and my brother.

Quick Digits was furious at being the source of the crowd's mockery. "Screw this. Let's go," he said through clenched teeth.

We all walked out in defeated silence, and Adrian suggested we go to White Castle and grab some burgers because she was hungry. The nearest restaurant was about nine blocks away, and I didn't want to go but knew the crisp night air would help us calm down and think of a backup plan for Quick Digits. We were all simply stunned at the way everything had unfolded. So many emotions were running through me that I didn't know whether to cry, scream or simply sit on the curb and hang my head. The first time I ever snuck out the house, I had to get into a brawl with a crazy project chick. Glancing down, I was upset to see the chocolate pudding and food stains that ruined my outfit. Touching my hair, I attempted to smooth the clumps that were sticking up. I probably looked like some type of scarecrow. Crap, JaRoli had seen me at my worst, and I shuddered to think what type of impression he had of me now.

Glancing over at my brother's grim face, I suddenly felt the weight of his loss. Damn, that wild chick had spoiled his chance of getting on the mic. It would have been a real big deal, for a producer to have heard him live, and I felt a twinge of guilt that somehow I'd played a part in messing that up. When we were within sight of the White Castle restaurant, Quick Digits broke his silence. "Bumping into you tonight was just total bad luck for me," he stated, his dark eyes glowing with anger.

"But I didn't do anything."

"Yeah, you did. You showed up at the party." Quick Digits fumed, watching Adrian walk through the door. "Damn, I can't believe I got kicked out when I was all set to get on the turntables."

"Everybody knows you're great, and I'm sure C-Ice will give you a second chance," I mumbled, not wanting him to level his full anger at me.

Quick Digits' expression remained grim, and he looked unconvinced. "Mom and Dad know about this party? Did you sneak out?" He stared at me for a moment, then added in a threatening tone, "Don't lie to me."

"What do you think? They never let me go anywhere," I complained.

Quick Digits blew out a disgusted breath of air, then unleashed a slew of angry words at me. Repeatedly pleading my case that the fight hadn't been my fault, he kept insisting that it was my deeds that had cost him a deal. Our argument was going in circles, so I decided to stick with my original plan to spend the night at Adrian's, then sneak back early tomorrow morning before my parents got home. No way did I want to go home to face any more questions that night. As long as Quick Digits didn't blow my cover, I could pull it off.

My brother digested what I said, glanced at his watch, then gazed into the well-lit restaurant. I studied his face and noticed the muscles twitching in his jaw from his clenching his teeth so tightly. He looked back at me and said, "You know, you really need to take your dumb behind home. Shayla and her crew are some real hood rats, and it's stupid for you to be hanging out in the projects. You don't know the streets, and anybody can tell that you're naïve." When I didn't respond, he continued, "You know what? I'm not going to worry, since you want to play the stubborn role. I'll be damned if I even lose a minute of sleep over your hard-headed ass." He opened the glass door to the restaurant and walked in.

I decided it was best to keep my mouth shut and not hurl any smart-mouthed comments back, because I felt guilty and sorrowful about his situation. Slowly I walked through the door after him. The tense, awkward smile I was wearing was beginning to hurt my face, and the spot above my left eye was starting to throb. I prayed that I wouldn't have a lump there and that the next day would be a much calmer one.

CHAPTER 8

The sound of merengue music coming through the open window from the next apartment woke me out of my sleep. Looking around, I blinked twice, trying to understand where I was. Cotton-candy-pink walls and Barbie dolls neatly placed on a shelf: Adrian's apartment. Then the memories of the night before came rushing back. The stupid fight.

Rolling over in the bed, I came face-to-face with Adrian. She was sleeping on her back with her mouth slightly open. A thin layer of drool was running down the side of her cheek. Gross. Since my mind was crazy wired, I needed to get myself together and jet. Easing out of bed, I grabbed my duffel bag off the floor, opened the door and tiptoed to the bathroom.

The apartment was eerily quiet as I made my way down the long hallway, past Adrian's mother's and brother's closed bedroom doors. As I entered the bathroom, I flipped the light switch on the wall, then cringed as my reflection suddenly appeared before me. I'd forgotten how many mirrors there were in Adrian's bathroom. Ms. Gomez was seriously vain and had covered the cream-colored room with mirrors. A full-length one on the bathroom door. Another on the shower door. And mirrors from the ceiling to halfway down the wall that wrapped around the rest of the bathroom. I closed the bathroom door, then shut my eyes and walked closer to the mirror on the wall. When I opened my eyes, I wanted to cry. It looked as if I were hiding a small rock under my skin right above my left eye. My fingers touched the sore lump, trying to mash it down, hoping it would disappear. No such luck.

Trying desperately to keep myself from crying, I unzipped my duffel bag and pulled out my toothpaste and tooth-brush, along with my face soap, washcloth and acne products. After brushing my teeth and washing my face, I quickly undressed and jumped into the shower. There was a bunch of yummy-smelling shower gels in the rack, so I picked the Bath and Body Works vanilla-scented one. The full blast of the hot water and vanilla-scented bubbles loosened my rigid shoulder muscles and made me feel a little bit better, and I didn't even mind that my hair got wet.

"Hurry up," Ms. Gomez called from the other side of the bathroom door. Then she started banging on the door.

Dang, she's rude, I thought as I shut off the shower. *People are still sleeping around here.* "Hold up a second, Ms. Gomez," I called out.

"That you, Angela?"

"Yeah," I grumbled as I grabbed one of the folded plush yellow bath towels off the stand-up vanity rack in the far corner. Drying off, I quickly got dressed in the outfit I'd worn over before the party.

"What are you doing? Getting ready for a beauty pageant? My bladder's about to burst."

"All right. I'm moving as fast as I can!" I exclaimed, getting annoyed. Now I could see why Adrian and her mother were always fighting. It was aggravating to get your bathroom time interrupted. Having a few minutes to get ready was crucial. Sometimes it meant the difference between having a good day and a bad one. Throwing my stuff into my duffel bag, I opened the door.

Ms. Gomez, standing in the doorway barefoot, wrapped in a blue cotton robe, instantly screwed up her face. "Wow, you look terrible. I hope whoever gave you that lump looks worse than you."

Why can't she just act motherly and say something nice? I thought.

"What the hell happened at that party? Were you fighting over a boy?" Ms. Gomez started frowning as if I were the ugliest thing she had ever seen. But the truth was, she wasn't looking much better with no makeup on. Her eyes were baggy and red, and her skin was real pale, almost ghostlike.

"Good morning to you, too," I said, sounding more snappish than I'd intended, and walked out of the bathroom. My feelings were hurt from her comments.

"Don't catch no attitude with me, little girl," she warned.

"Wasn't trying to," I replied evenly.

"I advise you to take your ass on home and put some ice on that lump. And you need to watch the tone of your voice. That's probably what got you in trouble," she snapped, and when I turned around to respond, she shut the door in my face.

Adrian was still sleeping when I walked back into the room. Combing my wet hair into a high side part, I pulled it over my left eye to hide the lump. The glued-in candy-apple-red weave piece was still holding up and looked good.

"Yo, you leaving now?" Adrian asked groggily as she sat up in bed and stretched.

"Yeah, I gotta sneak back in the house some kinda way."

"What's up with that hairstyle?"

"There's a lump there. I can't let my parents know I've been fighting," I stated sadly and threw my comb and brush into my bag and zipped it back up. She nodded. "All right, see you later," I mumbled, the weight of last night's madness hitting me again.

"Okay, just close the front door. It'll lock itself." Adrian lay back down and pulled the covers over her head.

My whole body was tense as I left the apartment and raced through the stairwell. My feet barely hit the steps. When I got out of the building, I pulled my cell phone from my bag to check the time. It was only seven o'clock. Feeling paranoid, I glanced around quickly and noticed a guy in a wife-beater and baggy jeans leaning against the front of the building smoking a cigarette. Damn, if he wasn't the spitting image of a cousin of Shayla's, and I involuntarily shivered, thinking he was going to jump me. I needed to get out of enemy territory and practically racewalked out of the complex.

Surprisingly, the streets were empty, but maybe that was because it was Sunday. As I hustled to my block, my mind kept doing a flashback to the fight scene with Shayla. How had I ever gotten mixed up with a crazy female from the projects whose second home was juvie hall? Was it possible that my karma was that bad, or was the universe punishing me for sneaking out?

Finally, my family's redbrick three-story house came into view. As I got within a few feet, out of the corner of my eye I spied my nosy neighbor, Mr. Keith, on his porch. He had his binoculars glued to his eyes, and he was looking up and down the block in a sweeping motion, as if he were working a stakeout for the police department. That cranky old man was one of the last people I wanted to see.

"You walking the streets this early by yourself? That's not safe," Mr. Keith called out without taking the binoculars from his face. What a nosy old fart. I wanted to tell him off but knew he would just rat me out to my parents.

"Have a wonderful morning," I answered sarcastically without looking at him. A sense of relief engulfed me as I bounced up the front steps to my door.

It was disappointing to see the Cappuccino Blast in the

driveway, which meant both Mama and Daddy were home. Still, I hoped I could sneak into the house without bumping into anybody. Reaching into my duffel bag for my keys, I was upset that they weren't there. As I shook the bag, hoping for a jingling sound, it occurred to me that I had probably left them on my dresser.

Starting to feel really paranoid and exposed, I was determined to get inside the house without anybody questioning me. Then it dawned on me: I could use the pull-down metal fire escape ladder my father had installed in the back of the house to get to my room. Daddy had ordered it last summer after watching a late-night infomercial on fire safety. Quietly I headed to the backyard, being careful to not make a sound. Although I had never used the ladder before, how hard could it be? I thought.

Our backyard was the prettiest one on the block. It was actually my father's favorite spot. He had planted azalea bushes in the rear of the yard, daisies and impatiens on the borders and rosebushes in the rear corners. We had a cement patio where we had a seven-piece chair and table set, with a massive umbrella for shade. I looked up at the metal ladder, which extended from the attic to the second-floor window. It was out of my reach, but there was a rope hanging from one of the rungs. I figured all I had to do was pull the heavy braided cord and the ladder would slide down to the cement patio. Since the cord was out of reach, I dragged over one of the heavy metal patio chairs and placed it under the ladder. I stood on my tiptoes on the back and arms of the chair, grabbed the rope and yanked real hard. The chair fell over with a loud clang, and I knew I was busted as I dangled there. It was as if somebody had clashed cymbals. When I glanced down, the distance between me and the cement porch seemed terrifying. I was afraid to let go, so I just held on, like a trapped fool.

A moment later, I felt a whack on my back, and the surprise blow caused my hands to slip free.

"What the hell is wrong with you?" Quick Digits yelled at me.

"Ow! You made me fall," I whined, rubbing my sore elbow and noticing the broom in his hand.

Quick Digits glanced from the fire escape to the overturned chair, then to me. His expression was hard and cold, his eyes like black marbles. "What's your problem? Are you completely stupid?"

Scrambling off the ground, I was furious that I got busted. I took a hard look at my brother and noticed that his eyes were red and he was wearing the same clothes from the night before, except now they were wrinkled, as if he'd slept in them. "Don't call me stupid. You're stupid. I just wanted to get in the house without seeing anybody, including you."

Out of nowhere, Quick Digits pushed me so hard I stumbled, nearly hitting the ground again. "Girl, you better get your dumb ass in the house right away before I tell Mom and Dad everything."

We held our ground, looking angrily at each other for a minute, two gladiators poised for a showdown. Suddenly his demeanor changed; the thirst for punishment had evaporated, and he turned to go back in the house. Even though our standoff had ended, he still had the upper hand, and I was out of choices, so I followed him through the side door into the kitchen.

My hand was on the banister, and I was headed to the safety of the attic when I heard my name. "Angela, is that you?" my mother called from her bedroom just as I passed the second-floor landing. Her voice caused me to stomp my foot in frustration. It was upsetting that I just couldn't catch a break.

"Yeah, it's me," I reluctantly answered.

"Get down here." Mama stepped into the hallway, still dressed in the white uniform she wore when taking care of Mr. Levy. "Why does it look like you just stepped in this house?" She was rubbing lotion on her hands and had a concerned look on her face.

"D-didn't Omar tell you?" I said, my voice shaking slightly.

"Tell me what? I just stepped in the house a few minutes ago."

"Oh. I spent the night at Marcy's house. I told Omar to tell you." My face grew hot from the lie, and I tried to keep my eyes steady on her face.

"Why didn't you ask me first?" Mama questioned, her eyes full of suspicion.

As I rambled my excuse about staying with Marcy, I added that I knew Mama liked her and her aunt because they were big churchgoers. My little speech didn't stop my mother from going off on me. She was always real hard on me because I was the only girl and she lived in fear that I would end up pregnant at an early age. I wanted to tell her not to worry about that because I couldn't even land a boyfriend, but my smart comments might have led her to hit me. My mother had gotten pregnant with Quick Digits when she was twenty-one. She'd always had dreams of going to college and had wanted to become a registered nurse, but she had felt obligated to put everyone else's dreams before hers. After high school, she got a job and helped her family out. Then, when she finally applied for college, she met my father and became pregnant. Sometimes it felt as if Mama was putting too much pressure on me because she didn't get to live out her dream. Personally, I thought she was still putting herself last by purchasing the restaurant. That business was like a quicksand trap, and I feared she might never see any happiness from it.

After Mama ranted for a few minutes, she stared so hard at my hair I was surprised the glue in my weave didn't melt. "And why are you wearing that ridiculous hairstyle?"

"Oh, this?" I patted the hair over my eye, trying to buy

time as possible excuses flooded my mind. I didn't want her to make me undo it, so I scrambled for a lie. "Uh, Marcy put my hair this way. All the girls are wearing it."

"Every style isn't for everybody. Don't wear it again. It looks foolish."

"Oh, okay," I said quickly to avoid an argument, and headed back up the stairs.

"Your father is cooking breakfast this morning. It'll be ready in about twenty minutes," she yelled after me.

Boy, I was so glad to be back in my own room. I eased myself across the bed. My movement woke up Smoky, who got up from the foot of the bed, stretched, then nuzzled my cheek with his nose. Scooping him up I hugged him, sinking my face into his soft, warm fur. He purred affectionately, and I was happy that at least somebody was glad to see me.

When I went down to the kitchen thirty minutes later, my mother, father and brothers were all seated at the table. There were dishes of waffles, eggs, sausages, toast, Canadian bacon and oatmeal, and a glass pitcher of orange juice sat in the center of the table. "Good morning, everybody," I sang out sweetly, and took a seat. I figured it was best to fake a positive attitude so no one would suspect I was hiding a painful lump under my bangs.

Mama cleared her throat, which was the signal that she was about to say the blessing. She had changed into her black Liz Claiborne short-sleeved shift dress. The dress was one of her favorites and looked good on her. Meanwhile, Daddy was suited up for a workout. Dressed in a green nylon tracksuit, he looked ready for a serious sweat session. Mama bowed her head and everybody did the same. "Lord, thank you for this wonderful food and the opportunity to share it with our loved ones. Some folks don't have parents, so we should all love, appreciate and obey ours. And children should always tell their parents where they are going at all times. When they do, it shows they respect the rules of the house. Amen."

Dang, Mama knew how to throw around a guilt treatment.

Everybody seemed to breathe a sign of relief when Mama finished her speech and helped themselves to the food on the table. "Just pass me the oatmeal," Daddy said to Mama. "I don't want any of that high-cholesterol, fattening food. I'm in serious training."

"Dad, you're starting to sound like one of those diet-crazed females. Men don't worry about things like that," Quick Digits chuckled.

"They should. High blood pressure and clogged arteries can cause strokes. It can make you taste the mat faster than a right hook," Omar said as he spread jelly on his toast.

"You guys can snap on me all you want, but I'll have the last laugh when I bring home the championship belt," Daddy replied.

"Daddy, you gonna fight somebody?" I asked, surprised that he was stepping back into the ring after all these years. His announcement alarmed me because boxing was a serious sport. Many fighters ended up with brain injuries from staying in the game too long. Permanent memory loss and slurred speech were dangerous side effects of that business, and I didn't want anything happening to my father.

"I got myself on the card for a fight in two weeks. Lightning Fists Jenkins versus Rockman Altronda at the Harvey Gym in Forest Hills," Daddy said with a delighted grin.

"Rockman? He's good. I caught one of his fights on the public access channel. The last guy who fought him got a concussion," Omar said seriously, "and he was younger than you and in much better shape."

"Do you always have to be a jerk?" I said, cutting my eyes at him. Omar's words could deliver such a sting, and I wished he would keep his mouth closed for the rest of the meal.

"Only when I'm trying to imitate you," Omar threw back.

"How come this is the first time I'm hearing about this fight?" Mama inquired, her voice dead serious.

"Because this match is something that's very necessary for me," Daddy answered, then started eating his oatmeal plain without putting any butter, sugar or cinnamon on it. "There was no discussion necessary. This is something I have to do."

"Are the promoters making you sell tickets?" Mama asked.

"That's the business when fighters are trying to make a name for themselves," my father stated nonchalantly.

"Dad, you gotta watch out for that. There's a lot of scamming going on where promoters are pocketing all the money from ticket sales and giving the boxers nothing," Quick Digits warned.

Ignoring Quick Digits, I said, "Are you going to be on television?" I popped a slice of crispy bacon in my mouth, savoring the smoked flavor. The idea was growing on me that my father could become a famous heavyweight champ. Even though I was frightened about the dangers, I never wanted to express any doubts to my father. He was the one person who never criticized my fashions or self-expression. I felt a deep sense of loyalty to him in that regard. He needed a strong supporter, especially if he had to warm Mama up to the idea.

"Not yet." Daddy laughed.

"I don't trust your management. You're already paying your coach and sparring partner, now you've got to sell tickets for your own fight," Mama spat out, then banged her fist on the table. The vibration was powerful enough to wobble the pitcher and send a few drops of orange juice splashing down the side.

"Nobody said getting back into the ring was going to be a bushel of roses. I'm trying to do this the best way I know how." Daddy blew out a sigh. He looked from me to Quick Digits to Omar in earnest, then cleared his throat. "If I had listened to my parents, I would be farther along in life, but I hung out with the wrong crowd and didn't get my education like I should have. Now I'm tossing garbage cans and getting beat upside my head in the ring, trying to make a living. You kids need to listen to what I say and learn from it. Appreciate the love and good advice me and your mother give you all."

The kids-should-listen-to-their-parents speech was one my father loved to preach. When Daddy was in his last year of high school, life had been sweet. He had a part-time job at the grocery store, drove a red Ford Mustang and was all set to go to college. His family always warned him about hanging with his first cousins, Rob and John, who were, in his mom's eyes, two bad seeds. But Daddy felt they were cool people who just didn't have the financial advantages his family had. So one Friday when Rob and John suggested they go by the convenience store for cigarettes, he didn't think twice. It didn't alarm him either when they told him to stay in the car. Daddy never knew they robbed the place until a police cruiser stopped them a mile up the road. Sadly, Daddy got five years in jail for being an accessory. The sentence would have been longer if his parents hadn't spent all his tuition money for a lawyer. He never did make it to college after that incident. Daddy honestly believed that his conviction stopped him from finding a successful career path. Through the years, he applied for jobs with the federal, city and state agencies. He longed for a position with good security and benefits. But after the initial interviews, he never got callbacks. Although my father now worked with the private trash company, he would have been more satisfied working as a New York City sanitation man because the pay and benefits were better.

"We do appreciate you, Daddy," I said.

Daddy looked directly at me. "Good. Then don't pull any more stunts like staying out of the house all night. You clear that with me or your mama first."

"Okay," I answered quietly, dropping my eyes to my plate.

"I really wish you wouldn't take that fight. My gut is telling me something's not kosher," Mama said, shaking her head. She threaded her fingers together and placed them under her chin.

"Cora, you need to stop worrying and let me handle my business," Daddy said confidently.

"Mr. Mannie Jenkins, it becomes my business when you use money that should have gone to our household or business expenses for boxing lessons," Mama retorted. "Do you know we're fifteen hundred dollars short on Omar's tuition? What am I going to tell the school?"

"There is no need to bring this up in front of the kids. I just miscalculated some things. Don't worry, baby. I've got a plan to come up with the money." My father, slightly embarrassed, waved his hand as a sign to end the conversation. He was a proud man and hated to show weakness. He always wanted to portray himself as a strong father who could take care of the family.

"Between the restaurant, you spending money like water and these kids, I'm about to lose my mind!" Mama screeched, ignoring the aggravated look on my father's face.

"Please, do not put me in that equation," Quick Digits stated. "Everybody knows I pull my own weight around here. My gigs pay my portion of the rent, and I don't ask anybody for anything. In fact, I almost had a record deal, but some fool blew it for me." Quick Digits cut his eyes in my direction. The venomous stare he threw my way nearly made me choke on my toast. It was very obvious that he was real angry with me, and if everyone hadn't been distracted by the conversation already going on, they would have questioned Quick's hate-filled look. Throwing him a pleading glance that said let's talk about this later was useless. Finally, I dropped my eyes and stared at my plate again, hoping he wouldn't tell everyone at the table about my wild night out.

"Cora, I don't understand why you are jumping all over me when that new catering van you invested in is still sitting in the lot," Daddy countered.

"We actually got an event booked for next Saturday," Mama replied in a smug tone.

"Good. It's about time. Okay, I got this money shortage problem all figured out. I'll sell some food at the West Indian Day parade and have Omar help out." Daddy looked directly at Omar. "Even though you'll already be in school, I'll come and get you that holiday Monday." He paused to take a sip of coffee. "Angela, you can help out, too."

My head shot up at the mention of giving up my holiday in order to pay Omar's tuition. I blurted out my thoughts before I could catch myself. "Daddy, why do I have to work on Labor Day to help pay Omar's stupid tuition? That's not fair. I put in enough time at the restaurant."

"Angela, get that twisted look off your face. Your behind is on cracker-thin ice with me," Daddy roared. "You've got some nerve sneaking out last night, then telling me what you don't want to do."

Mama held up her hand to cut off all further outbursts. "Everybody finish up. Things don't feel right to me, and it's time for some prayer. We've got enough time to catch the nine o'clock service, and I'm on the program to sing today." Mama looked around the table as if she dared anybody to say they didn't want to go.

CHAPTER 9

After Mama made her announcement, the table got real quiet again. My father, brothers and I didn't want to go to church, but nobody had the guts to say it first. My mother was normally a pushover, but on certain topics like church, she could be Queen Bossy Bee. Back when she was the president of the Women's Group, she used to have all of us kids heavily involved in church activities, from singing in the youth choir to visiting the sick and shut-in at nursing homes. She even dragged Daddy along for a lot of events. But when her schedule got too hectic between the restaurant and her job, she slacked off. It took just too much energy to persuade everybody to help out.

Finally, my father spoke up. "Cora, I'm going to take a pass on church this morning. I'm due for a session at the gym." He threw her a smile, hoping to soften her mood.

My mother said nothing, just narrowed her eyes and took a sip of her coffee.

"Honey, come on, now. Let's not argue about this," Daddy reasoned.

"We're not. We're all going to church, and you can hit the gym after that," my mother said with a plastic smile on her face and a determined look in her eyes. My father just let out

a sigh and didn't say anything more. Once Mama got a
certain tone in her voice, Daddy knew it would be pointless
to argue.

An hour later, we had all piled into the Cappuccino Blast.
Everybody was in a grouchy mood. I was especially mad
because Mama made me wear a stupid plaid dress that she'd
gotten from her employers. The Levys' daughter had a
clothing shop, and when stuff went out of style she sometimes gave us the outdated merchandise. Mama made me
keep the extra clothes as backup for church since she hated
a lot of my stuff.

When she pulled out the boring gray and blue plaid dress
that I had tucked way in the back of my closet, I started
getting loud. Then she gave me the choice of wearing the
dress or losing my hairstyle. No way was I going to let her
see that lump, so I shut up and slipped on the dress, which
seemed better suited for a seven-year-old.

When we finally arrived at Calvary Olive Baptist Church,
we were lucky to find a parking spot since we were running
late. Our church was very popular and did a lot for the community, like offering senior-citizen housing, job counseling
and placement, and self-help courses. We had to weave in
and out the church lot, which was filled with shiny Benzes,
BMWs and chromed-out Caddies, in search of a space for
the longest time. When we finally parked, our van looked
like a junkyard reject compared to all those pretty cars and
trucks in the lot, and I knew that bothered my father. He
claimed that a lot of people at that church were hypocrites
and liked to toss their wealth in your face.

"Everybody come on, we're running behind schedule,"
my mother announced as my father turned off the van. We
all reluctantly got out.

Our church was built like a triangle. The front of the
building consisted mostly of huge panels of glass that
allowed the brilliant sunlight to stream in. The rest of the

structure was white stone and stained glass windows. We walked up the concrete walkway, the smell of the freshly cut lawn still wafting in the air. Church members volunteered to keep the hedges clipped and flowers watered, and the grounds looked really neat and well taken care of. We made our way up the concrete steps and opened the heavy oak door of the church. A short, plump female usher with a determined look in her eyes stepped into view and held up a white-gloved hand, blocking us from walking down the aisle. Since there was someone speaking at the podium, we would have to wait to be seated until the usher gave us the all-clear signal to be seated. A few people turned to look back at us and smiled because we'd gotten caught by one of the ushers who took her job way too seriously.

The person at the podium seemed to yammer on forever, and I was getting mad about having to stand around in my stupid plaid dress. I wanted to sit and hide. Noticing that the last pew on the right-hand side of the church was half empty, I tried to sneak around the usher and ease myself into that pew. The usher suddenly grabbed my arm and pulled me back. There were beads of sweat rolling down the sides of her face, and from the wild look in her eyes, I wouldn't have put it past her to put me in a headlock if I really tried to resist.

"Angela, behave yourself," Daddy whispered, and reached out to put a hand on my shoulder. I could hear both Quick Digits and Omar snickering behind me.

Finally the person at the podium finished speaking, and the usher held up one finger in front of her and put her other arm behind her back. She started walking down the aisle, which was the signal that we could join the rest of the congregation.

"Angela, go sit with your father and brothers. I need to go down to the basement to change," Mama instructed, then headed toward the stairs. Resisting the urge to follow her, I instead walked straight down the aisle. I squeezed into the pew to sit next to Daddy, and Omar and Quick Digits sat on his other side.

"It's so good to see everybody in church this morning," Reverend Edwards boomed from the pulpit. "God has indeed blessed us just by getting us up and bringing us to this holy place. Hallelujah!"

"Hallelujah! Hallelujah!" A woman sitting directly in front of me stood up and started shouting and moaning as if she were about to pass out. All eyes turned to look at her, which frustrated me because I was sitting directly behind her and didn't need to get caught in her cross fire. So I slid down a few inches in my seat.

"Angela, don't slouch," my father admonished quietly. "Your mother and I taught you better than that." A hint of a smile touched the corners of his mouth as he viewed the hymnbook.

"Thank you for that testament," Reverend Edwards said to the shouting woman, who calmed down, then took her seat. "It's always good to praise the Lord. And now it's time to hear a selection from the women's choir." Reverend Edwards took a seat in the huge red-fabric-covered chair off to the side in the pulpit.

"Yes, he knows just how much we can bear." I heard my mother's soprano voice leading the choir as they came stepping down the aisle to the beat. The choir was wearing new gold-and-emerald-green robes, which added a majestic touch to their look. Everybody in the pews seemed to perk up, moved by Mama's hitting high notes like an opera singer. Nobody in the choir could touch her range, and she could tear up a gospel song. Her voice was so amazing she could make it sound like a musical instrument. She really could have been a professional gospel singer, but when people brought that up, she waved them away. She would state that she just liked to sing for the Lord in church.

Glimpsing over at Daddy, I wanted to laugh at the sappy, crooked smile on his face. Daddy loved bragging about Mama's singing. "Can't nobody touch Cora when it comes to singing." That was Daddy's favorite saying during family reunions or when we had a lot of people over at a party. He was so proud of her. Daddy would also brag about her being a business owner and a strong mother. Glancing back and forth between them, I realized how lucky I was to have them. Those thoughts made me feel less anxious and gave me the patience to get through the three-hour service.

The choir worked their way up to the chairs situated in the section behind the pulpit. Members of the church were standing up, screaming out Amens. Daddy stood, his face beaming with pride, looking handsome decked out in his Stacy Adams cream-colored linen suit with a tobacco-and-white-striped tie and Stacy Adams tobacco-brown leather shoes. His mood swing was amazing to me. Just a few minutes ago he was upset with Mama, but now he was so happy. He could flip his feelings like that, then flip them right back. It had to be one of those grown-folks things.

After the choir finished singing, Reverend Edwards walked back up to the podium. Reverend Edwards was a little taller than Daddy but much bigger around the waist. If you saw him sideways, his body resembled the letter D. "Church, the women's group will be hosting the fellowship hour. They put together a surprise picnic lunch for us in the park across the street. I want to give a special thanks to Miss Thomas, the president of the women's group, for spearheading this event."

My eyes widened when I heard that and suddenly remembered. Miss Thomas was Marcy's aunt, and she always dragged Marcy to church with her. Sitting up straighter in my seat, I looked around, trying to spot Marcy. If I didn't find her and hit her off with the details of my alibi, she might blow my cover about being at her house last night. The possibility of Mama's hearing about my misdeeds on church grounds made my blood run cold. She loved this place and never wanted anyone to know anything negative about the family. She was truly all about image, and I didn't want the truth to unfold here. I tapped my father's arm. "Daddy, I don't want to go to that picnic after church."

"Your mother will probably want you to be there because she's in the women's group, but I'm not going. I've got to get to the gym," Daddy answered.

My heart sank and I desperately tried to pull together a plan that would let me skip out on the picnic, but I couldn't think of any solid excuses. After what seemed like forever, the church service was over. I really wanted to find Marcy, but with everybody rushing the doors at the same time, there was no way that was going to happen. Following my brothers and father down the aisle, we all shook Reverend Edwards's hand on the way out, then walked down the cement steps to wait for my mother.

Panicked, I pulled my cell phone from my purse and scrolled for Marcy's number in the directory. After Marcy's voice mail clicked on I said, "Marcy, give me a call when you get my message. I know it's Sunday and you're at church, but I need to tell you something real important."

My father overheard the message. "Why are you wasting your minutes? Marcy should be around here somewhere." I didn't bother to answer, just shrugged and closed my phone.

By the time my mother came out of the church about ten minutes later, Daddy was restless and back in the same grouchy mood he'd been in when we first got there. It was good to see her because I was tired of looking at Daddy staring at his watch and bunching his face into a frown. Quick Digits and Omar were waiting a few feet away from us, standing in the shade of a tree, talking really quietly, as if they didn't want anybody to hear what they were saying.

Studying them, I wondered if Quick Digits had revealed to Omar what happened at the party last night. As I chewed on my thumbnail, I threw glances at them, finally deciding that my secret was still safe, because Omar would have immediately said something stupid if he'd known.

Mama was beaming as she walked up to us. "That was a nice service today, wasn't it? Come on. Let's go across the street for the fellowship hour."

"Cora, I've got to spend some time with the punching bag," Daddy said with determination. He shoved his hands in his pants pockets. By the firm set of his jaw, he knew my mother was going to throw a fit.

"Mama, can I leave with Daddy?" I asked as Quick Digits and Omar walked over to our group.

"Hey, I gotta bounce, too. I need to hit the studio," Quick Digits interjected before she could reply.

"Mama, I'll stay with you for the picnic. You can always count on me to be by your side," Omar stated in a voice that was laced with phoniness.

"You're such a little brownnoser," I blurted out in disgust.

"Angela, hush your mouth," my mother snapped. "We all need to attend the church picnic as a family." Her complexion was flushed and her temper rising in anticipation of the revolution.

"Listen, I've already booked my gym time, and I'm not going to lose that money." Daddy crossed his arms and gave my mother a stern look.

"Yeah, Mom, I can't afford to lose any more of my hard-earned Gs either. I've got to finish some tracks today," Quick Digits added.

Mama looked like she wanted to scream at the top of her lungs, but there were too many people around for her to start arguing and acting like a fool. Our attendance at church events meant so much to her. They gave her status and bragging rights in the eyes of the female members. She pushed her lips together in a hard line in an attempt to calm herself down, then effortlessly formed a smile as Miss Thomas walked by.

"Cora Jenkins, you and your family are joining us in the park, right?" Miss Thomas peered over her glasses. It was hard for me to like Marcy's aunt. She was a tiny, bossy woman with dull gray skin, and her eyes were that weird shade of blue you sometimes saw on old people. From her sensible black rubber-soled shoes to her stiff, straight stance, that old woman reminded me of a retired military sergeant. She seemed capable of whipping a whole platoon into shape.

Daddy cut Mama off just as she was about to speak. "We're in discussion about that right now." Daddy didn't like Miss Thomas. He always said that just because she was eighty, he wasn't going to jump out of his shoes every time she said so.

"Uh-hum," Miss Thomas said, and walked away. She knew she had been dismissed.

"Mama, can I leave with Daddy?" My panicky feeling was back after seeing Miss Thomas. My plan was to leave and catch up with Marcy later to give her the scoop.

"No, you can't," Mama insisted. Then she looked at my father. "Why are you trying to embarrass me? You didn't have to answer Miss Thomas for me. That was rude."

"Cora, I'll leave you the van. I'm catching a cab home." Daddy was clearly tired of arguing and had made up his mind. He turned and walked toward the cab stand on the corner of the boulevard.

"Pops, I'm coming with you," Quick Digits said defiantly and ran after my father.

"Quincy Jenkins, you listen to me and get your hard-headed behind back here!" My mother screamed out my brother's birth name to show him she meant business. She raised her right hand, motioning for him to come back, and suddenly seemed to remember where she was when several members of the congregation whipped their heads around in her direction. She hastily pulled her hand down and pretended to smooth the nonexistent wrinkles from her dress while watching Quick Digits and my father fade into two dots in the distance. An air of defeat seemed to settle over her as we watched them disappear. "Come on, you two. Let's get across the street to the park," she stated to Omar and me without making eye contact. She lifted her head high and led the way.

If I'd had the nerve, I would have run full speed behind Quick Digits and my father as if I were in the Olympics, but I was too scared, so I obediently followed my mother across the street. The cotton plaid dress I was wearing suddenly felt like wool. The cheap, itchy fabric was like a hundred ants marching across my back. I patted the hair over my eye, and knew it was starting to lift and lose its straightness. Jeez! Why couldn't this day be over?

As soon as we passed through the gray chain-link fence around Spadonia Park, I spotted several wooden tables covered with red-and-white-checkered tablecloths. On each table, the committee members had placed trays of hot dogs, hamburgers, barbecued chicken, baked beans, potato salad and snacks like Cheez Doodles and cupcakes. There was also an assortment of sodas and bottled waters. I scoped Karen a little distance away, standing by one of the tables with a group of girls from the youth choir, including Marcy. "Mama, I got to catch up with somebody," I declared, and ran off before she could tell me no.

Karen was standing at the head of the table wearing a beautiful crisp white Chanel suit with gold buttons. She was talking and laughing loudly, holding a can of Welch's grape soda in one hand and a mustard-covered hot dog in the other. It was amazing that she hadn't spilled anything on that white suit. Jealously, I wished somebody would drop a big glop of something on her. "Hey, everybody," I said, and gave a wave before I turned to Marcy. "Can you come with me for a minute? I need to speak to you about something…in private." It was important for me to get Marcy away from the table in case Karen decided to bring up the fact that I had been thrown into a dessert table last night. Also, it was humiliating for me to be in her presence because I felt she had some dirt on me.

Marcy was working on two plates piled with hot dogs, hamburgers, baked beans and potato salad, and frowned as she looked at me. "I'm eating. Can't you talk to me here?"

"Some people don't have any manners!" Karen interrupted, then whipped her perfectly pin-straight hair over her shoulder. "How are you gonna just come over here and pull Marcy away from her food?"

"Yeah, at least wait until I'm finished eating," Marcy added, then took a bite from her burger.

It took all my willpower to keep from telling Karen to mind her own business. I was still mad that she had snubbed me at the party, but I didn't want to hear her tease me about losing that fight with Shayla either. Instead, I plopped down on the bench. "All right, finish stuffing your face," I said grumpily. Everybody's attention went back to Karen, who was bragging about what her parents were planning for her birthday in November. No invitation was going to show up in my mailbox, so I ignored the conversation. I started watching some boys who were flying kites in the park. The day was beginning to turn windy, and the boys were having a hard time keeping their kites from getting tangled in the trees.

"What happened to your face?" Latrice Miller, a member of the junior choir, who was sitting directly across from me, tapped my hand and gazed at my forehead. "You got a big bump right here." She pointed to a spot on her own forehead. Grabbing the chunk of my hair that was puffing up, I pulled it back over the lump.

"Oh, that. I bumped my head," I said to quickly cut off further questions. I opened my imitation Prada handbag to quickly search for a hairpin.

Just then Miss Thomas and my mother came walking up to the table. "It's good to see you young people bonding. How is everybody enjoying the fellowship hour?"

"This is very nice," Karen answered, and put a megawatt smile on her face. "The women's group did a great job on all the food." She threw her arms out wide, as if she were onstage. "They did a fabulous job in pulling this off." She was really good at being phony, I thought in disgust as I pinned my bangs in place and wished my mother and Miss Thomas would move on.

My mother glanced over at Marcy, hunched over her plates of food. "So, Marcy, did you and Angela do anything fun yesterday evening?"

Marcy had just finished putting a big spoonful of potato salad in her mouth and looked at my mother with a confused expression.

My heart instantly went into a gallop, and I could see my future disappearing before my eyes. "Yeah, yeah…we had a great time watching some movies," I cut in, hoping Marcy would catch on and not blow my cover. "We were watching some old Jackie Chan movies, remember?" I said as I gave Marcy a slight wink. Marcy was such a Goody Two-shoes I wondered if she would play along with my lie.

"Are we talking about yesterday?" Marcy asked with a completely clueless look on her face. "'Cause it was only me and Latrice at my house."

"Yeah, we were rehearsing some gospel songs," Latrice chimed in. "Marcy and I have to perform solos next week." At that moment, I really hated them both. Were they both that dense that they couldn't catch my hint? I wanted to keep talking, to make them take back what they were saying and act as if they'd been mistaken. But I didn't say anything more because I really didn't think those two—or anybody else—would have my back if I made up another lie.

"Sister Jenkins, you're mistaken. Angela wasn't over yesterday. I might have been at a committee meeting until midnight, but I do know what's going on in my house," Miss Thomas stated loudly.

"Oh," my mother said, realizing what was going on. She wringed her hands together and took a deep breath. "I must have my days mixed up." I was so embarrassed for Mama and me that I wished I could zap myself and disappear.

Marcy's aunt was not fooled by her excuse. A judgmental gleam appeared in her eyes as she looked at me, then directed her gaze at my mother. "Sister Jenkins, I advise you to keep a closer watch on your daughter. Today's children will deceive you and then destroy you if you don't chastise them properly. That's one thing I don't have to worry about with my grandniece, Marcy. She's a well-behaved child." Miss Thomas glared at me again before walking over to another table.

My mother took a deep breath and composed herself, pulling her shoulders back and lifting her chin up. She was not going to put on a shameful face in public, wasn't going to show how deeply she was hurt. "Angela, I'm going to find Omar and then we're going to head home. Meet me by the van," she calmly stated before walking off.

"Marcy, why didn't you cover for me?" I demanded, feeling as if I wanted to cry. "You're supposed to be my friend."

"I am your friend, but you should've said something. How was I supposed to know your mother was gonna grill me like that? I told you not to go to that party," Marcy said, then dropped her eyes to the table.

"Girl, you caught trouble at that party and you're catching more now. You really should have stayed home if you knew you couldn't hang." Karen neatly popped the last of her hot dog into her mouth.

Nobody said anything else as I got up from the bench. They knew I was busted and didn't need to hear more from them. I headed across the street to the church parking lot, feeling as if I were walking toward my doom, all the while wondering what punishment Mama was going to dream up.

CHAPTER 10

"BOY, are you stupid!" Omar spat out the insulting words as we rode back home from church. We were sitting in the last row of our van, as far away from Mama as possible. Not bothering to respond, I just rolled my eyes and looked out the window. "How are you gonna tell Mama a lie like that and then don't tell Marcy to have your back?"

Once we got back in the car, Omar kept insisting to know the story behind Mama's wrath. He was the last person I should have confided in. But he got on my nerves so badly I finally broke down. As I revealed the details, I hoped he would be sympathetic. No such luck. Now he was grilling me like a prosecutor. I was fatigued from all the drama and getting cranky from his questions, so I decided to simply ignore him. Mama had one of her gospel CDs on full blast and didn't say a word to us after we got in the van. Whenever she was really mad, she cranked the gospel music up. Way up. Neither Omar nor I had the nerve to ask her to turn the volume down a little, even though we were sitting near the speakers and had to almost shout to hear each other.

When we finally pulled up in our driveway, Mama turned the music off and turned around to look at us. "Omar, you can leave. Angela, I need to talk to you." Omar hustled out of the van as if somebody had told him a bomb was about to explode.

"Angela, I now know you weren't at Marcy's house last night. Where were you?" I sat silent, thinking the truth would get me in worse trouble and it was best not to snitch on myself. My mother assumed that I was out with Adrian and began to lecture me on how she didn't approve of my best friend's behavior but let me hang around her because she had a good heart, just needed more home training. "That poor child is at such a disadvantage because her mother wants to run with her. I've never seen a grown woman try and wear the same clothes as her daughter. She's foolish."

Her comments made me want to laugh out loud because it was true. But when Mama got to the part that I should know a whole lot better because I had two sensible parents, I became uncomfortable, feeling sure she was about to drop a wicked punishment.

My mother cleared her throat and paused after making her speech. Panic gripped me, and I felt shrouded with gloom.

"You won't be getting any more paychecks or allowances from me or your father until I say so. I'll hold on to your money until I feel you deserve it."

"Mama, no!" I wailed as if I had just gotten hit with a pail of scalding hot water. "That's foul! I'm owed a paycheck right now. If you hold it, I won't be able to do my back-to-school shopping or buy material."

"No, what's foul is you embarrassing me at church today. When you run the streets, anything can happen to you. It's dangerous. Maybe you will learn to obey the rules."

"You've always treated me harder than the boys," I cried.

"I have to be careful with you. You're my only daughter," she reasoned, a serious look in her eyes.

"No," I hollered. "You treat me mean and unfair. Daddy is the only one who looks out for me."

"Your father has indulged you long enough. He agrees with me that once you start disobeying the house rules, all privileges are taken away. That goes for all you kids."

My mouth flew open to protest some more, but she held up her hand to silence me. "We're done. Get out and go to your room." The look on her face matched the hard tone in her voice.

Clamping my lips shut, I flew out of the van and into the house. I purposely stomped on each step as hard as I could, so my feet were vibrating when I reached the attic. No new school clothes. The worst punishment I could have gotten. I wanted to scream at the top of my lungs from the unfairness of it all. Distraught, I walked in circles trying to think of a way out of it. But it was hopeless. Sitting heavily in the chair at my work desk, I put my head on the wooden table and burst into tears. After crying in defeat for a few minutes, I felt myself getting a headache and knew I had to stop. My gaze rested on my machine, and I decided that sewing would calm my nerves.

Forcing myself to get up, I grabbed some tissues from the box on my nightstand and dried my tears. Shuffling over to the wire CD rack that stood next to my nightstand, I selected my Fabolous *From Nothin' To Somethin'* CD and popped it in my stereo. The "Baby Don't Go" single instantly lifted my mood. Kneeling before my big blue plastic bins, I rifled through scraps of fabric before selecting some black lace. A few weeks ago I had spotted a real funky dress in a magazine, so I'd torn out the page and stuck it on my bulletin board. I decided to add my own little spin to the dress. Soon I was sewing and piecing together a black lace bustier on my mannequin and sidekick, Ms. Understood. This had the potential to be one of my back-to-school outfits, but I still needed money to buy some additional material. All I could do was pray Mama would change her mind about my punishment.

"Angela," my mother called.

I walked out of my room and stuck my head over the landing. "Yes, Mama?"

"Go and find out if Omar is packed and ready to leave for school. We're all supposed to get on the road in a little while."

There was no way I wanted to ride for more than an hour in the van with Mama and Omar, and I asked to stay home.

"I need somebody to ride with me for the drive back. Either you or Quick Digits, I don't care who."

"Okay," I replied, and dashed down the stairs, intent on getting Quick Digits to take my place.

Omar's bedroom was down the hallway on the opposite end from Mama and Daddy's. His door was closed, so I knocked on it a few times. "Yo, Omar you finished packing?" He didn't answer me, so I started knocking harder, determined to get a response.

"Enter," Omar called out from the other side of the door.

When I opened the door, I saw Omar spraying starch on a pair of khakis that were on an ironing board. There was a whole pile of wrinkled khakis on the bed, plus a few white shirts. A bunch of neatly pressed ties hung from the back of a chair.

"You've got to iron all that? Why don't you wait until you get to school?"

"No way. In the future, I'm going to be a successful professional, so I've got to set standards and be prepared at all times," Omar stated, as he sprayed a generous amount of startch on the pants.

"Mama doesn't have time to sit around all day and wait for you to iron all this crap." I stared at the clothing on his bed in disgust.

"That's the difference between me and you. I'm a perfectionist—you're a slob."

"Am not. You always go overboard, and that's stupid."

"Going overboard got me a scholarship, and that's way more than your dumb behind ever got," Omar teased.

"What's all that fussing about?" my mother called out. She had suddenly appeared on the second-floor landing.

I walked out of the room and closed the door. "Omar's not going to be ready for a while. He's just now ironing all his clothes when he should've done that days ago."

"Let me come and see what that boy is up to." Mama walked into Omar's room without knocking and closed the door on me. Moments later, she came out with an armful of his wrinkled clothes. Mama had stopped ironing for us a while ago, stating that we all needed to be more self-reliant. Now she was going to do it for him? It was unbelievable how she bent the rules for Omar. No way did I want to take that trip with them. I headed down to the basement to see if I could beg Quick Digits to take my place for the ride.

Quick Digits was jamming some old-school beats in the music room. He had the door wide open, and I peeked in and saw him standing behind the two turntables, headphones on and eyes closed, lost in the melody. The music was sounding good, and Quick started spitting out some fierce rhymes. My head started nodding, and I moved from side to side, dancing to the beat.

Quick Digits must have felt my presence, because he opened his eyes and stopped rhyming. "What are you doing down here spying on me?" His expression was neutral as he lowered the volume.

"Man, I wasn't spying on you. I came down to ask you something, but I got caught up in the music. That sounded really good, what you just did. Is that part of your demo tape?" I hoped my compliment would dissolve whatever bitter feelings he had toward me.

"You've got nerve to come down here and try to butter me up. I'm still mad at you for making me blow that gig."

The solemn expression on Quick's face made me lose a little confidence.

"Oh c'mon, you still mad at me over something that wasn't my fault?" I smiled and hoped my expression came across as sincere.

"Yeah. You and Adrian are bad luck. Now say what you got to say and leave."

"Um, Mama wanted you to ride with her to Omar's school. She'll feel safer with you in the van for the trip back home." I crossed my fingers behind my back, hoping he'd agree.

He didn't say anything for a few minutes, just put his hands on the vinyl records on the turntables and started spinning some old Run DMC. "King of Rock" and "It's Like That" boomed from the speakers, expertly blended by Quick Digits. He must have been in the zone, because his long fingers were flying from record to record, scratching and spinning, never dropping the beat. Then he stopped abruptly and gave me a mean look. "Too bad. You're going to have to play the role of guard dog today. I'm not going. Nobody said jack to me before, so don't try to con me into taking your place."

"Wait…" I tried to scramble a sentence together, but Quick Digits turned the music back up to drown out my words. He picked up the microphone. "Get off my turf," he boomed. I sucked my teeth and left.

An hour later, Mama, Omar and I were in the van on a crowded turnpike, headed to Poughkeepsie. Mama was once again playing gospel music, but at least she didn't have it so loud that we couldn't hear ourselves. Omar and I were playing Ms. Pac-Man on a handheld video game. I had convinced myself to be nice to him for the ride, because I wouldn't see him again until Thanksgiving, and that fact helped me tolerate his presence.

When we finally drove through the gate of Norman James Tisch Preparatory, Omar got real quiet. He dropped his controller and turned to stare out the window, so I shut the game off. It was my first time visiting the campus, and I was amazed by the sprawling green hills and important-looking buildings. Gazing over at Omar, I could tell he was nervous, because he was blinking too many times.

My mother pulled into the visitors' parking lot and we got out. Omar pulled out his one big suitcase, which was on wheels, and lifted the handle. As I looked around, I noticed that there weren't very many brown faces. And I also noticed that all the other kids getting out of their SUVs and expensive cars had more than one suitcase. In fact, they seemed to have lots of electronic stuff, like laptops, CD players and flat-screen plasma televisions.

Suddenly I felt sorry for Omar. Our family might have owned a restaurant, but we were still people who were just scraping by. I felt nervous for him because I knew your game had to be really tight to get in here.

"These kids better watch out for the O man. You're smarter than a lot of them," I said. My comment erased the worried look from Omar's face, and he started grinning, which made me happy.

"Where's building A?" my mother asked as she scanned the campus.

"Over there." Omar pointed to a gray building, and we headed in that direction.

We arrived at the entrance, and a security guard in a dull brown uniform sitting behind a desk and holding a clipboard stopped us. He was an ancient-looking white man with snow-white hair and steel-blue eyes. He held his arm straight out in front of his body like a school crossing guard before asking for Omar's full name. The security guard scanned the list on his clipboard, slowly flipping the pages and tracing the names with his finger. When he looked up, a sneer appeared on his face as he vigorously shook his head, signaling that Omar was not on the list.

It was humiliating to get turned away by the impolite security guard, who was probably clocking minimum wage. Mama knew Omar's tuition was short. She should have straightened that out before we arrived. For a moment, she seemed unsure what to do and remained rooted to her spot. When other parents and their children started crowding the entryway, I tugged on her sleeve, anxious to get out of there.

"Let's go to the registrar's office," Omar whispered. I nodded my approval. It was starting to get too embarrassing to stay.

After spending a few minutes in the registrar's office, we were directed to see the dean of admissions, Dwight Krauss, whose office was in the same building.

Dean Dwight Krauss seemed pleasant as he ushered us into his sunny office. He looked like a typical professor, dressed in a starched white shirt, tan slacks and brown loafers. There were several important degrees hung in a vertical line on one of the walls and family portraits placed on the various flat surfaces. The black leather couch, matching leather chairs and zebra rug on the floor gave the room a relaxed feel. And the pictures of waterfalls were a nice touch. As I eased onto the couch, I found myself appreciating the buttery soft texture. I loved leather furniture, and when I got older and got my own apartment, I intended to invest in some expensive pieces.

"Ah yes, I'm familiar with Omar." Dean Krauss leaned back in the plush leather chair and stroked his thick mustache as he reviewed the file. "That's a brilliant young man you have there."

"Thank you. My husband and I strive to teach our children the importance of education. My daughter, she's not as smart as Omar, but she tries," my mother said, smiling nervously.

I looked at Mama in shock. *Why'd she have to say that?* I thought. She knew I might not have been as smart as

Omar, but one day I was going to hold my own as a famous fashion designer. Deciding not to protest her comments, I stared straight ahead. She was nervous at the thought of her precious Omar getting tossed out of his precious prep school, so I'd give her a pass. This time.

Dean Krauss put the file down and looked directly at my mother. "Mrs. Jenkins, I'm sorry for your situation, but the school is tightening its financial belt. It is our policy for all tuition to be paid in full before the student arrives. The administration tries to be very accommodating. We even offer online payments." He clasped his hands together on his desk and gave my mother a sympathetic look.

My mother pleaded her case about Omar being a scholarship student and her understanding that his tuition was covered one hundred percent. Dean Krauss patiently explained that it was totally covered for the first year only. After that, only 75 percent was covered. When Mama mumbled that she hadn't realized the facts, the dean raised his eyebrows as if he'd heard that one before.

Omar and I were starting to get real embarrassed as Mama pleaded for a one-week extension. Damn, she should have had Omar's tuition payments on point. That should have been her number one priority, above the restaurant, above everything, since her world revolved around him. The bitterness was taking me over, and I needed to get out of that office. I glanced at Omar, and even though he sat there expressionless, his cheeks had a ruddy glow and his back was ramrod straight, and I knew he was humilated to the core.

"As I said, usually we require that tuition be paid in full at the start of the semester, but I'll make the exception and give you a one-week extension," Dean Krauss said. "We love having dedicated students like your son attending our institution, and we don't want to put a damper on his enthusiasm because of a misunderstanding."

"Thank you so much," Mama said, looking as if she wanted to jump out of the chair and do a hallelujah shout.

The dean gave us a handwritten note, and after we straightened things out with the registrar's office, we headed back to the dorm. Omar had a look of total devastation on his face, and I actually felt sorry for him.

"We're going to room 1C," Mama said smugly to the guard as she handed him the paper. He glanced at the note and nodded for us go in.

When we entered the dorm room, there were two other boys already there—an Asian kid typing on a computer and a blond kid wearing a blue blazer, striped shirt and khakis. Dang, didn't these brainy kids ever chill? I thought. They already had their beds made and their bookcases stacked with textbooks and novels. Their work areas were already personalized and set up with their computers, photos, papers and other stuff.

The blond boy walked up to us. "Hi. I'm Christopher O'Malley." There was so much maturity in his voice and stance that I pegged him as a future world leader.

"Well, aren't you a little gentleman," Mama cooed. "I'm Mrs. Jenkins, and this is Angela and Omar."

"That's Jai on the computer," Christopher said, and pointed. The Asian kid turned around to wave.

"Well, you guys can leave now," Omar stated with a touch of impatience.

"Do you want us to help you unpack?" I asked.

"No. You can just go," he insisted.

"Omar, don't be silly. Let us help you." Mama seemed oblivious to Omar's somber mood. She began to unlock the suitcase.

"No, I don't need any help. I can do this by myself," Omar said sharply, and put his hand over the lock to halt Mama's actions.

"Well, okay." Mama bent down to kiss him on the cheek, but he did a quick sidestep and she ended up kissing the air.

My mind was reeling from his snub and I knew it was time to go. "Okay, Omar. We'll catch up with you later." I grabbed Mama by the wrist, but she wouldn't move. Bravely, I put my hand on her upper arm to give her a pull. Mama needed to get out of there before she erupted. Her body was tense, and I was afraid she would uncoil at any moment and lash out like an angry cobra. She finally followed me out the door, and I waved goodbye as we left the room.

Mama didn't utter a word as we walked back to the van. She was hot with anger, and I couldn't really blame her. Her favorite son had just dissed her. For once the shine was off the mighty and brilliant Omar. At that moment, I should have felt like doing cartwheels, but right then, I didn't feel like celebrating the moment I had been anticipating for so long.

CHAPTER 11

Finally my big day arrived—the official first day of high school. I was kind of nervous because I didn't feel on top of my game after I got dressed. As I left my house, I braced myself for the wisecracks that surely would be coming my way. Everybody knew me as a person who always wore new stuff that got attention. Due to my money crisis, I had to settle on wearing my black-and-white-horizontal-striped stockings, a black balloon skirt and a pink blouse with a row of black ruffles down the front, accessorized with pink and black flowers in my hair—last year's stuff I hoped nobody would notice, but I knew somebody would, since a lot of the kids who had attended my junior high were going to Kressler. Even though I had good intentions for finishing the outfit still hanging on my mannequin, due to my lack of funds and my inability to get the materials I needed, my mental vibe was completely gone.

Adrian had sent me a text message earlier that she would meet me on the corner down the block from my house. She looked really cute in her skintight dark blue Baby Phat jeans and white Bebe T-shirt. "Shoot, you wasn't lying when you said your moms wasn't getting you nothing new," Adrian said, giving a critical eye to my outfit.

"Money's been real short in my house," I said defensively.

"Money is tight in my house, too, but my mom or my men always step up and come through with some fresh gear for me." Adrian kicked up her foot to show a high-heeled, open-toed black suede shoe. "You like?"

"Ooh, those are so cute. Did your mom buy you those?"

"Heck no. Kenny did."

"No! You lying!" I said, feeling a little jealous of the pretty shoes and a little peeved that Adrian would be seeing Kenny like that. It just didn't seem right. Growing up around Kenny made him seem more like a brother to us than anything.

Not wanting to express how I really felt, I quickly changed the subject and we began our ten-minute walk to school. As we drew closer to Kressler High School, I looked at the massive gray brick building and felt grateful that I was going to get a chance to take courses here. It felt great to be on the right path for my fashion career, and I was determined to make a name for myself at the school. My positive feelings were short-lived when I started observing all the kids around me. It seemed to me that everybody had on fresh new sneakers and clothes, and I instantly felt insecure.

"Guess who?" a girl's voice sang out as a pair of hands covered my eyes.

"I don't know," I said, grabbing the person's hands and swinging myself around.

"It's me, Tia." Tia looked so cute in her green gypsy skirt, green tank top and matching olive-green ballet flats. Her hair was supershiny and straight and smelled like Pantene hair spray. Self-consciously I patted my massive Afro with pink and black flower decorations and wondered if I should have blown my hair out as well.

The school bell suddenly rang. All the ninth graders were supposed to report to the auditorium at eight forty-five to hear a message from the principal. The freshmen students had received a letter about a week ago welcoming them to the new school. We were told we would get our class schedules after this meeting. Adrian, Tia and I walked to the auditorium and sat together in a half-empty row a little distance from the stage. A few seconds later, Marcy appeared and took the empty seat next to me.

"Hey, y'all," she said. Marcy was in a cheerful mood and smelled like maple syrup, and I could bet she had enjoyed that breakfast.

"Hey, Marcy," we all replied.

A silver-haired woman in a navy suit walked from behind the heavy red curtains on the stage and stood behind the podium. A hush fell over the auditorium as she tapped the microphone to test the volume. She smiled and introduced herself as Ms. Steinberg, the principal of Kressler High School, and began informing us that the freshman year would be a challenging one because we would be meeting new people, taking more advanced classes and starting to mature into the leaders of tomorrow.

Straining my neck, I scanned the auditorium for a glimpse of JaRoli, but he was nowhere to be found. Then I noticed Karen and a couple of her girls coming down the aisle, their high heels loudly clicking against the linoleum floor. I got so caught up in staring them down that I had to tear my eyes away just to concentrate on what Ms. Steinberg was saying.

"As all of you know, Kressler is a school that has a creative arts emphasis, especially on the fashion side. We encourage our students to be independent, strong-minded leaders who boldly go after their dreams, and we start nurturing this way of thinking starting with our freshmen. Traditionally, the ninth-grade class puts on a holiday fashion show. We'd love everyone to participate in one form or another, but unfortunately there are only a limited number of slots, so we will hold elections for the key position of director. The director will set the theme of the show and choose a team, and is basically responsible for the whole organizational flow. The road to capturing the role happens this way: first, there will be a primary, and the top two vote getters will face off in a general election about two weeks later. The winner of that second election gets the spot. So if you want the director position, you will have to campaign. We're going to begin early this year, so check out the posters that list all the details in the hallway right outside the auditorium doors. Oh, be sure to pick up your schedules first at one of the tables also on the other side of the doors. Okay, everyone, enjoy your first day."

My ears were pricked up. I was ready to bolt into the hallway for my schedule, then check out the posters before heading to class. Impatiently, I waited for Marcy to maneuver herself out of her chair and into the aisle. I practically race-walked through the throngs of students in my quest to view the materials.

There were several tables set up outside the auditorium with alphabetized manila folders taped to the front of them. You had to locate your last name by the folder on the table, then pick up the card that detailed your schedule. I got mine easily enough, then pushed my way through the crowd to read the holiday fashion show announcement.

"Why is Angela Jenkins reading that poster? She's got some nerve wanting to run the fashion show when she ain't even wearing nothing new for the first day of school!" Candace yelled. "She recycled that mess from last year."

"Everybody knows that's the rule. You got to at least wear a new outfit for the first day of school," a heavyset girl I didn't know screamed.

"Chick's family owns a restaurant and she looks real broke on day one," Inez added, then started laughing and giving high fives to her group.

Karen stepped next to me to read the poster for a

moment. She was wearing a demin jacket with a rabbit fur collar, a denim skirt and sleek knee-high, pointed-toe, patent leather boots. Turning to me, she stated, "Nobody wants a weirdo in charge of the fashion show. I'm going to run for director, and I'm going to win." She had her hair pulled into a high ponytail, and it occurred to me that she looked like a model. Standing next to her, I felt unglamorous and dowdy. "Everybody knows I can rock a wardrobe better than you. Tell you what, you vote for me and I'll make you my assistant."

For a moment, I almost considered her offer: if I lost, at least I'd still be involved in the fashion show. Then my competitive spirit kicked in and I decided not to give up without a fight. "No way. How about you vote for me and I'll let you be my stage manager?"

Karen looked repulsed from my response. "You will never win against me. Nobody is going to vote for somebody with bag-lady style. You're wasting your time trying to win against me," she warned, then snapped her fingers in the air and pranced toward her crew.

Tia, Adrian and Marcy walked over to me at the bulletin board. From the shocked looks on their faces, I knew they'd overheard Karen's insulting comments. They offered me some words of comfort and told me not to pay any attention to her.

"So, are any of us in the same classes?" Tia asked. We compared schedules and noticed that we all had the same gym and lunch period. Marcy was also in my homeroom.

"Oh man," Adrian whined. "Look at this—gym is split in two parts, dancing one week and swimming the next."

Because I was worried about my hair getting messed up in the pool, I wasn't too happy about that class.

We all went our separate ways since none of us had the same first-period class. On my way to English, I felt a little depressed. Just because I had bold fashion flair, why did it seem everybody was against me, always clocking me and memorizing my outfits? *They're all jealous, that's why*. This year I vowed to show them all. My talent was going to help me capture the director title.

The first day went real quickly, and at two forty-five everybody had to report back to their homeroom for final attendance before the three o'clock dismissal bell rang. After Ms. Oliver took attendance, I pulled out my crossword puzzle book when a tall girl with an orange Afro entered the room. Squinting in disbelief, I refused to believe my eyes. No way could that be who I thought it was.

Ms. Oliver asked to see her schedule and announced that she was definitely in our homeroom. As Shayla went to take a seat at an empty desk in the front row, I shrank a few inches in my seat in an attempt to hide from her view.

Marcy was sitting next to me and passed me a hastily scribbled note that read she wished Shayla was not in our homeroom. I glanced at Marcy, and she looked completely terrified.

The bell rang, and everybody raced for the door. Marcy and I waited for the other kids to leave first, including Shayla. We made it down the three flights of stairs and were racing past the first-floor lockers when I felt somebody shove me in my back. I stumbled, and fell, dropping my bags. Quickly turning around, I looked up from the floor into Shayla's mean, twisted-up face.

Marcy let out a shriek as if she had been hit with hot oil, then said, "Please don't beat up my friend. She's a really nice person."

"Mind your business and I won't kick your ass, too," Shayla spat, and Marcy shrank back from her glare. Scrambling to my feet, I was upset that this was the second time Shayla had thrown me to the floor. Blinded by anger, I gave her a hard shove back, which sent her flying into the gray metal lockers. Damn, this was high school! I wanted to make my mark as a fashionista, not constantly fight like a first grader.

At that moment, Mr. Keith, my history teacher, pushed through the crowd of kids who had gathered to see the fight. "Ladies, what's going on?" he demanded.

"She pushed me," I howled, expecting Shayla to hit me again.

"You pushed me first," Shayla lied.

Mr. Keith seemed to be a real mellow teacher. He wore badges and pins that read *No War* and *Love the Earth*. He instructed me and Marcy to go out the front exit and Shayla to depart by the side door. He also threatened us with a suspension if he heard about any more fights between us. Picking up my book bag and purse, I raced with Marcy out of the building. I hoped what Mr. Keith said had rubbed off on Shayla, because I was getting tired of brawling with her.

CHAPTER 12

The end of the second week of school came fast, which I was glad about. The first official meeting about the fashion show was supposed to happen after the last class on Friday in room 101. Earlier I had asked Tia, Adrian and Marcy to come to the meeting with me so I could represent as if I had a crew, but nobody could make it. Instead, they promised to meet at my house Saturday around noon.

"This will be the most exciting show yet." Ms. Yetti was standing in front of the classroom greeting everyone coming in. She had been a fashion designer in both Paris and Milan years ago, and now she taught sewing. She was really nice, and I was so glad to be in her intermediate class. And I was thrilled that she was coordinating the fashion show.

I think she had a lot of power at the school, because the room where she taught was painted in geometric squares of chocolate-brown and aqua-blue, while the other classrooms were boring beige or white. There were also huge black-and-white photos of popular fashion models and European landmarks like the Effiel Tower and the Leaning Tower of Pisa hanging around the room. During class, Ms. Yetti always stated that it was important for a room to give you inspiration. That it got your creative juices flowing. One of her other mantras was to avoid aligning yourself with negative people and things, because it definitely blocked your process.

There were thirteen bright orange chairs placed in a semicircle in front of Ms. Yetti's desk, and I took one on the far end. Karen, Inez and Candace walked in together, giggling loudly. It figured. Karen never went anywhere without those two trailing behind her. About ten other girls walked in after them, and I recognized two of them from history class.

"All you losers can leave right now. Karen's gonna win this competiton," Candace said in my direction as they all took seats on the opposite end. A contented smirk appeared on Karen's face, as if someone really had announced her the winner. Enviously I noted that she was wearing a khaki shorts set from the Gucci collection. As I stared in Karen's direction, it occurred to me that Candace and Inez were more like ass kissers than friends to her. There was no way Karen could really appreciate them as friends. She was such a snob, I bet she thought of them more as her entourage.

"You wish. This competition is mine," I said with bravado.

"My offer is still good until Monday," Karen stated smugly. She pulled a steno notepad and several copies of *Vogue, Allure* and *InStyle* out of her bag and set them on her lap. She kept throwing sneaky glances my way throughout the session and I knew that heifer was trying to intimidate me.

Ms. Yetti stood in front of the classroom and cleared her throat. She was a petite woman with frizzy, shoulder-length red hair and pinched features and had a tendency to express herself with wild, sweeping gestures. "In the spirit of a healthy contest, we are going to run this like a real campaign," she told us. "I'm going to require all competitors to come up with a theme for the show and create an outfit for the presentation."

"The other kids are going to have to vote us in, right?" I asked.

"Yeah, but you still gonna lose," Candace sang out. She irritated me so much that I gave her the finger when Ms. Yetti turned her head in the other direction.

Ms. Yetti picked a piece of paper up off her desk and read from it. She was excited to fill the group in on the details. My mind tuned out a bit because I knew the prize list by heart. The winner of the director slot would get to spend some quality time at a famous designer's showroom. That was great because we would get an up-close-and-personal look at exactly how they put their fabulous collections together. The experience would be like striking gold for me. The winner would also receive a bunch of other prizes: a laptop, a video game system, a sewing machine, patterns and an assortment of CDs and DVDs.

When Ms. Yetti finished, I blurted out, "What do I need to do to win?" Then I rolled my eyes at Karen's group.

"Campaign!" Ms. Yetti said, getting even more excited. "I want to see posters created, and we'll have a primary day when everyone gets to give a speech and state why they're the best candidate. After the votes are cast, the two contestants who get the most votes will go head-to-head. The winner of that election will be director of the holiday fashion show."

I knew my crew could come up with some creative posters. Marcy's strength was drawing, and Tia could create some catchy slogans for the campaign.

Karen and her friends started grinning, mumbling among themselves as if they were coming up with a blow-your-mind multimedia strategy. Their tight unit really made me doubt myself. My girls should have shown up. How was I going to win when she had such a strong crew?

Ms. Yetti talked for about twenty minutes more; then the meeting was over. Hopping up, I quickly gathered my things so I could be the first to leave. Anxiety and doubt were clouding my mind, and I didn't want to hear any more junk from Karen's butt-kissing friends. I left the building, and as I was walking through the courtyard, I noticed somebody standing off to the side by the garbage cans, slightly hidden by an oak tree. That struck me as suspicious, and my radar instantly went on alert.

"Yo, stuck-up chick," a girl called.

Turning in the direction of the voice, I couldn't believe it. It was that madwoman, Shayla. How could my luck be so bad? She was dressed in a black tank top, black jeans and black sneakers. Her hair was cornrowed to the back and gathered in a ponytail at the nape of her neck. It was odd, but she reminded me of someone who was dressed to commit a crime. "You again?" I was annoyed and tired of her. She slowly approached me and stood so close that I noticed her green eyes had specks of yellow in them. "What do you want? I ain't got time to waste with you." Shifting the strap of my schoolbag higher on my shoulder, I braced myself for a sucker punch. I really wasn't prepared to fight, because I was wearing a dress and my gold T-strap high heels. Even though I bought the shoes a year ago, I had never worn them, and the bottoms were slippery because I hadn't gotten a chance to put taps on the soles. But no way was I going to run from her. Huh, I'd kick the shoes off if I had to defend myself.

"Ain't got time to waste on you either." Shayla paused a moment, then asked, "You got any cigarettes?"

"No, I don't smoke," I replied, and braced myself for some crap to jump off.

"You pretty tough for a bourgeois chick," Shayla stated.

Her comment surprised me because it felt like a compliment. I said nothing and wondered what she really wanted.

"You was at that fashion show meeting, wasn't you?" I gave her a puzzled look. "I saw your name on the sign-up sheet posted outside the room." Shayla paused for a second, then continued, "Most of them broads in that competition are wack. Why you gonna do all that campaigning?"

"'Cause I have to in order to win. What's it to you?"

"I can help you win real easy." Shayla and I heard laughter and noticed Karen and her girls walking toward us. "Come on, let's go. I don't want them to hear what I got to say."

I hesitated for a moment. This was crazy. She was the enemy—I wondered if she had somebody waiting to jump out of the bushes to pounce on me and tell me it was all a joke. Shayla was doing a 360-degree personality change on me, and I didn't know what her game plan was. After a few seconds, curiosity got the best of me, so I decided to follow.

"How can you help me win? You want to be on my campaign team?" I asked.

"Hell no. I ain't doing that stuff. I'd only work in the background—help you get some votes—but I'll need some cash."

"What? You bugging." I stopped walking and glared at her.

"Naw, seriously. I got a rep. Everybody knows me. If you pay me a fee, I'll guarantee that you win. Big-time politicians do it all the time." Shayla waved me on to keep pace with her.

I started biting the nail on my thumb. This was all too much to compute and digest. Things didn't seem right—felt really shady. A little voice inside my head told me to take the inside sure track to winning, at any cost. Another voice, the logical one, said to walk away, I didn't have the money.

"All politics is like that, but hey, I'm not twisting your arm. I'll just make the same offer to Karen Frasier's team and she'll leave you in the dust. It really don't matter to me who wins," Shayla stated nonchalently.

"No way. She doesn't need any extra help," I said

abruptly as the image popped into my head of Karen and JaRoli holding hands in victory after she won the director title. Then another image of them onstage and hugging at the holiday fashion show nearly made me choke.

"How much you want?" I asked, feeling the desperation kick in.

"Two hundred dollars."

"Two hundred dollars! That's a lot of money," I shrieked.

"It'll be worth it."

We walked in silence for a few minutes as I thought about her offer. How in the hell would I get two hundred dollars? Mama had me on serious punishment, so I wasn't going to see a paycheck for a while. Quick Digits would be too stingy to lend me the money without grilling me and then having me sign a contract. Omar was out of the question. Adrian was the only person I could approach, but I wanted to keep this particular transaction to myself. I was so busy concentrating on it that I didn't notice we had walked to the projects and were actually standing in front of building D.

A dark-skinned man wearing a dirty blue shirt and oil-streaked overalls called out to Shayla. Even though he looked sleepy, he had a tight grip on a forty-ounce of Olde English. He was leaning on the hood of an old banged-up Buick. A girl who looked about eighteen and a little girl who was about three years old were perched on the hood as well.

"Aiight," Shayla called out to the man. Then she said to me, "Hey, come over here and meet my people." The last thing I wanted to do was meet them. But I didn't want to make her mad if I said no. We walked over to the car and Shayla said, "This here is Big Bruce, Leela and her baby Lil Jo."

I gave them all a wave, then started feeling a little uncertain.

Big Bruce took a swig from the bottle and wiped his mouth with the back of his hand. "You look real familiar," he stated in a gravelly voice.

"That's 'cause her family owns the Island Shack. She works there sometimes," Shayla explained.

"Oh yeah. And your brother's a DJ, right?" Big Bruce asked, pointing one finger at me with the same hand holding the beer.

"Yup. DJ Quick Digits," I confirmed.

"Well, y'all are all right people." Big Bruce smiled at the recognition. He belched loudly and rubbed his stomach. "One day when I have a party, I'm hiring y'all to cater and havin' your brother do the music."

"Oh, please stop lying. You ain't got no money to hire nobody," Shayla snapped, and they started laughing.

"The Island Shack. Damn, y'all make some good food at that joint. That red snapper is whipping!" Leela exclaimed. She seemed out of place with her floral sundress and purple J. Crew flip-flops. Her shoulder-length blond dreadlocks and light brown eyes gave her an exotic look. I wondered if Big Bruce was her boyfriend, but for her sake I hoped he wasn't. They didn't seem like a good match at all.

"Thanks," I said, and started feeling as if maybe I should get home when they all started staring at me. "Well, I'll catch up with you later, Shayla," I said, and walked off.

"Think about what we talked about and get back to me. I'd hate for you to miss out." Shayla watched me as I walked away, her face devoid of emotion.

On my way home it hit me. I couldn't believe it. What had just happened felt straight-up crazy, and I became a little light-headed. Shayla wanted to be on my team. Maybe she really liked the way I stood up to her. Deep down I was torn between feeling laugh-out-loud happy and totally apprehensive. How could she change like that? Did she really respect me? Maybe. I pushed the negative thoughts aside and tried to concentrate on the positive. Having a gangsta girl in my corner would give me power and street cred, and I probably could win that contest easily. That would really be awesome, I thought, and began to whistle as I headed home.

CHAPTER 13

"**Your** daddy is going to knock somebody out tonight," my father yelled as he came down the stairs and entered the living room still dressed in the navy sweatsuit with the Spark's Gym logo emblazoned across the chest and down the sides of the legs. He had walked into the house an hour ago but was still in a jubilant mood after a sparring session with his trainer.

Daddy was bouncing on his toes and gliding his feet back and forth across our freshly waxed floors as he threw air punches around the living room. As he danced between the living and dining room, throwing uppercuts and left hooks, I hoped he wouldn't accidentally break anything. Our black teakwood dining room table was always formally set and ready for company. The white Lenox china plates trimmed in gold, Farberware flatware and Mikasa water goblets and wineglasses sat on a peach tablecloth. The dishes were cleaned every two weeks, whether we used them or not.

I was sitting on our gold-and-brown, floral-patterned couch with my legs crossed and feet tucked under me, watching an interesting program about global warming on the National Geographic Channel. Mama used to get on me when I sat like that, but our couch was now worn and ready for replacement, so she didn't nag anymore.

The program ended, and I focused my attention on my father. "Daddy, I want you to wear this tonight for good luck." I gave him a bulky brown paper bag that I had hidden behind the couch pillows.

"What's this?" he asked as he reached for the bag.

When I'd gotten home from school, my thoughts were completely scattered. My mind was still swirling from Shayla's offer, and working with material always helped me focus. When I searched my fabric bins and came across the red-and-black satin material, I knew it would make a perfect boxing robe for my father. I'd even stitched *Mannie "Lightning Fists" Jenkins* in gold letters across the back.

My father pulled the garment out of the bag and smiled broadly as he viewed it. "This is beautiful, honey!" he exclaimed. He slipped on the robe and strutted around the room. I was proud to see that it was a good fit. "Oh boy, my baby girl has got talent!" He kissed me on my cheek, then went back to shadow boxing.

"Mannie, you better cut out all that prancing around before you catch a cramp." My mother laughed as she leaned against the archway that separated our living and dining rooms. She was wearing an olive-green apron tied around her waist and had a towel hanging off that. Even though she worked two jobs, she liked to cook the Friday supper. The aroma drifting through the house smelled like lemon pepper chicken.

Quick Digits came up from the basement with Marlon, who was holding a stack of albums under his arm. They walked into the living room, and my eyes locked on Marlon. He was so cute, and second on my list of guys I would have loved to have as a boyfriend, JaRoli being number one. He had hung with my brother for years, helping him out on the music production end, but just lately I had developed a serious crush on him.

Marlon greeted my parents and smiled in my direction.

And I felt like melting. Marlon had skin the color of banana pudding. He wore his hair in a low cut with waves and had dark eyes and a shy smile. Even though he was seventeen years old, he was so quiet and laid-back that I felt I could connect with him.

"Hey, Marlon," Daddy said. "I haven't seen you around the house in a while."

"Me and the Quick man been busy getting ready for some real important gigs."

"Yeah, we've been jamming in the basement all day. So, what's going on?" Quick Digits asked.

"Don't you remember? Daddy has a fight tonight," I answered.

"Boy, don't tell me you forgot the most important evening of the year. Lightning Fists is making a comeback," Daddy shouted and threw a playful punch at Quick Digits.

Quick put his hands up and took a step back. "That's right, you got a boxing match at the gym on Queens Boulevard. Sorry, but my mind is wrapped around this mega-music gig Marlon and I have got lined up at Randall's Island—the Super Music Fest."

"Oh yeah? Who's gonna be there?" I asked.

"A lot of top acts in hip-hop, reggae and R&B. And I'm going to be the opening act before the big willies hit the stage."

"Can you get extra tickets? I wanna go." I clasped my hands together and placed them under my chin. Quick Digits had finally lost his anger toward me, and we were back on good terms.

"I'll see, but I can't make any promises," Quick Digits stated.

"Excuse me, but I've got to go and meet up with some people. Good luck with your fight tonight, Mr. Jenkins. I'll let myself out." Marlon headed to the door.

"How much are they paying you?" my father asked, and crossed his arms.

"Straight-up professional rates. This is no hot dog and corn bread show. I'll be eligible for the union after this gig." Quick Digits grinned proudly.

"That's terrific, Quick!" my mother cried and gave him a hug and kiss. "You are so lucky. Now let's hope this luck will spread around for your father's fight."

"Luck! I don't need any luck. This fight is mine. I have to tell you all, I feel so good about this. It's about time for me to stop hiding my talent and get some prize money for this family," Daddy stated confidently.

"Won't it bother you to get hit?" I asked.

Quick Digits gave me a light shove. "What kind of question is that to ask somebody who's about to get in the ring? What are you trying to do? Mess with his head?"

"Sorry," I said.

My father laughed. "There's nothing to be sorry about. My intention is to not get hit."

My mother started teasing my father, and he ran after her and grabbed her by the waist, and they both fell on the couch howling and laughing. It was good to see them so happy; it seemed as if the bad vibes we were catching lately were finally disappearing.

"Okay, Dad, don't tire yourself out before you get in the ring," Quick Digits called.

Daddy got up from the couch and pulled Mama up. "I've got to get ready. The boxers have to check in at least an hour before the audience arrives."

"We'll all be there for you," Mama said, looking from me to Quick Digits.

"You know, I don't get to say this enough, but I love you all," Daddy solemnly stated.

"We love you, too," Mama, Quick Digits and I said.

"Sometimes a man gets lucky by having a supportive

family. You all mean so much to me, and no matter what happens tonight, just know I'm going to give it my best," Daddy vowed.

"Honey, we don't doubt you," my mother reassured him with a loving look on her face.

"That I know. But other folks have been on my back about me getting in the ring. People have been laughing at me, especially at work. They tell me I'm too old and slow, but sometimes you can't be afraid to do things that shake folks up, no matter how much criticism you get." Daddy went upstairs to get his stuff to leave, and the three of us just looked at each other for a few minutes, wondering what that big speech was all about.

My cell phone started vibrating and I pulled it off the waistband of my jeans. Adrian's number popped up on my screen, and I walked into the kitchen to talk. After I told her about my father's boxing match, she wanted to come and bring Kenny with her. I wanted to say no, come alone. There was no way I could sit there and watch them kiss and hug all evening. Maybe the clutches of jealousy had gotten to me, or perhaps they struck me as a weird couple. Dang, I didn't know. We'd known Kenny for too long, been through too much. Finally, I relented and agreed to meet them at the gym.

Sometimes Adrian was just too much of a flirt, I thought as I pulled an outfit out of my closet. Tonight I would wear my wedge-heeled silver shoes, silver-and-pink-striped stockings, a black skirt with pink polka dots, a white shirt with a black-and-white-striped tie, and a black sweater with tiny hand-sewn silver roses on it.

At seven forty-five my family and I were walking through the doors of the Harvey Gym. It was a musty-smelling place that wasn't quite what I'd pictured. The walls were mustard-yellow, and the boxing ring was surrounded on all sides by bleachers instead of chairs. I'd thought it would be much bigger, but I guess I had watched too many boxing matches on HBO.

"Hi, Angela," someone called.

Turning around, I was stunned to see JaRoli dressed in a royal-blue basketball jersey with matching royal-blue basketball shorts that hung past his knees. His shoulder-length braids were wet, as if he had just gotten out of the shower.

"JaRoli!" I screamed, then threw my hand to my mouth. Felt a bit embarrassed because I had said his name so loud. The last time I had seen him was the Rochdale party, and I hoped he wouldn't bring that up.

"What you are doing here?" he asked.

"I was going to ask you the same thing." I could feel myself blushing.

"My dad has me taking boxing classes here. I just finished my session, and my coach told me to stick around to catch tonight's fight."

"Oh, that's so funny, 'cause my father is fighting tonight."

"Word!" JaRoli said as his thick black brows flew up. "Wow, that's funny."

"Yeah, I know."

"Angela, come on and take your seat," my mother called out. She was sitting in the second row with Quick Digits beside her.

"Come on, sit with me," I told JaRoli, and he followed me. I introduced him to my mother and brother and hoped nobody would say anything stupid.

"So how you like Kressler so far?"

"It's okay. I tried out for the soccer and football teams and made it."

"Like you didn't think you would? You were all up in the sports section of the newspapers last year."

"Yeah, but it's a different game now. Those juniors and seniors play rough. During football practice I got tackled so hard, I got the wind knocked out of me."

The serious look on his face made me smile. "I guess everybody is playing rough because they're all trying to catch the eyes of the college recruiters."

"Uh-huh, but just because you can cripple a brother don't make you NFL material. If anything, it may make you eligible for the penitentiary." We both started laughing, and I really began to feel comfortable talking to him.

"Let me ask you a question. Have you heard about the Super Music Fest at Randall's Island?"

"Yeah. I wish I could go, but they're sold out, and right now only the radio stations have the tickets."

"My brother is going to be the opening act," I stated happily.

"Word? That is awesome. You going?" He grinned, and deep dimples appeared in his cheeks.

"Yeah." I figured now was as good a time as any to find out about Karen. "Let me ask you...hmm...are you and Karen a couple?" I studied his face for a reaction.

"Naw, we're just friends. We're just tight because I've known her for a long time," JaRoli said, never dropping his gaze.

"Well, in that case, if you want to come, I can try and get you a ticket," I said, hoping that Quick Digits could get both of us in.

"Are you kidding? If you get me a ticket, I'm there." JaRoli smiled wide, and I noticed that he had the most perfect teeth. He grabbed my hand and kissed it. "Thanks so much." He was still holding my hand when Adrian arrived with Kenny.

Adrian came into the gym holding a can of grape soda and a bag of hot cheese popcorn. She raised her eyebrows when she saw JaRoli let go of my hand. Kenny was walking behind her eating a bag of cashews. I introduced everybody, and Adrian and Kenny took a seat next to JaRoli after saying hello to my mother and brother.

"Whoa, is that your uncle Clyde wearing a fur up in this place?" Adrian howled, and pointed to the other side of the ring.

I was horrified to see that it was. Uncle Clyde noticed us at that moment and came walking over with some female who was wearing an identical silver fox jacket. It was a warm evening and I couldn't understand why they were wearing fur.

"Hello, people." Uncle Clyde smiled. "Cora, how are you?"

"Clyde, what are you doing wearing that ridiculous fur coat?" Mama gave him and the woman by his side a disapproving look.

"I'm a grown man with money in my pocket. That means I can wear whatever I damn well please." Uncle Clyde gave Mama the evil eye, then put his arm around the woman. "Hell, I got so much money people come to borrow money from me."

He was hinting at the fact that he'd loaned Mama and Daddy the money for Omar's tuition. He'd even made both of them sign a promissory note, which had infuriated Daddy. "I don't care if Cora is my sister. I've watched too many episodes of *The People's Court* to let this much money leave my hand without some paperwork," Uncle Clyde had stated as they sat at the kitchen table.

Uncle Clyde proudly introduced us to his new girlfriend, Regina. Regina was tiny. She looked as if she was barely five feet tall. She was wearing heavy foundation, gold eye shadow, blue contacts and a curly weave that reached her waist. The neckline of her short dress was low cut, and her jiggling boobs were on the verge of spilling out. I loved my uncle, but he had some messed-up taste in women.

The announcer entered the ring and told everyone to take their seats, and Uncle Clyde and Regina settled themselves in the row ahead of us. He announced my father's name; then the theme music from *Rocky* came on and my dad came strutting into the gym wearing the hooded robe I had made. My family and friends all stood and started chanting, "Lightning Fists! Lightning Fists!" Daddy's trainer parted the ropes for him, and I noticed there was a sheen of perspiration on my father's face and upper body. I had read somewhere that that was a good thing because it meant he was really warmed up.

Once Daddy's music died down, Rockman Altronda's name was announced. The song "Mama Said Knock You Out" by LL Cool J came on, and the crowd went wild.

"What is this, the battle of the theme songs?" I said aloud. "Daddy, knock him out!"

Rockman came marching down the aisle, and my mouth dropped open. He was huge, with muscles on top of muscles, and looked as if he could put a whipping on Mike Tyson.

"Are you sure your father's ready to take him on?" JaRoli asked. "That guy is a major contender in the heavyweight division."

"That man looks like a monster," Adrian said in awe.

"My daddy's gonna take care of him," I said confidently, although I felt scared.

After the ring announcer gave the instructions, Daddy and Rockman each went to their corner; then the bell rang and they came out slugging.

"Yo, this ain't no fight, this is a war," Adrian said gleefully, and begin clapping her hands in appreciation.

"I can't watch," I cried, and covered my eyes after Rockman gave my father a fierce right hook. When the bell rang, I uncovered them and was horrified to see my father with a bloody nose.

"Mannie, don't let that washed-out boxer beat your ass. Fight!" Uncle Clyde called out.

Daddy went to his corner, where his cut man worked on his bruised nose while his trainer shouted tips at him. The bell rang again, signaling the start of the second round. Daddy jumped off his stool and came out like a warrior, but everybody could clearly see he was losing.

The fight was becoming too brutal for me to watch. A feeling of resentment rose up inside me. What was Daddy trying to prove? He was past his prime and not in top condition to take on Rockman. What if he really got hurt and ended up brain damaged? Those thoughts caused me to shudder. My breathing become irregular, and I prayed I wouldn't start hyperventilating.

JaRoli looked at me with concerned eyes. "Are you okay?"

"They need to stop the fight," I whined.

JaRoli grabbed my hand to comfort me. "The ref's not going to stop the fight unless somebody quits." He paused before adding, "Or they get too injured to defend themselves."

Just then a roar buzzed through the crowd as Rockman landed a solid punch to Daddy's chin, sending him to the mat. The referee started giving my father a ten count, but he struggled to his feet. He grabbed the rope to help himself up.

"Mannie, I did not come to this fight to see you get your ass kicked. Get up and show him what you got!" Uncle Clyde yelled. "You need to win that prize money, because you owe me."

"He doesn't need to hear that right now," Mama screamed at Uncle Clyde.

"If not now, then when?" Uncle Clyde threw Mama a defiant look.

"You can quit, Daddy. We still love you," I called out.

Quick Digits leaned over and told me, "Mama said Daddy can't quit until after round three or he won't get paid."

"Man, that's kind of bogus," JaRoli said. "I hope that's not true."

"Screw that. Your father should throw in the towel. He can't beat that man," Adrian said, grabbing a handful of popcorn out the bag. Her gaze was fixed on the ring as she ate the popped kernels one by one.

"If he had a bat he could," Kenny quipped and choked back a laugh. If JaRoli hadn't been holding my hand, I would have smacked Kenny on the back of the neck. There was nothing funny about my father getting a beatdown.

Daddy managed to stay on his feet for the third round and put on a good show. In the fourth round, it seemed my father's confidence was renewed, and he was on a mission to prove something. He went after Rockman as if he was a chump. The crowd started cheering my father on, and I was really happy for him. If he could just manage to get in a lucky shot and knock Rockman out, he could probably win the match.

As these happy thoughts were going through my head, Rockman caught my father on the chin with a right hook that was so powerful it knocked him through the ropes and onto the judges' table.

CHAPTER 14

The day after my father's losing fight, Adrian, Tia and Marcy came over to help with my campaign. Ever since I'd gotten busted by Mama in the park, Marcy and I had become a little closer. She had called a few times, apologizing for blowing my cover. It was easy to forgive her because it wasn't really her fault. The three of them arrived together, catching a ride in Tia's father's Cadillac Escalade, which he had tricked out with chrome dubs and a chest-pounding stereo system. Everybody was pitching in and bringing something we could use to create the posters. Tia was responsible for the cardboard we would use to write the slogans on. Marcy arrived with a stash of colored Sharpies in different sizes, and Adrian was in charge of glitter and glue to give the posters some pizzazz.

"So how's your father doing?" Adrian asked as she walked through my bedroom door and took a seat on the guest twin bed.

"He's in pain, but he'll be okay."

"What happened to him?" Marcy inquired as she sat on the floor and handed me a bunch of Sharpies.

"I'm surprised you don't already know, Miss Eyewitness News," I teased, and took the markers.

Marcy grinned. "Yeah, I'm outta the loop. I usually know all the details, but my source has been out of town." My mouth gaped open at her admission, and I wanted to nudge her for details on who this might be, but I knew her lips would stay tight as a vault on that one.

"He had a fight last night and got knocked out the ring," Adrian interjected before I could explain.

"Really?" Tia exclaimed, her eyes wide with the news as she took a seat at my desk. "Here's the poster boards." She propped the stack of oversize paper on the floor against the wall.

I gave everyone a piece of the poster board and a Sharpie, then sat cross-legged on the floor next to Marcy. Taking a deep breath, I paused then painfully revealed the horrible details of the fight. The room was filled with quiet awe when I told them how my father ended up on the judges' table. He came away with a fractured collarbone and a bruised rib, but he was expected to be fine in a few weeks.

Adrian, who was printing Angela's Got Style on a poster, broke the silence with a giggle. "Angela, I just love Uncle Clyde. He's a true gangsta, I swear, but he looked like a straight-up old-school pimp in that fur jacket he had on at the gym." Marcy and Tia began giggling as well.

"Yeah, you can talk, but I bet you wish you had a fur jacket," I snapped as I outlined my name in glue on the cardboard.

"And you know that. I'm going to have to get somebody to hook me up," Adrian said. A smile creeped across her face, and she seemed smug about that fact.

"Who? Kenny?" Marcy called out from the floor.

"Nah. I've got other names in my phone that y'all don't know about," Adrian said.

"Dang, Adrian, you turning into a big-time ho," Tia complained. She nervously pulled her bangs from her face after Adrian shot her an evil glare.

"Oooh, them some fighting words," I howled as I brushed red glitter over the glue.

"I don't know why y'all hating. Do any of you have any men?" Adrian narrowed her hazel eyes and gazed at each of us. She held a purple Sharpie between her fingers and flicked it back and forth. "Angela, what's up with you and JaRoli? Have you snatched him away from Karen yet?"

"Umm, not yet. But they're not really a couple. He told me that he just hangs with her." I wanted to tell them that I'd invited JaRoli to the Super Music Fest but was afraid I might jinx it.

"That may be what he says, but Karen acts like he's her possession," Tia said.

"Angela, you'll never get him if you don't push up on him. Yo' ass is always going to be sitting on the sidelines if you don't listen to me. And you two," Adrian said, focusing on Marcy and Tia, "y'all ain't got nobody and don't look like you'll ever have nobody, so stay out my business."

The tension in the air was thick, so I spoke up. "Okay already, let's change the subject. I'm so glad that you heifers came over today to help me out with this campaign 'cause yesterday I was mad that none of you showed at the first meeting. Karen and her crew were there, and that made me look bad."

"Oh please. Karen and her skanky friends ain't nobody," Adrian grumbled, and turned her attention back to her drawing.

"I don't know why you're mad. I told you I couldn't miss choir practice," Marcy said. She was meticulously writing the words *Vote Angela Jenkins Director Of The Holiday Fashion Show. She'll Bring Attitude And Edge.* Her lettering was so fancy it resembled calligraphy.

"Yeah. Why you bugging? I couldn't miss my salon appointment. My father's girlfriend would have gotten all on my back," Tia said as she hunched over the desk, furiously coloring.

"Dang, what do you do? Go to the salon every week?" I asked. Tia looked up from the desk and glanced over at me, hooking a lock of hair behind her ear.

"As a matter of fact, yeah, I do," Tia said. "My father's girlfriend owns the shop, and she gets mad if I cancel because she does my hair for free."

"Well, you one lucky witch," Adrian snapped. "Most people lucky if they can get their butt in the beauty parlor chair every two weeks."

"So, have you worked on your speech?" Marcy asked me.

"Not yet. I been too busy working on my theme. I'd love to do a fashion show on the Victorian era."

"The Victorian era?" Marcy said, and they all wrinkled up her noses.

I expressed to them that I was thinking ultracool Victorian. When I was browsing the Internet, I came across some back-in-the-day photos of Prince. He looked superhot and sexy with his ruffled shirts and velvet jackets. It gave me the idea to do a rock-and-roll Victorian fashion show.

Scrambling to my feet, I walked to my desk to retrieve my sketch pad out of the drawer. As I flipped the pages, I studied their reactions, but they all seemed a little uncertain. Deciding it would be best to show them an actual outfit, I walked over to Ms. Understood, who was covered up with a sheet. I pulled it off to reveal a man's military-style purple velvet jacket with gold buttons, a red ruffled shirt and purple velvet knickers with gold buttons on the side. They were mildly impressed.

"How are you going to present the outfits? Put them on hangers and hold them when you give a speech?" Tia asked.

"If I can't get people to actually model them, then I'll put them on mannequins."

"You better go with the dummies. Even though your stuff is cool and you're my girl, I ain't getting in front of an auditorium and modeling nothing," Adrian snipped.

"Me neither," both Tia and Marcy chimed in unison.

"Y'all supposed to be my girls. Down for whatever. How y'all gonna do me like that?" The way they brushed me off made me angry.

"Look, we your girls and all, but I ain't modeling for them kids at school. Some of them are stuck on stupid," Adrian said, and went back to writing on her poster paper.

When I confessed that I was thinking of asking JaRoli to wear the outfit, all three of them looked at each other, then burst out laughing as soon as the words left my mouth.

"No real guy would do that for a stupid campaign," Adrian teased.

"Yeah, what if you lose? The guy would have made a fool out of himself for nothing," Marcy added. Their lack of support made me angry and all the more determined to ask him.

"Please don't," Tia pleaded. "Your stuff is just too high fashion, not for the everyday guy."

"Besides, JaRoli's gonna look like a jerk in that costume," Adrian said, and they all burst into giggles.

They made me so mad. "Now, see, y'all are thinking real negative. A real crew who's down for me would never throw doubt my way." After my reprimand had hung in the air for a moment, I blurted out, "Shayla thinks I could win." Everybody got real quiet after I made that admission.

"What?" Marcy cried, her eyes bugging from my announcement.

"Angela, what you talking about?" Adrian said, with an edge to her voice. "I know you're not talking about the same roughneck Shayla from the projects."

"Yeah, I am. She met up with me after the fashion show meeting and said she could help me win," I retorted, not mentioning that Shayla wanted money.

"How is she gonna help you win? By beating everybody up?" Tia snapped. She was normally a sweet, good-natured person who rarely got angry, but now her mood was like rumbling thunderheads right before a huge downpour.

"Angela, you stupid if you think that girl could be your friend. She's bad news," Marcy warned.

"All she likes to do is fight. And in the end she's gonna screw you over," Tia added.

"Whatever," I spat. "I just need a crew who's gonna have my back all the time, and Shayla seems like she'll have my back."

"We do have your back," Adrian said loudly. "We're here working on these posters, right?"

"Yeah, but I bet if I asked Shayla to model an outfit, she would."

"You know, I'm not staying here and listening to this." Tia threw down the marker and pushed aside the poster she was working on. "All I got to say is if you bring Shayla on this campaign, count me out."

"Me too," Marcy said, abandoning her poster. "I'm not down to hang out with thugs."

As they got up to leave, Adrian went to the bathroom. I didn't feel like fessing up and telling them the whole story about Shayla since I wasn't sure yet what I was gonna do, so I kept quiet. When the front door slammed, I went to check on Adrian.

I called to her through the bathroom door. She didn't answer, and I heard the sounds of her throwing up. I banged on the door to try to get her to respond.

After a few seconds, Adrian came through the door looking terrible. She was wiping her face with one of my washcloths. "My stomach's been bothering me lately."

She looked awful to me, real washed-out and pale. "You okay?"

Adrian shrugged and lay down on the spare twin bed with the washcloth over her forehead. I sat down on my bed facing her, not saying anything. After a few minutes, she sat up and swung her legs over the side of the bed. "I gotta get going. Carmen is going out tonight, and I told her I would babysit."

Questions I wanted to ask her, like how she felt about the whole Shayla thing and whether she was angry with me stayed on my tongue. "I'll catch up with you later," I said as Adrian walked out the door.

Sliding farther up on my bed, I pulled my knees to my chest and laid my back against the headboard. Damn, what if Adrian was pregnant? I really hoped she wasn't, because everybody knew your life got much harder once a baby was on the scene. Even though Adrian had money now for gear, all that would have to go toward the baby. During all the years I'd lived at the projects, I noticed that when the pretty, cool girls whose clothes and hairstyles were on point had a child, their lives usually took a turn for the worse. It just became harder for them to compete once they had to tote their little bundle around. Sadly I thought about Adrian and how she wouldn't have time for me if she was pregnant. Our friendship would definitely change.

Suddenly, I felt real lonely, as if everybody had deserted me. It would have been wonderful to have somebody to talk to about the whole Shayla situation. The house was empty because Mama was working an extra shift for the Levys and Daddy was doing overtime desk duty at his job since he couldn't ride the trucks due to his injury. Quick Digits wasn't around because he was hanging out at somebody's studio.

All of a sudden it hit me and I knew what I had to do. I had to take a chance. After all, that was what successful people did—they took chances when everybody else told them they'd never make it. I creeped downstairs to my parents' bedroom. As I pushed open their door, I felt a tidal wave of guilt. Swallowing the huge lump in my throat, I made my way to Mama's side of the bed. Mama kept spare cash in a bronze metal security box under their king-size bed—called it her emergency fund. *It's okay,* I thought. *I'm gonna put the money back.* As I dropped to my knees and pulled the cold metal box from under the bed, I almost lost my nerve. I needed to make sure that I won. Promising myself I would put the money back, I opened the box and pulled out two crisp one-hundred-dollar bills. The box was empty after I took the cash, and it made me feel paranoid. As I stuffed the money in my bra, I knew I had crossed a line and wasn't quite sure I would find my way back.

CHAPTER 15

I didn't see Marcy, Tia or Adrian for several days after we had our little blowup and wondered if they were mad at me. On Tuesday, the homeroom teacher announced that Marcy was out sick, and apparently Adrian hadn't felt like coming to school for the past two days.

Gym on Wednesday was the one class period we all shared, and this was the designated week the girls used the pool. I'd sent Adrian a text message this morning, but she hadn't responded. When none of them showed up for class, I knew that the next period—lunch—would be a lonely one. As I got dressed in my black knee-length denim capris with glued-on armed forces patches, a red T-shirt with big pink hearts splashed across the front, red-and-black-horizontal-striped tights and my Kitson canvas sneakers—which I loved because they were designed with multicolored patches—I decided to skip the cafeteria scene. I combed out my hair into an Afro and figured it would be best to go outside and read my Italian *Vogue*. The European designers were always way ahead of the Americans, and I loved to know what the next trend would be. Checking my Kenneth Cole book bag to make sure the magazine was still safely tucked inside, I headed to the graffiti-scratched wooden bleachers.

There was a bit of a breeze blowing, so I planted myself in a sunny spot. As I flipped through the glossy pages of the magazine, I heard my name called. To my surprise, it was JaRoli.

"Hey, Angela, I like your 'fro," he said, and sat next to me.

"Oh, thanks," I replied, and self-consciously patted my hair. "I just got out the pool."

"You got swimming, too?"

"Yeah, and I hate it. So, what you doing for lunch?" I asked, peeking over his shoulder and wondering if Karen was hovering nearby.

"Me and a couple of my boys are going to hit the basketball court."

"JaRoli, c'mon, man, we ready to start," a guy wearing a Yankees baseball cap yelled out. JaRoli held up his index finger to signal he needed a minute.

"Hey, I wanted to exchange numbers. I meant to ask the night of the boxing match, but it got crazy. How's your dad doing? Is he okay?"

"He bruised his rib and fractured his collarbone but he's gonna be okay."

"Great. Give me your cell so I can store my number." Rifling quickly through my pocketbook, I found my phone and handed it to him. JaRoli skillfully hit a few buttons and was done. He pulled a BlackBerry out of the back pocket of his Guess? jeans. "Now tell me yours."

I rattled off my number, and the image of Karen having a hissy fit if she ever saw my name in his phone made me smile.

"Don't forget me if the Fest tickets come through. I'd love to hang out with you." JaRoli kissed me on the cheek and gave me a beautiful smile before he raced off to the basketball courts. The smell of his Michael Jordan fragrance enveloped me, and I closed my eyes, savoring the scent.

"Wassup, Angela?" Shayla startled me when she plopped down heavily in the spot next to me.

"Where you been? I haven't seen you all week," I said accusingly.

"Around. So are you down with my deal?" Shayla pulled at the strings on the hood of her beige terrycloth jogging suit. Her eyes shone with anticipation.

"Maybe. But how can you guarantee that I'm going to win?" The thought of forming a partnership with Shayla and giving her the money still made me nervous.

Shayla started laughing. "Shoot, you must be the only chick who don't know nothing about my rep. 'Cause I know people who know people who know how to get stuff done."

"What kind of stuff?" I asked.

"Designer pocketbooks, sneakers, jewelry, smokes, whatever. Anything you want or need, I can get."

Twisting my lips to the side, I thought that if she could get her hands on all that kind of stuff, she should be able to nail a victory for me. Then again, most of her family had the criminal connections to get merchandise. Did I really want to get twisted up in her schemes? A feeling of despair came over me as I mulled over my situation. What did I really have to lose? My friends had basically abandoned me. This win would surely put me on top. Nailing the title would give a lot of people an attitude adjustment. I stuck my finger into my sneaker and slid out the folded bills I had been walking around with all week. "Here. Now make sure I win," I said as I handed her the money.

Shayla peeked at the bills before putting them in the pocket of her pants.

Suddenly, a girl called out Shayla's name. Shayla scanned the handball courts and noticed her cousin LaQuita coming through a hole in the metal gate.

What is LaQuita doing here? I thought. *She doesn't go to this school.*

"Hey, LaQuita, T-Bop!" Shayla waved the girls over, and I felt nervous as they headed toward us. The girl called T-Bop wore a cheerful expression on her round face. She was dressed in a tangerine-colored denim skirt and tank top. A FUBU skullcap covered her short braids.

Throughout the years I had heard scary stories about LaQuita terrorizing the projects but had never really been that close to her. It was clear that even though she played the hardcore role, she was going for the sexy look. Her boobs, which looked to be about 36C, were on full display in a low-cut V-neck T-shirt. The tight green jeans she wore could hardly contain her plump behind. LaQuita was only a year older than Shayla and looked a lot like her—in fact, they looked more like sisters than cousins. They both had that same tough expression, those exotic green eyes and similar skin coloring, but LaQuita's complexion was more red and yellow, like a nectarine.

LaQuita threw me an intimidating look as she checked out my ensemble. She scanned me from head to toe and rolled her eyes as if she disapproved. Fortunately, Shayla introduced me as a cool person, and she seemed to loosen up a bit.

"Let's play some handball," T-Bop stated, and glanced toward the far end of the playground. I noticed that all the courts were full and figured lunch period would be over before we got a chance to play. Just as I was about to voice my opinion, they all began walking in the direction of the crowded playing area. Not willing to get left behind, I gathered my stuff and followed them.

There were four girls playing on one of the courts. LaQuita marched into their playing area and stood squarely in front of the cement wall. "Y'all need to bounce."

"Why you stopping our game?" one girl wearing braces protested. "We just have a few points to score before we're done."

"Yeah. You have to wait until we're finished," said a second girl, who wore ponytail puffs.

I really wanted to tell Shayla and LaQuita that we should let the girls finish their game, but from the looks on their faces, they weren't trying to hear anything.

"Get the hell off this court now," Shayla stated in a hard tone.

"You wanna make us?" the girl with the braces said. Obviously, she didn't know about Shayla and LaQuita's reputation.

Shayla walked up to the girl and punched her so hard in the stomach she fell to her knees. "Still wanna fight? Y'all four against us four."

"Wait up. Let's not fight," I interrupted nervously. "We can all work this out." The last thing I needed was to be involved in a brawl. That was not the expectation I had for freshman year.

"That's all right. We're leaving," the second girl said solemnly as she helped her injured friend to her feet. The girl with the braces was hunched over holding her stomach as she left the court. From the pained expression on her face, I could tell she was on the verge of tears.

As they walked off, I turned to Shayla and wanted to scream at her about hitting the girl. All three picked up on my thought and looked at me as if I were an alien. "When people see us coming, they need to step first and ask questions later," Shayla stated viciously.

"If they know what I know," T-Bop added, and started giggling hysterically.

"Everybody knows we rule this area. Sometimes chicks need to learn a lesson," LaQuita snarled.

Shayla pulled a handball out her jacket and announced that I would be her partner. As we played an all-out fierce game, I started thinking about them. Although I hated to admit it, I was a tiny bit impressed that people gave Shayla and her crew respect. That was something I could get used to. Shayla and I got beat by LaQuita and T-Bop by four points. I hoped Shayla wouldn't turn into a sore loser and start cursing up a storm, or worse, turn on me. My stomach suddenly began to gurgle from missing lunch, and I wondered if the cafeteria was still open. The bell rang at that moment, signaling the end of lunch and the start of a new class.

"I'm hungry. Let's go to Sterling Soda Shop," LaQuita commanded.

"I can't go. I gotta get back to class," I said, which made all of them give me a dirty look.

"Girl, you can miss one lousy afternoon of class. I'm treating, and I got Sonny's Benz," LaQuita stated.

"Sonny lent you his Benz?" Shayla said with a questioning expression.

"He ain't have no choice. LaQuita grabbed the keys from him and took off." T-Bop laughed.

"Come on, let's go," LaQuita said.

It took a moment for the idea to grow on me. All the kids raved about Sterling. It was a place that had homemade ice cream sundaes and banana boats, but I never got a chance to go over there because I was always at the Island Shack. Figuring it couldn't hurt to miss classes this once, I picked up my book bag, pocketbook and magazine off the ground. Following them through the hole in the gate, we walked over to a brand-new shiny Mercedes-Benz E350. We all got in and LaQuita turned the car on and blasted Jay-Z's latest album. LaQuita started singing the hooks of the track before hitting the gas and pulling out with a loud screech.

Sterling Soda Shop was on the other side of town, and it only took us about fifteen minutes to get there because LaQuita was breaking all kinds of speed limits. When we walked into the shop, I noticed the customers were mostly mothers with their preschool kids. The restaurant was decorated like a fifties diner. It had pink leather booth seats, a counter you could sit and eat at and all kinds of old-fashioned candy in glass jars displayed behind the counter in front of a huge mirror. Plus, the waitstaff dressed in clothes of that era: cigarette pants, poodle skirts and monogrammed shirts. They also had a jukebox that played classic songs like "Blue Moon" and "Under the Boardwalk."

"What y'all want? I'm treating," LaQuita announced after the waitress seated us at a booth in the back of the store and left us with menus.

"Uh, the banana splits sound good, but it's six bucks. This place is kinda expensive. I might have to borrow money from one of you," I said as I studied the photos of dishes on the menu. I tried to remember exactly how much money I had in my purse.

"Girl, are you deaf? I already told you I'm paying," LaQuita said.

"Don't worry about no bill," Shayla chimed in. "LaQuita's got this."

"I want a double cheeseburger, a chili-cheese hot dog, fries and a milk shake," T-Bop said.

Shayla called T-Bop greedy and started laughing really loud. It became embarrassing when the other customers turned and looked in our direction. I hoped nobody was there who knew me and could rat me out to my mother and father. My parents hated when kids acted rowdy in public and would always get angry if my brothers or I showed off in public. When their conversation started growing even louder, the waitress and counter person threw anxious glances in our direction.

"Hey, guys, let's keep it down before they get mad and ask us to leave," I said nervously.

LaQuita got pissed and banged on the table. "My money is green and nobody is gonna make me leave." I sat quietly, not wanting to say anything more to rile her up. She made me uncomfortable and I hoped one of the other girls would be able to calm her down if she erupted. LaQuita raised her hand and started waving for service. Our waitress appeared with a nervous smile, ready to take our orders.

After our food arrived, our table got mellow, and I could feel the tension leave my shoulders. They all joked around and cracked on each other, but nobody got really loud after that. The sundae was excellent. The vanilla ice cream tasted homemade and fresh and the chocolate syrup was rich and sweet. As I savored the last spoonful, I decided it was the best ice cream I had ever had.

The waitress came back over and dropped off the check. LaQuita picked it up and examined it, then passed it to T-Bop for verification. T-Bop looked at the bill, and the way her eyes looked so puzzled, I wasn't sure if she could add up the numbers. She nodded her approval. It made me wonder if either one of them could read. I had heard that LaQuita had dropped out of high school, and I didn't know T-Bop's story.

LaQuita pulled a wallet out of the back pocket of her shorts. When she unfolded it, I saw a driver's license flash, and it definitely wasn't her picture. There was a chunk of cash in the wallet, and she pulled out two twenty-dollar bills, a ten and a bunch of ones. "I'm ready to pay," she yelled to the waitress, who I was sure would be glad to see us go.

When we got back in the car, I looked at my watch. "Man, it's three o'clock. I gotta get to the Island Shack."

"Why you so nervous about being late? Your family owns the joint," Shayla said.

"I'll drop you off over there, but I ain't running no red lights to do it," LaQuita said. "The last thing I need to be doing is conversating with the po-po."

"Oh, you don't wanna run red lights, but you had this Benz doing eighty a little while ago," T-Bop quipped.

"Shut up." LaQuita laughed.

As we pulled into the Island Shack parking lot, I thanked

LaQuita for the treat. Then I hung my head low as I exited the backseat and prayed that nobody would notice me getting out of a Mercedes-Benz with LaQuita at the wheel.

Armani was on duty when I walked through the glass door. "Angela, do you know if your mother is coming in today?" she asked as I approached her.

"I dunno. She's been working every evening for the Levys."

"Well, Mr. Clyde said the paychecks are going to be late today, and I need to speak with your mother," Armani snapped. She had her hands on her hips and a deep frown on her face.

Alarmed, I said, "Today's not payday. Payday is on Fridays."

"I'm not dumb. I know that. We didn't get paid last Friday or the Friday before that. Mr. Clyde said we would get paid by three o'clock today, and now it's after three-thirty."

Unable to come up with an answer, I shrugged and headed down to the employees' locker room. It made me wonder what was really going on. Mama always gave out checks every week, and if she'd missed two payrolls that wasn't a good sign. I brushed aside the uncomfortable thought that maybe she could use the two hundred dollars I'd taken from her box. Since I wasn't getting paid, hopefully that took some of the heat off the payroll.

When I walked into the changing area, Marcy was standing in front of an open locker and turned around to me, an accusing look in her eyes. "I saw you getting out of that Mercedes-Benz. Angela, you need to stay away from Shayla. She's going to get you in trouble."

"I know how to handle myself," I retorted as I quickly changed into the black T-shirt and black jeans that the wait-staff wore.

"The people Shayla hangs with are street. You're not like them," Marcy said, grabbing my upper arm.

I pulled away. "Marcy, you are such a baby. Sometimes you've got to step up your game in order to be on top."

Throwing my stuff in the locker, I slammed the door and ran upstairs.

Armani was still standing near the register when I walked back upstairs. "I called your mother and told her to get over here." Uncle Clyde came from the back office at that moment. He was wearing a deep purple suit that I had seen before, but had removed the jacket. The vest and tie were a black and purple design, almost like a Pucci print. He had the sleeves of the light purple shirt rolled up, and an unlit cigar was in his mouth.

"You called Cora? Armani, why'd you do that? I told you I would take care of everything," Uncle Clyde stated harshly.

"How am I supposed to survive? On air? I need my money," Armani said, her accent getting thicker and her nostrils flaring as if she were a wild bull ready to stomp somebody into a dust cloud.

The few customers who were eating at the tables paused and directed all their attention at the two of them getting into it. Uncle Clyde immediately noticed the hush that overcame the dining area. He told me to handle the orders and the register while he spoke to Armani in the back room.

I noticed that I was the only one working the floor, but I felt confident about handling everything. The early dinner crowd was slow, and my shift was not going to end until nine o'clock. Usually I didn't work that late, but Mama had asked me to do it as a favor to her.

At about seven-thirty, a tall man and a woman, both wearing dark shades, came walking into the restaurant. Grabbing two menus, I went over to greet them. The smile quickly disappeared off my face when I saw that the girl behind the man was Shayla. I hadn't recognized her because she was wearing a kente cloth scarf that hid her hair.

"Shayla?" I said in surprise.

"What's up? Give us a table. We're hungry," Shayla answered nonchantly.

"Sure. Follow me," I said, and gave them a table in the center of the restaurant.

As they sat down, Shayla said, "We know what we want. Some of those spicy buffalo wings and mozzarella cheese sticks for appetizers, two red snapper dinner specials, two Cokes and a slice of sweet potato pie. And you can bring everything at once," Shayla instructed. Since the pecan-complexioned man she was with never spoke, I figured she was his mouthpiece. I scribbled their orders on my pad and headed to the back.

As I walked to the kitchen area, I noticed that Marcy was sitting behind the register. "Your mother is headed over to straighten some payroll stuff out." She kept her eyes on the register as she spoke, refusing to look at me.

Shortly thereafter, the dinner bell rang, which meant the order I had put in was ready. Sauntering over to the food pick-up, I grabbed the appetizers, two steaming fish dinners and the slice of pie and put them on a platter. Then I grabbed two Cokes out of the fridge and put them on the platter as well.

"Enjoy your dinners," I said as I dropped off the food to Shayla and her friend. He never removed his shades, just gave me a nod.

About twenty minutes later, Mama came walking into the restaurant with an aggravated expression on her face. It seemed like the situation was about to explode, and I hoped she could solve the money problem the restaurant was having without having to dip into the metal box under her bed and discovering that it was empty. Anxiety hit me. I really wanted to replace the money before she knew it was missing but hadn't figured out a way to do that yet. It was time I sought Adrian out for help. I would have begged Marcy, but I knew the answer would be no.

I kept tiptoeing to the back, trying to eavesdrop on Mama and Uncle Clyde's conversation from outside the closed office door. Finally it occurred to me that I should check on the dinner guests. When I stopped by Shayla's table, I saw that the man with the shades was gone. "Is everything okay here?" I asked, wondering if he was in the men's room.

"Oh yeah. That red snapper was off the hizzy. I need to learn to cook like that," Shayla said as she dabbed her mouth with a paper napkin.

Noticing that both plates basically had fish bones and gravy, I said, "Y'all want anything else—another soda, tea or coffee, or you ready for the check?"

"No, nothing else. Umm, about the check. I need a favor. This is kind of embarrassing, but that dude that was just here...we just had an argument over me seeing somebody else on the down low. He got mad and left without leaving me any money to hit this bill off," Shayla said sheepishly.

"You mean to tell me you can't pay?" I asked as a weird feeling ran through my body. It was a mixture of panic and fear. My mother would have a fit if she found out I got stiffed.

"No, I'm short by a few bucks. I'll just owe you, okay?" Shayla asked. She propped her shades on her head and gave me a sincere look.

"What about that money I gave you earlier today? Can't you use that? The bill is only fifty dollars."

"Nah. That money has to pay people for you to win that campaign, remember?" Shayla said loudly.

Grimacing, I waved my hand to shush her. I didn't need her to broadcast my business. Turning my head in both directions, I glanced around, hoping no one had overheard our conversation. "All right. You owe me fifty dollars," I said dejectedly.

"Cool. I won't forget," Shayla said gratefully as she got up from the table and threw me a peace sign. She walked out as if she didn't have a care in the world.

Dragging my feet, I slowly made my way back to the cash register. Marcy held out her hand for the money. "There's a little problem. She didn't have the money," I mumbled, and looked in the direction of the office.

"She just scammed you, didn't she?" Marcy's voice was laced with irritation.

"Nah. She just had an argument with her boyfriend, and he walked out. She'll give me the money later and I'll put it in the register," I said quietly.

"Now I gotta tell Mr. Clyde that you let somebody walk out of here with a free meal. Make that two free meals." Marcy frowned and crossed her arms.

"How was I supposed to know he was going to skip out and not leave her with any cash?" I whined. I hoped what Shayla had told me was true. We now had a partnership, and I really wanted us to be good friends.

Marcy shook her head. "She's playing you. Big-time."

"No, she's not," I said, thinking about the fashion show competition. "I'll get things straight. Just cover for me just this once, okay?"

"Don't ask me to do this anymore," Marcy said angrily. "It's bad enough nobody's getting paid without you giving away free meals."

It'll all work out, I told myself. *Once I win the competition, it'll all be worth it.*

CHAPTER 16

My mood was foul that evening as I put the key in the front door of my house. Armani found out that Shayla and her friend didn't pay, and she yanked me off the floor and sent me to the basement to clean fish. Marcy swore she didn't say anything, but I still couldn't figure out how Armani knew. Bob Marley's song "No Woman No Cry" greeted me as soon as I opened the door, and my spirit lightened.

I wondered if it was my brother or my father jamming in the basement, and I called out a hello as I walked through the kitchen and descended the steps.

The door to the music room was open. Quick Digits had on a pair of headphones, and both of his turntables were spinning. He was bopping his head and scratching records and spinning at a superfast pace. At the same time, he began rapping reggae-style over the music. Quick Digits was in the scratch and mix zone, his head down in concentration, his hands flying over the vinyl records. I took a seat in an old fabric-covered recliner that was positioned off to the side of the turntables to watch him jam.

"Wow, Quick. That was awesome!" I clapped when he finished a five-song session.

My brother started grinning this real big cheesy smile, then picked up a white hand towel off the table and wiped the sweat off his face. "I'm so happy. The moment I've been dreaming about is finally gonna happen."

"What are you talking about? Tell me," I said, feeling just as hyped as he was.

Quick Digits turned the music off and removed the headphones. "Remember the Super Music Fest gig I told you about at Randall's Island? Where I'm set to be the opening act?"

"I would have to be brain-dead to forget. That is the most awesome gig you ever landed. Is that still on for Friday night?"

"Yeah. Marlon called me earlier to tell me that some big-label executives are going to be there. Big-timers. They've already heard my demo tape and like my style, but they want to come out and hear me perform live." Quick Digits wiped his brow again and threw the towel around his neck.

"Really? Which label are they from? Sony? Columbia? Who are you going to sign with?" I asked excitedly.

"That's all confidential information, little sister. I'm not spilling anything to you yet."

My eyes started to mist up with tears of happiness. My brother had strived for years to get a break in the entertainment business. He was so dedicated, going to school and deejaying on the side to tighten his skills. And he didn't even care about hanging out and socializing. His music came first. A knot of guilt formed in my stomach as I flashed back to C-Ice's party. I still felt bad about my part in blowing Quick's opportunity. I threw my palms to my eyes to hold back the threatening tears as I asked Quick to forgive me again.

My brother held up his hand and gave me a halfhearted laugh. "That disastrous night was totally not all your fault. You know, I've learned out of every bad thing something good comes." A look of doubt crossed my face at his remark.

"Okay, I'm putting it out there. I was nervous about playing that party. Stage fright was making my life a complete hell." His face grew serious with his confession.

"You?" I was shocked by my brother's revelation.

"Can you imagine, me, the Quick man, losing his cool? Somebody hipped me to some special classes given by this psychologist." He gave a halfhearted chuckle.

"Wow. So now you don't get stage fright anymore?" I found it amazing that he had been struggling with that problem. No wonder his performances had been so uneven.

"If I feel the attacks come on, I do deep breathing exercises to relax me and keep myself calm. Man, finding out about those classes was one of the best things that ever happened to me."

"I'm really glad for you, too. I really wish you could rub some of that calmness off on Mama. Uncle Clyde has got those books at the restaurant so jacked up that ain't nobody got paid, and Mama's on the warpath."

"Mama's got to learn how to handle her own business. She wants to be a black Martha Stewart, but how's that going to happen if she's too scared to take charge?"

"She can't take charge at the restaurant. Not if she's always taking care of the Levys," I reasoned.

"That's the point. Mama doesn't have to stretch herself thin by working at the Levys. If she just worked at the restaurant, she could handle the books, the menu, everything."

"But we need the money," I insisted.

"The money's there. It's just not being handled right."

"Daddy and her get into it all the time about that."

"Being scared can hold you back. If you rely on other people to make you successful you'll never make it, because they'll always be calling the shots. You've got to believe in yourself if you want to be on top. Personally, I believe it's a mistake for Mama to listen to Uncle Clyde for business advice. Yeah, he's really lucky at gambling and collecting bets, but a restaurant is an entirely different ball game. Our place isn't some exclusive hangout. We shouldn't have a laundry contract, and we shouldn't have all those different uniforms for the employees, and we damn sure shouldn't be making payments on a van when the catering service hasn't gotten off the ground."

"I know. Daddy was fussing with Mama before about how high that monthly bill is."

"That's my point. She's trying too hard to impress, and she's digging herself deeper in the hole."

"Wow, Quick Digits you sound so smart."

"Only because I am," he said, grinning. "I've been thinking about doing something to help out at the restaurant."

"Like what? Volunteer for cleaning fish?" I joked.

Quick Digits explained that he was going to play at the restaurant Saturday after next to help draw a bigger crowd. As he revealed his plan, I knew it would really give our business a boost. My brother could create a nice vibe with some slow jams while folks ate. Then, later in the night, he could get wicked and turn it out. It would be wonderful to have a packed house on a Saturday night. We could definitely create a buzz in the neighborhood with our event.

Quick Digits got quiet for a moment, then rubbed his hand over his stomach. "I'm hungry. Did you eat at the restaurant earlier?"

"No. I was so sick of smelling fish guts that I had to get out of there."

"Come on. Let's grab something to eat. My treat."

Getting up off the recliner, I said, "Mr. Cheapo is treating? I've got to mark this on my calendar." My brother came from behind the turntable and gave me a hug, then bopped me on my head.

"Yeah, and remember I'm going to keep that nickname

even when I become a millionaire, so don't dial my phone begging me for nothing."

"Well, I got a favor to ask you now while you're still broke. Can I get an extra ticket to the Super Music Fest?"

"For who? Adrian?"

"No. My friend JaRoli."

"Never heard you mention him before. Is he your little boyfriend?"

I started blushing. "Naw, it's not like that yet. We're just friends."

"Okay. I'll get both of you tickets as long as y'all don't cause a riot and get me kicked out, because if you do I'm removing your name off my family tree."

"Hmm," I said, and put my chin in my hand. "That's a tempting thought."

Quick Digits grabbed me by the shoulders and shook me. "Just kidding," I yelled, and we laughed and headed up the stairs.

The next morning I woke up with a nervous fluttering in my stomach and a fresh set of pimples on my chin and cheeks. It was primary day, and I was feeling the stress. All the candidates were supposed to give a presentation to the ninth-grade classes at first period in the auditorium. Last night when I came in from dinner with Quick Digits I had written my speech. Now I was mentally kicking myself because I knew I should have worked on it earlier. My mind was not straight, and a full week of practicing in front of the mirror would have done me good. Public speaking was not one of my strengths. But that two hundred dollars I'd given Shayla practically guaranteed that the contest would be mine.

It was do-or-die time, I thought as I gazed at my image in the mirror. At least I felt really good about my outfit. I was wearing an aqua-blue leather miniskirt that was covered in tiny pink and blue rhinestones, a black beaded lace top, pink-and-blue-vertical-striped stockings and pink-and-black-tiger-striped high-heeled shoes. To add maximum pizzazz to my outfit, I loaded on pearl necklaces of all different lengths.

Pulling my cell phone out of my mini aqua-blue purse, I called Adrian's number. Her voice mail clicked on, and I left a message. I reached into my closet and grabbed the two outfits that were wrapped in plastic and my book bag and laid them on my bed. Feeling slightly hungry, I headed downstairs.

When I walked into the kitchen, Mama and Daddy were sitting at the table with plates of grits and egg-whites in front of them. Daddy was in his usual spot reading the *New York Times,* and Mama was reading her Bible. An old gospel song by Aretha Franklin was playing loudly on the living room stereo, and I hoped everything was okay, because loud spiritual music meant Mama was in one of her moods.

"Don't you look pretty today?" Daddy said, placing the newspaper on the table and giving me a smile.

"Thank you, Daddy," I said, and kissed him on the cheek. "Morning, Mama." I leaned over and kissed my mother on the cheek as well.

"You do look gorgeous," Mama agreed as she closed her Bible and placed it on the table. "Anything special happening at your school today?"

"As a matter of fact, yes. Today is primary day. The kids are going to vote for director of the holiday fashion show. The two who get the most votes are going to go head-to-head for the election," I said, as I opened the cabinet door and grabbed a granola bar.

"How could we forget," Daddy said as he slapped himself on the side of his forehead. "You've made hourly announcements every day." He chuckled.

"I could do an awesome job with that show." I crossed

my fingers and kissed them. "Wish me luck that I'll make the final cut."

My mother laughed. "Angela, you're incredibly gifted, and even folks who don't have twenty-twenty vision can see you were blessed with a wonderful talent. In my opinion, you've already won, because you're the best designer that school's probably got."

"Mama, how come you never really said this before?" I said, anticipating a punch line behind her compliment. This was news to me. I unwrapped the granola bar and took a bite, savoring the chewy texture.

"I never wanted to give you too much praise in that area because you tend to get too wrapped up in the fashions and the clothes. You sometimes get so emotional that you go overboard. It's almost like you set your gears to all or nothing, and that's a lot of pressure to put on yourself. You've got to remember there's more than one prize to get out there in life. Never sell yourself short by focusing all your energy on one thing." Mama gave me a serious look.

"Maybe, I guess," I said, feeling a little confused. It was as if she was giving me a message, but I couldn't decipher it without the codebook.

"Learn to appreciate the gifts that you've got, otherwise God can take them from you," Mama added. "You need to remain humble and sincere. Everyone knows you're a smart girl, but don't feel that if you don't win your world is going to crumble." I nodded, hoping that she wouldn't launch into a long-winded sermon. Her words somehow made me feel down. Life had left her a little disappointed, but I wasn't about to let anyone stop me from accomplishing my dream. I had to win, second place just wasn't good enough.

Daddy pulled his wallet out of his back pocket and picked out a twenty-dollar bill. "Here, this is for you. I already know you made that cut," he stated proudly.

"Ooh, Daddy, thanks." He put the money in my hand, and I placed another kiss on his cheek.

"That reminds me, Mannie, I meant to ask if you took any money out of my emergency fund," Mama said, and put down her forkful of egg whites. My heart dropped. She'd found out the money was gone. My intentions were to do a borrow-and-replace, but now it was too late. The bomb had dropped, and the explosion was going to happen in a moment.

"What are you talking about?" My father went back to reading his paper.

"The bronze box that I keep under the bed. Did you touch it?" my mother repeated, her voice rising by a few octaves.

"Why would I do that?" My father shifted his paper to the side to peer at my mother.

"Because the two hundred dollars I had in there is missing. I noticed it was gone last night," she stated bluntly.

"Woman, I didn't touch your money. If I needed anything, you know I would ask." My father folded the newspaper in three parts and laid it down on the table. His peaceful reading time was over.

"Well, it just didn't get legs and walk away. With you being involved in that boxing mess and all the people you owe, I don't know what to think." Mama placed her hands on her hips.

"Mama, maybe you took it out and misplaced it," I said, desperate to get her to change the subject and get off Daddy's case. This was a disaster. I never wanted her to accuse my father of taking the money. Why couldn't she doubt that the money was ever in the box? That had happened to me before—I was sure I had put a necklace on my nightstand but the next day couldn't find it. Turned out I had forgotten that I had placed it in my jewelry box. It was wrong to just accuse somebody like that.

"Angela, I'm not a fool. I didn't take the money out that box. Now, you go on to school and win that contest. I'm just a little confused right now about that money because I was going to use it to pay a bill at the restaurant."

Daddy angrily pushed his chair away from the table and jogged upstairs, never saying a word more. I knew he was hurt. Ever since he'd served that prison bid, Daddy hated to be falsely accused. My mother knew that was his number one sore spot. My soul ached at my being the cause of his distress.

Mama got up from the table and walked to the base of the stairs. "I didn't say you took it. Only asked if you touched it."

This was a horrible start to the morning! My stomach started hurting. I hated the fact that they were arguing and Daddy was getting blamed for something I was responsible for but couldn't confess to. I felt so bad for taking Mama's money. But if I fessed up right then and there I didn't think I could deal with their disappointment. Plus, they probably would have been so mad that they would have made me pull out of the contest. My world was in turmoil and I didn't have an easy solution, so I quietly ran upstairs to get the outfits I would present and then walked out the front door without saying goodbye.

When I got to the corner store, I waited ten minutes for Adrian and even buzzed her cell phone again, but no luck. This was the time I seriously needed to talk with her. Having no choice, I walked to school alone.

After I entered the school with the crowd of students, I headed straight for the auditorium. "Angela, are you prepared for the election?" I turned around and looked into the smiling face of Ms. Yetti, who was coming out of her classroom.

"I guess so. It's now or never." I sighed.

"Are you presenting those items?" Ms. Yetti pointed at

the plastic-covered pieces in my arms. I nodded. "Step inside for a moment. I want to take a quick peek and don't want to ruin the surprise for any of the other students." I followed her into the classroom, and she grabbed the hangers and hung them on the back of the door. The smell of freshly roasted coffee filled her office. An automatic coffeemaker sat off to the side. The aroma was intoxicating, and I was tempted to ask for a cup.

"Beautiful, just beautiful!" Ms. Yetti exclaimed after she lifted the plastic and ran her fingers along the stitching of the outfits. "You've got a great eye for detail and an innovative mind." She re-covered the outfits and handed them to me.

"So, you really think I got a shot at the director title?" I asked nervously. For some reason, I needed to hear some reassurance.

"Angela, win or lose, you've got the talent to go far. Just believe in yourself and don't compromise."

I nodded. "Okay, I won't. Nobody is modeling these for me today. Do you think I could borrow some mannequins from the sewing room?"

"I don't see why not. Those outfits are so beautiful they deserve to be shown properly. Are you headed to the auditorium now?"

"Yes. We're supposed to start giving the speeches in twenty minutes," I stated as I glanced at the big black-and-white clock on the wall. My heart began to race from the impending deadline.

"You hurry along. I'm going to call maintenance and have them deliver two wire-frame mannequins so you can display your outfits." Ms. Yetti walked over to the phone on her desk and began dialing.

"Thank you so much," I said gratefully. Ms. Yetti smiled in response as I left to face the crowd.

After entering the auditorium, I went directly backstage.

There was a total of twelve girls competing for the director title, and everyone was there. All the girls looked on point. Their attire was impressive, and everyone's hair looked as if they had just stepped out of a salon. It was going to be a war. The air was filled with static and nervous energy.

A guy holding a clipboard introduced himself as Ron. He was a senior and gave us the order we would be presenting. My name was fifth on the list. The bell rang to signal the start of class, and a rush of kids filed into the auditorium. I noticed a maintenance man wheeling in the wire-form mannequins. He left them near the heavy red curtains on the left side of the stage. I thanked him and quickly got the outfits on the forms and covered them up with the dark plastic.

Karen was chosen to be the third presenter, but I was too nervous to listen to her or anyone else's speech. Even as the other girls viewed one another's outfits, I chose to stand in my spot and not interact, focusing all my attention instead on my speech, written in green ink on blue-lined notebook paper. As far as I was concerned, none of these girls were my friends. This was a competition, a battle, and victory would be mine.

After what seemed an eternity, it was finally my time to present. I wheeled the two mannequins out and was greeted with silence, which unnerved me. "Greetings, everyone," I said as I walked behind the podium and unfolded the paper, which was getting moist from my sweaty hands. "I'd really like to be director of the holiday fashion show, and I think I could do a fabulous job if you'd just give me a chance."

"No way, not you," a girl yelled. I ignored the comment and kept going.

"Why keep doing the same old thing year after year? I want to do a Throwback to the Victorian Age fashion show set to rock 'n' roll and R&B music."

"That sounds stale. This ain't the eighteen hundreds," another girl called out. "Get off the stage!"

I paused for a moment, gripping the edges of the podium to steady my rattled nerves and rubbery knees. The bright stage lights made it hard to figure out where the insults were coming from. Suddenly I wondered if everyone felt the same way as the rude girls and if I had any chance to win. My confidence started to plunge. For a brief moment I thought about walking off the stage, calling it quits.

"Y'all better give her a chance to speak and stop interrupting or I'm going to start kicking somebody's ass." I trained my eyes on the spot where the familiar voice was coming from and noticed that Shayla was sitting directly in front of me, in the third row. It was great to see her there. I didn't know if my other friends were there or not, but Shayla had my back for sure.

"Okay, students, settle down and let the candidates finish. We want this to be a fair election, and I don't want to hear any more profanity or shouts or that person will be asked to leave," a teacher called out from the side of the stage.

The rest of my speech went well because nobody booed, and I didn't trip and fall on my face when I unveiled the outfits. It actually shocked me to hear some aahs from the audience, so I was really ecstatic when it was over. When the entire presentation was finished, I walked off the stage and looked around for Shayla or one of my friends but couldn't find anybody. The ninth-grade kids were going to vote at lunchtime, and I knew it was going to be hard for me to concentrate on anything else that day. We were told the winners would be announced in our homeroom class.

At the end of the day, in homeroom, my heart was racing, and my hands felt too slippery to hold a pen. Shayla didn't show up for attendance, and for a brief moment I felt panicked that she had taken my money and was playing me for a sucker.

"Class, settle down. I have an announcement to make," Ms. Oliver said. "As you know, an election was held today to see which two candidates will battle it out for the position of director of our holiday fashion show."

My mouth was dry, as if I were sucking on cotton balls, and suddenly I felt as though I was going to faint like one of those corny movie actresses.

"Dang, Angela, you look like you losing color," a kid named James said.

The class broke out in laughter, and Ms. Oliver shushed them. "I'm pleased to announce that the two candidates who received the most votes and will go head-to-head are Karen Frasier and Angela Jenkins."

The light-headed sensation that threatened to overcome me passed. "I made the cut!" I yelled, and jumped out of my chair. The rest of the kids starting laughing at me, and some even yelled out congratulations. "Thanks, y'all!" I exclaimed as the bell rang.

"Congratulations, Angela. Make us all proud," Ms. Oliver said as I walked out the door. She looked so happy for me that I wanted to run back and hug her, but I didn't.

My cell phone vibrated as I walked out of the school: it was a text message from Adrian. "Congratulations. Meet me in front by the Q105 bus stop."

As I was waiting for Adrian, JaRoli walked really close by, startling me. "Hey. Congrats on the big win," he said. He looked so gorgeous with his intricately braided hair and golden-brown eyes that I felt hypnotized and was temporarily speechless. Suddenly he pulled me into a hug and I closed my eyes, lost in the scent of his cologne.

"So, are you excited?" he said, after our brief embrace.

"Yeah, but Karen's my opponent. A lot of people around here like her," I blurted out, and nervously searched his face for a reaction. It was time for him to spill the beans about whose side he was on. If he did, I could know if he liked me enough for girlfriend status.

"So what? You both are strong in your own way." His response somehow disappointed me. I really needed to know where he stood.

"Yeah, I know, but sometimes the other kids just don't get me."

"They got you enough to give you this win, right?"

I didn't bother to respond, because I wasn't sure if they had, or if Shayla had truly influenced the votes. That was something I never wanted him to know. He didn't seem the type who liked to get over. Even though we didn't share any classes, I knew he was a solid B student and he didn't hang with a rowdy crowd. He also had a tight family. His mom was always active in the PTA and his father was a fixture at his games.

"Angela, you're the only girl I know who's not afraid to be you. A lot of your clothes are on the wild side, but just keep doing you. It'll be aiight." JaRoli gave me a light tap on my shoulder.

"I guess. Umm, my brother was able to get that extra ticket for the music fest. You still want to hang out tomorrow?" I asked.

"Yeah. Hit me off on my cell." JaRoli grinned. "I gotta get to football practice."

"Bye," I whispered to his back. He was trying so hard to play the middle ground between me and Karen that I felt like the outsider.

Adrian showed up a few minutes later looking a little better than she had the last time we'd met. Her hair was pulled up in a high ponytail, and I could tell she had touched up her highlights. The bright red Tommy Hilfiger tennis dress she wore looked cute on her. I was delighted to see her. "I called you this morning to walk with me to school."

"Couldn't do it. I overslept and came to school around eleven o'clock," Adrian said evenly.

"Oh. Have you seen Tia and Marcy? I figured we could celebrate with some ice cream sundaes or something."

"Yeah, I've seen them, but they don't want to hang with you. Marcy told Tia that you're still hanging tough with Shayla. They're afraid some stuff is going to jump off."

Adrian looked me straight in the eyes as she delivered the news.

"That's not true. I'm not really hanging with her," I said, feeling disappointed. "So, do you want to grab some ice cream with me?"

"I'm not eating dairy right now. My stomach is still a little upset. I just wanna go home."

"Well, can't we grab some Mickey D's to eat at your house?" I pleaded, hating to think she didn't want to hang with me.

"Okay. I'm not gonna turn down a Big Mac and fries, especially when it's free." Adrian smiled at me and we headed toward McDonald's.

Later, as we sat in Adrian's bedroom eating the last bites of our Big Macs and fries, I felt our friendship was still tight enough for me to ask her some personal questions.

"Adrian, I want to ask you something, but it stays between us two. I noticed you've been sick a lot lately. Are you pregnant?"

Adrian's complexion seemed to turn a little gray when I asked her that. She took a few seconds to answer me. "I don't know. I'm a month late and too chicken to take a pregnancy test." She popped the last of her cheeseburger in her mouth and balled up the wrapper.

"Oh," I said, unable to think of anything reassuring to say.

"You know, I've been praying that I'm not. I'm afraid."

"Maybe you're not. You could just be late." I desperately wanted to offer her some comforting words. Hoped there was some truth in what I said.

"Yeah, maybe. I'm so scared. Carmen's been looking at me funny lately 'cause I've been sick. She's angry about me making the same mistakes she did. All she does is yell at me, telling me I better not be pregnant 'cause if I am she's kicking me out." Adrian tossed the balled-up wrapper into the garbage pail.

"She doesn't mean that," I said. "Your mother loves you and would never do that."

"I dunno," Adrian said, with a worried look clouding her features.

"No, she really does. She just wants you to have it easier than she did. Everybody knows a baby is a big responsibility." As the words slipped through my lips, I was surprised at how mature I sounded.

"Listen, I'm kinda tired. Do you mind leaving so I can get some rest?" A distraught look crossed Adrian's face.

"Sure, no problem," I said, feeling disappointed because it seemed as if she was kicking me out.

After leaving Adrian's building, I felt kind of sad and must have been walking with my head down, because I didn't see Shayla coming toward me. She approached me with a wide smile and congratulated me on the big win. I thanked her for all her help but didn't feel the happiness I should have. My mind was whirling with Adrian's problem, Tia and Marcy's not speaking to me and my mother's being angry with my father.

"You know I got in trouble when you and that guy left without paying at the restaurant yesterday," I said.

"Word? They caught an attitude over that little bill?" Shayla said, and dropped her mouth open in shock.

"Yeah. When are you going to give me the fifty dollars you owe me?" I asked.

My question wiped the smile off Shayla's face in an instant. A stony expression settled on her features. "You should give me that dinner for free. I helped you win."

"I already gave you money for that. That dinner wasn't part of the bargain," I argued.

"Right now, I ain't got it." Shayla patted the back pockets of her Jordache jeans.

"Damn, I thought you were going to give me that money back right away," I said, getting upset.

"Look, I'll make it up to you. You like to sew. How about I get you some material?" she asked.

"You want to pay me back with material?" The offer struck me as crazy.

"Yeah. Where do you get your stuff?"

"Khan's in the Coliseum." I thought for a moment and figured it might not be such a bad deal. "Well, I do need an outfit for the election next week."

"Bet. Let's go there tomorrow after school. I'll meet up with you in homeroom," Shayla said, and smiled.

Happily I agreed and walked off as I started to visualize what my next outfit should look like—shorts set, pantsuit, dress, skirt…I couldn't decide. The new material opened up a world of possibility. Then, like a freight train speeding down the tracks with no brakes, the memory of my parents arguing over the stolen money crashed into my thoughts, depressing me. I prayed what I had done wouldn't cause them to hate each other forever.

CHAPTER 17

Mr. Adams, my history teacher, stood at the blackboard scribbling facts about the Vietnam War. Usually I thought my history class was interesting, but that Friday afternoon I couldn't wait for the school day to be over. Hiding my cell phone behind the stack of books on the desk, I checked for any messages I might have missed. Tonight was Quick Digits' show at Randall's Island, and JaRoli still hadn't given me a call although he knew I had a ticket for him. I punched my directory and scrolled to his name before I closed the phone. Even though I was dying to speak with him, I refused to be the one to call. The feeling I got was that we were friends, and maybe we could be something more, but if I called it would give off a desperation vibe and I didn't want to scare him away. And besides, I was doing him the favor.

The bell finally rang, and Mr. Adams was still talking as the students got up and were gathering their things. He said that we would have a quiz next week on chapter five, and a few of the kids let out a groan when they heard the news.

To my surprise, Shayla was standing by the door when I walked out.

She was dressed in a gray hooded Gap sweatshirt, dark blue jeans and dark blue suede PUMAs. Over her shoulder was a canvas knapsack. "Let's go. I'm ready to get the material from the store," she declared.

"After homeroom is over, right?" I wondered why she was in such a rush.

"Naw, let's skip homeroom. LaQuita's downstairs, and she'll give us a ride to the Avenue."

"If we miss it, they'll count that as an absence. Three absences and they send those cards home to your house. I ain't tryin' to hear no noise from my parents."

"Oh, please. This will be your second absence. That's no biggie," Shayla countered, and grabbed my arm as she walked to the stairway.

"Can't LaQuita wait ten minutes?" I pleaded.

"No. She's out there with the car. She's doing me a favor, and another absence is not going to kill your record, Miss Perfect."

"All right, all right," I grumbled, and followed her out of the building.

LaQuita was sitting on the hood of the Mercedes-Benz, laughing and talking to several thugged-out-looking guys. LaQuita was a straight-up ghetto chick who was good-looking enough to pull guys, but that day it was that E350 that had the guys' attention. She had on a yellow tank top and denim cutoff shorts that showed off her tanned legs but barely covered her butt. It was a warm fall day, but it was not hot enough for that outfit.

I called out a hello to LaQuita, but she either didn't hear me or pretended not to, because she didn't acknowledge me.

"Quita, what you doing, trickin'?" teased Shayla. I was thinking the same thing, that LaQuita looked like a ho sitting on that car.

"Catch up with y'all later. Peace," LaQuita said as she waved goodbye to the guys and got off the hood and into the driver's seat. Shayla got in the passenger seat, and I got in the back.

"So, where we going?" LaQuita asked as she turned the car on and the radio up to blast T.I.'s latest record.

"Coliseum. I got to stop by Khan's and get some material for Angela."

LaQuita pulled the Mercedes out of the parking spot and did a U-turn. I noticed a lot of kids were enviously watching us as we drove off. "What do you need?" LaQuita asked as she looked at me in the rearview mirror.

"Some new material so I can make a slamming outfit. I've got to give a speech again in the auditorium for the general election." LaQuita looked puzzed. "Didn't Shayla tell you? I'm running for director of the holiday fashion show, so I've got to make a good impression in the next go-round."

"Oh, that. You trying to go Hollywood," LaQuita said.

"Yeah, if Angela wins, she gets to hang out with a celebrity designer," Shayla stated.

"Well, hook a sista up with some Dolce and Gabbana or some Christian Dior," LaQuita laughed.

"Yeah, and some Burberry and Fendi." Shayla howled and gave LaQuita a high five in the front seat.

As I leaned against the soft red leather seats, I thought that this was all nuts. I tapped Shayla on the shoulder to ask her if she could really afford the purchase, but she waved me off. So I just relaxed in my seat again, enjoying the new-car fragrance and the head-nodding beats. The traffic on the Avenue was congested as we snaked our way to the Coliseum. Since LaQuita couldn't find an available meter, she parked illegally by a hydrant on the side of the building.

"Don't take too long in the store," LaQuita called as Shayla and I stepped out of the car. "This Benz pulls a lot of attention, especially with me behind the wheel."

"Oh, just roll the tinted windows up," Shayla shouted nastily as she pulled open the heavy glass door of the Coliseum and walked in with me trailing her.

"Now, don't act like we're together when we get in the store," Shayla said as we rode the escalator downstairs.

"Why?" I asked, confused, my hand twisting the single strand of pearls around my neck.

"Because you go in there all the time and I'm sure they give you discounts. I know I can pull a better one than you, but they won't give it to me if they know we're friends," Shayla explained slowly, enunciating her words as if she were speaking to a five-year-old.

"That makes no sense."

"Duh, the owner doesn't want you to feel stupid. I'm a businesswoman who knows how to negotiate, so any discount I get is going to be more than yours."

That puzzled me and I struggled to understand how she could be so sure of that fact. I had been a customer of Khan's for at least three years; there was no way she would get a better discount. Nothing she said made any sense. Her explanation felt like a put-down, and I felt an attitude coming on.

We got off the escalator and I stopped a few feet from the entrance of Khan's store. "You know what...forget the explanation," I said, feeling myself getting heated. "What's the brilliant plan? How will I let you know what fabrics I like?"

Shayla stated that she would keep her eye on me. We decided our code would be for me to touch the fabric between my fingers and then hold it up for a five-count. Since the store policy allowed customers to cut the fabric themselves, she would take three yards of everything I signaled. Still I was doubtful that she could afford the luxury fabrics that I intended to signal to her that I wanted.

After taking a few steps in the direction of the store, I hesitated. When I turned around to face Shayla, she had a look of annoyance on her face. As if she anticipated my lack of confidence about the scheme, she held her hand up to stop my questions. "Chick, I've got this under control. Stop blabbering," Shayla said, rolling her eyes. "One more thing. Once you've picked out three fabrics that you want, leave the store and stand in front of the main entrance."

I shrugged, entered the store and grabbed a basket, as if I were about to do some shopping.

It was enjoyable to stroll casually among the fabric rolls. The store had apparently gotten new merchandise in since the last time I'd visited. It was delightful to caress the yards of silk, suede and cotton-blend materials. The new jewel-tone colors of orange, purple and gold were especially eye-catching. Shayla was starting to get impatient, because I heard her loudly clear her throat several times. Mr. Khan was in the back because he had a delivery shipment, so his wife and son were on the floor. After all the money I had dropped on purchases at the store, Mrs. Khan still had not warmed up to me. She was a short woman who rarely smiled and looked at everybody suspiciously.

Finally I ran across some material that I felt would grab some attention. There was some cream-colored fabric that had white feathers stitched in rows across it. It reminded me of this ostrich skirt I'd seen an actress wear to an awards show. I also picked out a midnight-blue faux suede and a multicolor knit fabric that would make a good dress. As I exited the store, I glanced at Shayla, and she rolled her eyes and gave me a dirty look. *Yeah, I guess I did linger too long,* I thought smugly. *So what?*

While I was waiting outside, my cell phone rang and JaRoli's name popped up. Forcing myself to pause, I held back from answering until the second ring. I didn't want him to think I was desperate. Flipping open the phone, I said, "Hello."

"Angela, how you doing? It's JaRoli."

"Hey, man, where you been hiding out all day? You still going out with me tonight?" The words escaped my lips, and I mentally kicked myself for jumping to that subject first.

"Heck yeah. I'm calling to see how we going to get up there."

"My brother's friend Marlon is driving us. I'm sure he won't mind picking you up."

"That would really help me out, because taking the subway and bus to Randall's Island is no joke."

"What's your address?" I asked.

"I'm not far from the Avenue. I live in the big white house on the corner of Quinton Road and Leslie Avenue."

"Yeah, I know where that is. So, we'll pick you up at seven."

"Thanks so much for hooking me up. You my girl. Thanks for looking out for a brotha."

Smiling, I clicked off. *He said I'm his girl. I'm his girl*, I thought. Then I started to wonder if he really meant it or if it was a term he just loosely threw around. All I could hope for was that he meant it in the romantic sense. My blissful mood was cut short when I heard loud voices and turned to see Shayla running through the heavy glass doors, the canvas knapsack bouncing over her shoulder.

"They're trying to arrest me! Get to the car!" Shayla screamed to me, and like a dummy, I followed her and ran toward the car.

LaQuita was standing outside by the driver's door smoking a cigarette as we bolted to the car. She observed us with narrowed eyes and blew a puff of smoke out of the corner of her mouth before tossing the cigarette in the street.

Shayla screamed for LaQuita to get in the car. LaQuita stayed calm as she got back in the driver's seat and retrieved the keys from the console. I noticed that LaQuita was totally unfazed, as if this were an everyday situation for her.

"What the hell happened in there?" I screamed at Shayla.

We heard a bang on the hood and turned to see a Latino man wearing a navy shirt with a silver shield. He was the security guard from the Coliseum. He yelled for us to get out of the car and banged a few more times on the hood. The banging echoed loudly in my ears and frazzled my nerves. Visions of all of us in handcuffs getting hauled off to jail made me breathe in shallow gulps.

"Yo, get the hell offa my ride or I'ma hurt you!" LaQuita yelled. Her threats didn't stop the security guard, who started yanking at the passenger-side door handle.

"Police, police! Somebody get the police!" the security guard yelled, still banging on the hood.

People on the sidewalk stopped in their tracks with amused looks on their faces. "Damn, he takes his job real serious," a skinny dark-skinned teenage guy said. "'Cause if I had that job I wouldn't chase nobody outside of the building." Chuckles erupted in the crowd as they watched the dramatic scene unfold.

It seemed like an eternity before LaQuita was able to find the right key among the many hanging on her Coach key ring. She inserted it in the ignition, hit the gas and pulled away from the curb, with the security guard hanging on to the door handle.

There was a roar of disbelief from the crowd as they watched the security guard run alongside the Benz. I yelled for him to let go of the door handle and cringed at the possibility that he was going to end up under the wheels of the car. He ran alongside us for about half a block as the crowd hollered at him to come back. Finally he realized that LaQuita had no intention of stopping when she went through a red light without hesitating, almost sideswiping a green Honda Civic. He released his grip on the handle and tumbled to the ground, causing several other cars to hit their brakes.

"That security guard could have been killed. Shayla, what did you do?" I screeched, unable to believe what had just happened as I watched the guard struggle to get to his feet.

"You took too long picking out fabrics, that's what!" Shayla screamed back.

"They don't send you to jail for being in a store too long," I yelled, and looked out the back window for police cars. "What the hell did you do?"

"Bitch, what do you think she did?" LaQuita screamed. "Don't pretend you're that dumb."

"You stole the fabrics?" I whispered, and sank back in the seat, the awful truth hitting me hard.

"Yeah." Shayla turned around to face me. "Surprise. I helped myself to a five-finger discount."

"Why did you do that?" I wailed. "I didn't want you to shoplift. You could have just paid me back the money." Shayla didn't answer and turned to face forward.

Nobody said anything more until we pulled up in front of their building. Shayla stepped out of the car first and grabbed the knapsack off the floor. I cautiously looked around for any sign of an approaching squad car before opening the door and getting out. LaQuita stepped out on the sidewalk and hit the door locks. She threw us a disgusted sneer and gave a slight sideways nod. We knew the meaning behind her silent message. We needed to handle our misunderstanding. She sauntered into the building without giving us a second look.

Shayla walked over to me. "I took the fabrics because I thought we were friends. Since I couldn't pay you back right away and you were harassing me for the money, I did what I had to do. Here…" She pulled a bulging plastic bag from the knapsack and handed it to me.

"I really don't want it."

"But you want a fly outfit for the campaign. Shoot, after all I went through you better take it."

I reluctantly took the bag. "This is horrible. I didn't want you to steal the fabrics," I said in a low voice. It made me shudder to think about the trouble I was going to be in if Mama or Daddy found out. They would be furious over my getting locked up for stealing. One of their favorite dinner conversations was that they were so proud of all of us. We were good kids who stayed out of trouble. Not many people in our neighborhood could say that.

"Yeah, but I did it anyway. What's done is done. Hell, if I try to apologize and give it back now, they'll arrest me as soon as I walk in the store."

"Shayla, this is so wrong. I really like Mr. Khan. How can I ever shop there again? His wife is probably going to say we were together."

"How would she know?"

"Because she watches everybody like a hawk. She'll know."

"Well, it's too late to second-guess my plan. Now, since I put my neck on the line for you, I'm gonna to need you to spot me some money."

"Money! For what?" Shayla had a lot of nerve to let those words slide out of her mouth after what she'd put me through.

"For the campaign. That first two hundred dollars just covered part one. I'm going to need at least three hundred more to nail part two." Shayla's face was expressionless after she stated her request.

"Are you out of your mind? I don't have no freakin' three hundred dollars!" I shrieked.

"Your family owns a restaurant. Plus, I just risked getting arrested for you," Shayla said calmly.

"I didn't ask you to. I would never ask anybody to steal." My face grew hot as I struggled to keep my voice down.

"Well, if you know what I know you better find it."

"We ain't got money like that!"

"I'm serious. I proved I was a good friend to you. I'm on probation. If I got caught, they'd lock me up in the adult division. You'd better come through." There was a quiet fury behind her words.

Suddenly she didn't feel like a good friend to me. It

seemed I had made a bargain with the devil. Too late, I realized my mistake. A vision of Shayla wearing an orange county jail jumpsuit entered my mind. She was sitting on a bench in a locked cell. To my horror, I saw myself clad in an identical uniform, warming the spot next to her. I shook my head to clear the horrible image.

"This conversation is over. Get me some more money or else," Shayla threatened, her green eyes so full of anger that she would have made a great comic-book supervillain.

"Or else what?" I asked, thinking she was getting ready to fight me in the streets. But to my surprise, Shayla simply turned around and walked into her building, leaving me baffled about what her threat really meant.

My mind was confused and jumbled when I walked into my house. As I shut the front door, I realized I was still holding the plastic bag of stolen stuff. Not yet knowing what I was going to do when I heard footsteps, I quickly opened the living room closet door and tucked the bag deep in the back. Quick Digits was standing in front of me with a wide grin on his face as I shut the door. "So you still coming to the concert tonight?"

"Of course I am," I said, trying to turn off my anxious feelings and act normal.

Quick must have picked up on my tension, because he said, "Why are you so fidgety? You look real nervous. What did you do, rob a bank?" he joked.

I jumped and didn't immediately answer. My initial thought was that he somehow knew about the incident at the Coliseum. But then I figured I was just paranoid, because my brother would not have been in a pleasant mood if he'd heard what went down.

"I'm just real excited about tonight," I said, and forced a grin to my face.

"Okay. Now go ahead and get ready, because I know

you're going to need a zillion hours to go through your closet."

"No, I'm not."

"If you're bringing your little boyfriend you will," Quick Digits teased.

"Quick!" I forced a hollow laugh and took a swing at him.

He put his hands up in defense and took a step back. "I'm going to finish packing my records up. Marlon will be here soon, so don't hold us up."

As I ran up the stairs, the seriousness of everything hit me. *Man, this should be one of the happiest days of my life. I'm going out with JaRoli tonight,* I thought. Instead, stress had my stomach in knots, and my cheeks were starting to itch, which meant a fresh crop of pimples was arriving. My "friendship" with Shayla was over, I was in possession of stolen goods and I might lose the election. And to top it off, I still hadn't figured out a way to replace Mama's money. Damn, could things get any worse?

JaRoli and I had great second-row seats for the Super Mega Fest. As we sat with our shoulders touching, his Michael Jordan fragrance enveloping me, I was truly happy. We both stood up and screamed like lunatics when my brother and Marlon took the stage. They rocked the crowd with their slick dance moves and well-harmonized vocals. My brother took it to another level on the turntables with his lightning hand speed and rapid-fire wordplay. In my opinion, the other acts that followed, mostly hip-hop, dance hall and reggae performers, were good, but they couldn't upstage the opening act.

JaRoli was enjoying every minute of the concert and could hardly sit still. The crowd was lively, and we stayed on our feet with them, singing along with the performers and swaying to the beat. It was great when a female soloist slowed things down and sang a love song. JaRoli was so moved by the lyrics that he held my hand and sang the words to me. The butterflies were fluttering in my stomach, and my nerves were making my hands all sweaty. Even though I hated to let his hand go, I was glad the next song the band performed was fast-paced, because I was grateful to get the chance to wipe mine with a Kleenex.

During the concert intermission, JaRoli got up to buy us some candy and ice cream. In the few minutes he was gone, I had relaxed enough to just put my feelings out there and let him know what was on my mind.

"This concert is awesome! Thanks so much for hooking me up with a ticket," JaRoli said, and handed me a package of Skittles. He smiled at me, and I noticed how irresistible his pillow-soft lips looked. It was getting hard to resist the urge to lean over and kiss him. But I needed to get an answer to my question first.

"JaRoli, are you seeing anybody in a serious way?" I boldly asked. His lips twitched, and he seemed a little surprised by my question.

"Nah. I have a lot of friends that I hang out with for stuff like bowling, the movies and the arcade. But I'm not seeing anybody seriously." He took a bite off the corner of a Klondike bar. A chocolate flake clung to his top lip and he licked it off with his tongue. Unable to pull my eyes away, I found myself staring at him in awe. He was so handsome, and I really wanted him to be mine.

"Would you consider asking me to be your girlfriend?" I blurted out.

He took another bite of the ice cream bar before responding. "Angela, I like you. You're a really cool person, and it's great hanging out with you. But I'm not looking for a serious relationship right now."

"And why not?" I persisted. "Are you and Karen seeing each other?" I needed to know something more. Why couldn't I be his girlfriend? Was it because Karen was more popular? Was it my clothes? I had worn my three-quarter-length cow-print coat, a black-and-white-horizontal-striped skirt, a black shirt with silver circles on it, sheer stockings with bold black squares and my calf-high black leather biker boots. What was stopping him from making me the one? The hurt must have really shown on my face, because he leaned over and gave me a kiss on the cheek.

"Listen, I'm going to tell you the truth. I'm not ready for a steady girlfriend right now. My parents made me promise to wait until at least sophomore year before I got serious about a girl. They're afraid my studies and game will get sidetracked if I do."

I didn't know whether to believe him. Then again, he was probably telling the truth. His folks had their sights set on him going to college.

"My parents are really afraid of me bringing them a baby home. My older brother got a girl pregnant when he was a senior in high school," he confessed. "They just want me to take my time on that tip. You understand, don't you? We can still be friends, right?" His statement seemed sincere.

"I guess." My heart sank a bit. The friend thing? I was convinced that if I won the director spot, he would change his mind. My victory would put me ahead of all those hoochies who pursued him. His parents would be impressed with my ambition and talent and know I was the one for their son. So now the stakes had gotten higher for me to win.

CHAPTER 18

"HEY, everybody, I just got the best news!" Quick Digits burst into the living room, where Mama, Daddy and I sat watching *Rush Hour* on TBS. It was a rare occasion when we were all home on a Saturday afternoon. And after a morning of dusting the furniture and mopping and waxing the hardwood floors, we were all taking a break. Mama and I had our hair wrapped in scarves and were wearing old jeans and T-shirts. Daddy was wearing a pair of cutoffs and an old work shirt. The sweet citrus smell of Orange Glo polish still hung in the air.

"Why are you so excited?" my father said from his spot on the recliner. He had the footrest extended as he lounged and sipped a can of Coors Light.

"'Cause I'm about to blow up! An executive from C-Ice's label is interested in signing me. They caught my performance at the Super Mega Fest and want to make me a serious offer."

"What's a serious offer?" Daddy said, and cocked an eyebrow.

"A seven-figure deal for three albums," Quick Digits exclaimed.

"What! That's fabulous!" I yelled. "Your deal is so major!

The big dogs like Ludacris and Kanye West pull down that kind of paper."

In a split second, my mother leaped off the couch. Tears of joy filled her eyes as she chanted praises to heaven. She grabbed Quick Digits for a tight hug, and my father and I joined her.

Tears threatened to spill from my father's eyes, and he patted them back with his hand. "This is surely wonderful news. Now, we need to get you hooked up with a good lawyer. A shark!" he teased.

I was so happy for my brother. He deserved every bit of success coming his way. My only wish was that it would be my turn next with some great news—that I'd landed the director of the holiday fashion show position. This time I had written my speech well ahead of time, and could hardly wait for the final presentation and vote-off. Shayla no longer had my back, so I was in this all alone.

"And as a surprise to you, Mom, I'm going to play at the restaurant tonight." Quick Digits smiled as he broke the news to my parents.

"You really want to do that?" Mama asked. "You don't have to."

"Of course I do. And it's all set up," Quick Digits explained. "I've already asked Uncle Clyde to rearrange the restaurant this evening. We're going to push all the tables and chairs against the wall so we'll have room for a dance floor. I've seen some fancy restaurants do that on nights when they have private parties. And our place is spacious enough so no one will be cramped. I'll bring my strobe light and set my speakers up in the corners, but I won't blast the place out with the volume."

"That could be cool. It makes everything that much more special," I said.

"I don't know," Mama said. "I'd hate for it to seem like we're bragging."

"So what if it does? We've gone through a rough patch lately, but hopefully this is a sign that things are going to get a lot better," Daddy said. "Shoot, if Quick Digits gets that music playing good, I might hit the dance floor." He broke out in a joyful shuffle.

"Mannie, did you fracture your head, too, when you fell out the boxing ring?" My mother laughed.

The grin fell off my father's face real quick, as if he'd been slapped.

My mother put her hand to her mouth. "I'm sorry, honey."

"Yeah, Daddy. Mama didn't mean anything. Even though you lost, you're still our hero," I added.

"I had to be a fool to step into that ring," Daddy said, then sat down heavily in one of the floral-patterned armchairs. The mood in the room instantly darkened.

"Don't say that, Dad. You gave it all you had. That's worth a championship belt," Quick Digits said.

"No, I was a fool because I stepped in the ring for the wrong reason," Daddy confessed.

"Daddy, you wanted to be a boxing champ. There's nothing wrong with that," I said. "That was your dream."

"Kids, I want to tell you both a story. Years ago, I was a making a name for myself as an amateur boxer, knocking out big guys like they were chumps. I was a rising star, and I was real close to going pro," my father said, then looked down at the floor. He fixed his eyes on the beige throw rug in the center of the room. After a few moments, he blew out air that seemed mixed with sorrow. "My promoter told me that I could probably land some endorsement deals if I secured some major wins."

"Your father's telling the truth. He was really good, and everybody told him he had incredible potential," Mama said as she patted my father's arm.

"So why'd you stop?" I asked. "It sounds like you were about to blow up."

"It was a funny time back then for me. I had the potential, but I had so much doubt about myself. Not enough confidence. Even though I was a power hitter with a mean left hook, and people told me I would be the next heavyweight to break through, it was like I didn't really believe it. I had a self-defeating frame of mind."

"Why would that stop you? I don't understand," I insisted.

"The manager of this other boxer who wasn't as good as me wanted him to go pro. I was scheduled to fight their man, and they told me not to win—to throw the fight. They delivered their offer with a threat," Daddy said sadly.

"And you threw the fight?" Quick Digits asked.

"Because you were scared?" I added.

"Not really, but I convinced myself it was best if I took the money. My mind wasn't right back then. I hadn't too long ago gotten out of the penal system. That situation felt as if another dream was about to slip through my fingers." He paused for a moment in painful reflection. "Six thousand dollars. I gave up my dream for six thousand dollars. I wasn't sure if they would really come through on their threat. Still, that was no reason for me to give it all up." He sighed heavily in resignation.

"Well, at least you made some money out of the deal," Quick Digits reasoned.

"Yeah, that was hard to turn down," I added.

My father didn't comment. He went back to staring at the same spot on the rug. I didn't hold any hard feelings about what he did. His back had been to the wall, and five years of his life had just been unjustly snatched from him.

"Your father wasn't making much money in those days," Mama explained. "I wasn't working, and you kids were practically babies... We were going through some tough times."

"Yeah, but that's still no excuse. Taking a bribe messes

with your head, your character. I should have been strong enough to report them to the boxing commissioner," Daddy spat, and slapped the arms of the chair, grimacing from the memory.

"But that doesn't mean they would have believed you, or that the situation would have ended without violence," Mama said in a consoling voice.

"After that I lost all my excitement for the sport. I also lost the respect I had for my boxing career, because I let somebody else run me," my father spat, and stared into space.

"Angela and Quick, I want you to know that was incredibly difficult for your father to say. It takes a strong man to admit something like that," Mama said, her voice cracking.

"Yeah, that was a real painful chapter in my life," Daddy said quietly. "So when I got back in the ring it was for all the wrong reasons. I was chasing a ghost that was long gone." My father stood and pulled me and Quick Digits directly in front of him. "Don't ever let anyone steal your joy. If you run from folks, you're going to be running your whole life."

"We won't," Quick Digits and I said.

"Sometimes in life you got to take a stand. Either you keep bending over every time they tell you and end up falling flat on your face and never seeing your goals come to fruition, or you stand tall and firm and face the challenge with everything you've got." My father's eyes filled with water, and then he pulled us in for a tight hug.

"I'm so proud of you all," Mama said as she joined the circle and hugged us, too.

After a moment, Quick Digits pulled away and quickly wiped his eyes. "People, we're supposed to be celebrating a new future and new opportunities."

"Right. You're right," I said, feeling a little choked up.

My eyes swept the room and landed on our family photos on the wall unit. Happy pictures snapped throughout the years. My brothers and I grinning over a lit birthday cake. My father and I posing at the zoo. My mother and father embracing in front of the Christmas tree. It was hard to hear how my father had lost his dream. He'd made a decision. The wrong one. And now that dream was over. But it dawned on me what was really important: my father had us, and we loved each other. I realized that was what kept him from crumbling—the love and support he got from all of us.

"Okay. I've said my piece. It's time for a new beginning and a celebration," Daddy said, and smiled. "Everybody get ready. This family is going to par-tay. We'll leave for dinner around six."

"Yeah. We need to get this party started. I've got to get changed and bring my equipment over to the restaurant," Quick Digits said.

Jogging upstairs to my bedroom, I had the perfect outfit in mind for the party. Since I'd won the fashion show primary, I wanted to go all out with a fabulous outfit I'd created last year but never worn. A floor-length black skirt that poufed out a bit because of the layers of crinoline under the satin material, with a slinky champagne-colored top that had a huge bow and feather pinned to the left shoulder would definitely turn heads. I'd actually seen the outfit on a model in a magazine and re-created it on my sewing machine. After I laid the outfit out, I decided to chill and watch some television, then take a long, hot shower before getting ready.

Hours later, I was admiring myself in the mirror. I looked marvelous. I had flat ironed my hair, given it a side part and pulled it back behind one ear. Then I added fake hair and wrapped it in a huge bun the way I had seen celebrities do for awards shows. My look was completed with lots of chunky rhinestone jewelry around my neck and wrist.

As I stared at my glamorous image, thoughts about my night at the music festival with JaRoli flooded my mind. It had been a good date, but it had not turned out how I expected. I really liked JaRoli, but my sitting around waiting for him to ask me to be his girlfriend was no fun. I was just too pretty for that.

Daddy drove me and Mama to the restaurant in the Cappucino Blast. He and Mama were laughing, giggling and snapping jokes the whole ride like two kids. Their joy made me feel awful about what I had done. I desperately wanted to pay the money back, but I wasn't quite sure how I would explain its reappearance to Mama. Since she was in a happy mood, I felt it was a good time to ask about paychecks.

"Mama, is everything okay at the restaurant? The last time I was there, Armani and everybody was mad about not getting paid."

"Angela, don't you worry about that. Me and your father have figured it all out," Mama replied.

"Yeah, fracturing my collarbone has made me do things differently. Since I'm taking care of the books at my job, I convinced your mother to let me handle the books at the restaurant. It's time I got involved again."

"With your father taking care of that, it's a whole lot less stress for me," Mama said.

"And I can keep tabs on exactly where the money is going and what we should cut back on," Daddy said. "We'll most likely sell the new van because the monthly payments and insurance are killing our budget. There will probably be some layoffs coming soon, too. We feel badly about it, but it's better for a few to eat than a crowd to starve."

"Oh," I said. "Since you're reorganizing everything, does that mean I can get the paychecks you've been holding for me?"

"No. I'm not convinced you've learned your lesson yet," Mama replied. I didn't have the heart to argue since a small part of me felt she was right.

The mood was real festive when we walked into the restaurant. The lighting was dim, and soft jazz was playing on the speakers. It was packed, and a lot of our neighbors were there. Quick Digits had done a good job of getting the word out that he was deejaying that night. People also wanted to stop by because they had heard about Quick's record contract.

"How's my family doing?" Uncle Clyde came strutting over in a gray pin-striped suit and gave everybody hugs. "Angela, you look gorgeous, like a top runway model. That outfit is outta sight."

"Thanks, Uncle Clyde. I made it myself."

"Girl, you're just full of talent. Keep it up, and you'll be on top one day," he said before walking off. I was grateful because I knew Uncle Clyde was telling the truth. He always said he did not believe in lying to people about their talent. Too many people were walking around thinking they could sing or dance, making complete fools out of themselves because nobody told them the truth.

Mama, Daddy and I took a table together and enjoyed a seafood meal. People kept coming over to the table congratulating them on Quick Digits' record contract. Quick was doing a good job on the music, and a group of women surrounded him the entire time, plus lots of folks were hitting our just-created dance floor. At one point during the night Mama and Daddy got on the floor, slow dancing cheek to cheek, totally embarrassing me.

Finally, around two o'clock, there were only a few people left, and Mama was ready to call it a night—said she was tired and her knee was bothering her.

"I'm going to the bathroom first, then we can clear out of here," my father said.

A moment later, two men, one dark-skinned and tall and the other short and pecan-complexioned, both wearing baseball caps and white scarves that covered their noses and mouths, walked in.

"This is a stickup! Cut off that damn music!" the tall one yelled. He had a raspy voice and a mean look in his eyes... and held a gun straight in front of him. "Everybody hit the floor!" People started panicking and screaming when they realized the men were serious. "Shut up that noise or somebody is going to get a bullet. Everybody get your ass on the floor," he commanded.

People scrambled to get on the floor, but Mama stood motionless. The short gunman headed to the cash register, and the other, taller gunman walked over to her.

"Sir, please don't hurt anybody. We're just hardworking businesspeople," Mama pleaded with her hands out, palms up.

The shorter man by the register yelled, "Who is the manager of this joint?"

"I am," Uncle Clyde replied, and walked over to the register with his hands up. "Stay calm, I'm coming."

"Get over here and open this register," the short gunman ordered.

"Give me a minute. Let me get the key." Uncle Clyde threw him a look filled with disgust before reaching for the key ring on his belt.

"I said everybody get on the floor now!" the tall gunman snarled in our direction. I lowered myself to the floor and tugged on Mama's hand as a signal to follow me.

"Sir, I've got a bad knee and it's acting up. Can't I just stand?" Mama pleaded.

The tall gunman glared at Mama for a few seconds, and the vicious snarl in his voice terrified me. "Please don't hurt us. My mama's knee isn't so good. She can't get on the floor," I said.

The tall gunman never took his eyes off Mama as he in one swift movement balled his hand into a fist and hit her hard on the side of her face, knocking her to the ground. Stunned, I threw my body across hers.

At that moment, Daddy walked back into the dining area. "You hit my wife! I'll rip your head off!" he yelled out in rage.

The gunman by the register was holding a sack of money in his right hand; he pointed the gun he was grasping in his left hand in my father's direction. "Don't move," he said to my father.

Quick Digits came charging from behind the DJ booth with a murderous look on his face. I had never seen my brother so angry, and the rage that distorted his features scared me. The tall man saw Quick Digits running toward him and without warning fired the gun several times. Everybody started screaming, and I saw my brother fall to the floor bleeding as both gunmen raced out the door.

I was in shock as I watched my brother lie on the floor, writhing in pain. Uncle Clyde called for an ambulance, and it seemed only minutes passed before we saw the flashing emergency lights in our parking lot. The paramedics worked swiftly on Quick Digits before loading him onto a stretcher and racing to the hospital. We all prayed to God that we didn't lose him—he'd lost so much blood, even though Mama tried to stop the flow with some towels she got from the kitchen. Those white towels were soaked and red by the time the paramedics rolled him out.

One bullet hit Quick in the stomach. And now he was on the operating table as Daddy, Mama and I waited on hard, cold plastic seats in Mount Hope Medical Hospital.

"Daddy, do you think Quick Digits is gonna die?" I asked as I wiped the tears from my cheeks.

"The doctors feel since he's young he's got a good chance of pulling through, but we've got to stay strong and pray for your brother. This operation he's going through is pretty serious," my father replied, and gave me a hug.

A burly, redheaded police officer holding a pad came walking up to my parents. We all stood up. The police officer looked uncomfortable as he introduced himself and offered his well wishes for Quick Digits' recovery. "You know, I've been on the force seventeen years, and it seems people are getting more callous and cold-hearted. There's just too many guns out there in the wrong hands." Mama and Daddy nodded in agreement. "I've already gotten statements from your manager and several of the customers. I'm wondering if any of you recognized the men who robbed your establishment."

"We're a godfearing, respectable family. No, we don't know those hoodlums." Mama collapsed crying in Daddy's arms after her statement.

Officer Mahoney gave a sympathetic nod. "Why don't you all come down to the station house later and look at some photos? It might help jog your memory. Sometimes the people who commit these types of crimes have had some prior contact with their victims."

Then it hit me, but I didn't want to believe it. The tall, dark-skinned man looked and sounded just like the guy who'd been leaning up against the car in front of Shayla's building. Same complexion, same gruff voice, same height. And damn if the other one didn't look like the dude she'd brought to the restaurant for dinner. Was it true? Had Shayla sent them after my family for payback? Staring at the officer when the horrifying thoughts entered my mind, I quickly averted my eyes to gaze at the dull white and gray speckled hospital floor. I wasn't ready to be grilled about how I knew Shayla and those criminals.

Officer Mahoney noticed my expression. "Excuse me, young lady, but do you know anything about the men who robbed the restaurant?"

The right thing would have been to tell him yes. But I wasn't ready. Something told me to hold back. I shook my head.

The officer looked as if he wanted to say more, but he

closed his pad. He pulled a business card out of his breast pocket and handed it to Daddy, stating he would be in touch. He gave me a brief look before walking out the door.

When we arrived home from the hospital, I slipped into my pajamas and immediately got into bed. Hoping to grab a couple of hours of sleep; instead, I tossed and turned, unable to click my mind to the off switch. Finally, after three hours, I just gave up and jumped into the shower. I threw on my Ed Hardy terrycloth hooded sweatsuit and Nike sneakers. When I eased down the stairs the house was quiet, and I guessed my parents were still in bed since we hadn't left the hospital until 7:00 a.m., when the doctor informed us that Quick Digits had been moved to the intensive care unit.

The bright morning sun made the craziness of last night seem surreal. I walked out of the house and sat on my front steps for a few minutes, to give myself time to get my head together. Pushing off the stoop with my hands, I had determination in my stride as I headed toward the projects. As I rounded the corner to Shayla's street, I realized that I didn't know which apartment she lived in. Spotting a group of little girls playing hopscotch, I decided to approach them. "Hey, do any of you know which apartment Shayla Mercer lives in?"

One little girl scrunched up her nose, as if I had offended her, and I knew she wasn't giving up any information. Another girl in pigtails gave me a smile, then stated matter-of-factly, "She lives on the fifth floor."

A third little girl chimed in, "Shayla's not up there. I just saw her at the playground around the corner."

"Thanks," I said, and headed to the playground.

The projects playground had seen better days. There were empty beer and soda cans littering the patchy grass, and all the swings were broken except for two, and these looked fragile. Somebody had hooked a tire up to one of the loose chains and made their own swing. The seesaw needed a paint job and was full of splinters. It looked as if it could lead to a clinic visit if you tried to sit on it. It was good to see that at least the little kids had the slide to play on, and a sand pit was built around it so they couldn't hurt themselves.

Shayla was sitting on one of the swings smoking a cigarette. She was wearing a navy hooded windbreaker and dark blue jeans. A pair of white Adidas was on her feet. She seemed to be deep in thought and looked a little rattled when I stepped into her view.

"My family's restaurant got robbed last night. Know anything about it?" I asked. I decided not to be fake and bother with a hello, I just got to get straight to the point.

Shayla gave me a long, hard look before taking a drag on her cigarette and blowing out a perfect smoke ring. "This the ghetto. People and places get robbed all the time."

"Well, my brother got shot last night, and the person who pulled the trigger looked and sounded awfully familiar to me."

"A lot of black people look and sound alike." She shrugged.

"Yeah, but this black man looked exactly like that friend of yours, Big Bruce. And the other one looked like that fool you brought in for a meal. And you know what? I think you sent them to rob my family's restaurant," I said bluntly.

Shayla threw her cigarette down on the ground and got in my face. "You better watch what you say and what you accuse people of."

"I don't have to watch nothing if it's the truth," I said, not backing down. Our noses were almost touching, and I was so full of hurt and anger that I was ready to punch her with everything I had if she started some mess.

"Young ladies, please don't start fighting," a man walking

by with a reddish-brown pit bull called out to us, and quickly trotted over.

"Mind your business! I'm about to whip this ignorant bitch's ass," Shayla shrieked.

"Bring it on," I spat back, standing my ground.

The man grabbed my arm and dragged me away. Shayla reached into the pocket of her windbreaker. She pulled something out, and I could see the tip of a wooden handle sticking out from her closed fist. My guess was that she was holding a folded pocketknife. "I heard what went down at your family's restaurant last night, and I know your brother got shot. Don't give your parents more worry. Just go on home," the man said.

I looked at the man's face but didn't recognize him. "Yo, get off me," I said, snatching my arm away.

"Look, I don't mean you no harm. But I do know that Shayla runs with a tough crowd, and I don't want you to get jumped." The man had a concerned look on his face.

"Yeah, go on and take your punk ass home before you get it whipped," Shayla snarled.

I was so angry, I felt as if I could take on Shayla and her whole crew, not caring how things ended. But the man was right—Mama and Daddy had enough to worry about.

After a few seconds, I said, "Okay. I'm going home, but this ain't over, Shayla. If I find out you were involved, I'm going to make sure your ass gets locked up for life—you and your people who robbed my family and shot my brother. Believe that!" I yelled, and walked in the direction of home.

"Who's gonna believe you? Huh? You're not so innocent and sweet," Shayla shot back. "You cheated to win that school contest. That makes you a liar and a scammer."

Stopping cold in my tracks, I turned around. "Maybe. But that's not going to stop me from calling five-0."

Shayla just sat back down on the swing and shrugged. "You know where to find me. I'm not running anywhere."

She pulled a loose cigarette out of her jacket pocket and lit it with a match.

"Come on, let me see you to the corner," the man said, and yanked the chain of his dog, which had been patiently watching the whole scene. The dog rose to his feet and eagerly pulled in front of his owner, and I followed them.

When I walked back into my house, Mama and Daddy were sitting at the kitchen table drinking coffee. They wore identical white plush robes and looked weary and troubled.

"Have you heard any news about Quick Digits?" I asked as I entered the kitchen.

"I just got off the phone with the hospital. The operation went well. Praise God. He's conscious, and they downgraded his condition from serious to stable," my mother said.

"But he's not out the woods just yet. They've got to monitor him to make sure no infection occurs," Daddy said, then took a sip of his black coffee.

"Does Omar know what happened yet?" I asked.

"Yes. I spoke to him this morning. He wanted to come home, but I told him it's best to wait," Daddy said.

"Where have you been?" Mama asked as I took a seat at the table.

"To clear something up," I said, drumming my fingers on the plastic table mat.

"Girl, what are you talking about?" Daddy said.

"I think I know who shot Quick Digits." I pulled my hands into my lap and dropped my eyes to my feet.

Mama clutched the front of her robe. "You do? How?" she whispered.

"I've been doing some real stupid stuff lately. Really dumb stuff." I pushed my seat back from the table and took a deep breath. "My friends warned me against hanging with this girl named Shayla who lives in the projects, but I didn't listen."

"What did you do?" Daddy asked. Immediately I felt ashamed and found it hard to speak because of the lump that had formed in my throat. "Come on now and just get it all out. We need to know."

"Who is this girl?" Mama asked, her brow forming wrinkles.

"Shayla Mercer. Somebody I shouldn't have been hanging with. She spent time at juvie hall."

"Is she family to those Mercers where all of the boys made the news for robbing a bank?" Daddy asked.

"Yeah, she's first cousin to them."

"Why on earth would you want to hang with riffraff like that? Your father and I raised you better than that," Mama said angrily.

"I know I was wrong. I should have never hooked up with her. But it was after the first holiday fashion show meeting and I wasn't in my right mind. None of my girls showed up to support me, and Shayla told me she could help me win the election...but she would need some money to do it." It filled me with shame to confess those facts.

"You gave this girl money?" Mama asked with a pained look on her face.

"For what?" Daddy barked.

"To make sure I won the primary," I said.

"That was an absolutely foolish thing to do," Mama said.

"Yeah, and it's something I'm really sorry about. I don't know what I was thinking. I just wanted to win so bad."

"Where did you get the money from?" Mama asked quietly, as if she already knew the answer.

I paused for a moment. "I knew you kept money in that metal box under your bed...so I borrowed two hundred dollars."

"You stole from your mama? You were the one who took that money!" Daddy's eyes bulged in anger and shock. "You wanted to win so bad that you would steal?" he exclaimed in disbelief.

"I was gonna put it back," I said, my eyes tearing up. "But after I gave her the money, she started hounding me for more."

"Once you give a thug money, they'll never let up," Mama said, her eyes glistening with tears. "A person like that can never be your friend because it's not in her heart. She's too street, and all about getting over."

"Yeah, I learned that the hard way. Anyway, after I told her that I wasn't going to give her any more money, she threatened me…then this happened…" My voice trailed off as the image of my brother lying bloody on the restaurant floor filled my mind, and the tears started rolling down my cheeks. "And I think I know the men who robbed us. I've seen them with Shayla before. I think she sent them as payback because I wouldn't give her more money."

"I am so disappointed in you, Angela," my father said. "You have too much going for you to resort to lying, cheating and stealing. I don't understand why you did it."

"I don't know. I got caught up in winning. It seemed like I could never outshine Omar or Quick Digits. Nobody seemed to appreciate me… Then Shayla came along guaranteeing me the title if I gave her the money."

"That makes no sense. All of you kids are special," Mama told me. "I always pushed Omar because he was the timid one who couldn't cope with being teased by the other kids. Omar was always a target because of his small stature and glasses. I always knew you had the bravado, but he needed the push more. I knew you and Quick had more confidence." Mama shook her head. "I just can't believe this. Now your incredibly selfish and thoughtless actions have brought trouble to this family. Quick Digits could have died last night because you chose to run with hoodlums." Mama propped her elbow on the table and leaned her head in her hand.

My father had such a look of disappointment in his eyes after my confession. He looked as if he'd aged ten years as he left the table and headed upstairs. My apologies sounded hollow when I called out to him and my mother as she followed him out of the room. I prayed my mistake wouldn't cost my brother his life.

My parents left to check on Quick Digits and I went up to my room. I called Adrian and left her a voice message, asking her to stop by. After I clicked off, I decided to clean up my room. I had thrown all my pearls on top of my dresser when I came in from the hospital, so I unraveled them and opened my jewelry box to put them away. The blue glass bead bracelet that I had taken from Karen's parents' store caught my eye, and I picked it up; then I remembered the plastic bag of stolen material still sitting in the living room closet. I made up my mind to throw everything in the garbage because I knew I would never use that stuff and didn't want to be reminded of how I'd gotten it.

The doorbell rang and I grabbed my pocketbook, slinging it across my body, then ran downstairs to answer it, still holding on to the bracelet. Adrian was standing there when I opened the door. Her shiny curls looked like she had just gotten out of the beauty parlor chair, and she looked happier than the last time I had seen her. "Thanks for coming by," I said, feeling relieved by her appearance.

"No problem. It's all in the street about Quick Digits getting shot last night. How's he doing?" Adrian reached out and gave me a hug before she walked into the living room and took a seat on the couch.

"My mother spoke to the hospital this morning, and they said his operation went well. He's in stable condition. They think he's going to pull through and be all right." I took a seat beside her.

"That's great news. Do you have any idea who robbed y'all?" she asked, her eyes wide.

"Yeah, I do. Shayla introduced me to this guy named Big Bruce a little while ago who was hanging out in front of the projects. I really think he was the one who shot my brother."

"Damn, that's messed up if Shayla sent those guys to rob your family's business," Adrian said.

"I think she did. Boy, I am so stupid for thinking that girl could ever be my friend," I said.

"Well, I doubt if Shayla knows how to be a friend to anybody. I heard she was threatening a lot of the kids at school to vote for you in the primary."

"What? I would have never given her that money if I knew she was going to threaten to beat people up." It made me feel bad about how Shayla had made good on her promise to me. Then I recalled the handball court scene and was filled with remorse.

"Yeah, well a couple of people told me she stepped to them."

"Wow, I am so stupid." I wiped the hot tears blurring my vision.

"Don't hate yourself. You just got caught up in the game," Adrian said, and put her arm around my shoulders to give me a hug.

With a heavy heart, I confessed to Adrian about how Shayla had come to the restaurant a few days ago for dinner with some dude and hadn't paid the bill. How I thought that dude was one of the robbers. Then I also told Adrian about the incident at Khan's. I reached for the tissue box on the living room table to wipe the tears now rolling down my face.

Adrian patiently waited for me to finish, watching me with a sympathetic look in her eyes. Finally breaking her silence, she said, "Angela, those girls were out of your league, big-time."

"You're right. I don't know what I was thinking."

"It's crazy, but sometimes it takes madness to happen in order to learn a lesson."

"Man, did I ever! I'll never hang around anybody like that again," I said.

"I'm glad to hear that, 'cause the next time you try hanging around a hood rat like that I'm gonna kick your butt," Adrian said, and cracked a smile.

I smiled, too, grateful that things weren't worse. Then I decided to ask her the sensitive question. "So, how are you feeling lately? Is your stomach still bothering you?"

"Do you mean if I'm pregnant?" Adrian blurted out.

"Yeah," I confirmed, hoping she wouldn't catch an attitude.

She paused for a few moments. "The truth. Yeah, I was. Carmen took me to see a doctor at the health center after I started feeling worse. Turns out I had a miscarriage." Adrian glanced at the floor, then looked at me. "That was a scary lesson, and now I'm going to do a lot of things differently."

I was really happy to hear that. After a while I said, "Me too. From now on, I'm changing my ways, too." I opened my hand to show the bracelet. "I'm not boosting anymore."

"Cool." Adrian smiled.

I smiled back. "Friends forever?"

"Triple A is best friends for life," Adrian responded warmly. "So when are you going by the hospital to see Quick Digits?"

"Now," I said.

"Want me to come with you?" Adrian said.

I paused for a moment. "Not this time. There's some stuff I need to tell him, and I want to do it alone."

"Sure," Adrian said. "Just tell him I said hi and I hope he feels better soon."

"I sure will."

"Do you want me to walk you to the bus stop?"

"Yeah," I said, and got up and walked to the living room closet. I reached way in the back to retrieve the plastic bag containing the stolen fabric. Opening it up, I threw the bracelet in. That was something I didn't want in the house anymore. It was trash, and a reminder of the wrong turn I had just taken.

Adrian nodded in approval as we walked out the door. After I dumped the bag in a public garbage container a few blocks away, I felt a little lighter. Then a heaviness weighed on my heart as I wondered how I was going to tell my brother that I was partly responsible for his winding up in the hospital.

CHAPTER 19

The bus ride to Flushing was a long and crowded one. Even though the September temperatures had been mild, today the thermometer was hovering in the high eighties. The air-conditioning system on the bus was busted, and the seats in the rear seemed to grow hotter as we crept along. When the vehicle finally pulled to the curb at the Main Street stop, I felt a little light-headed from the exhaust fumes. I exited the bus and stood outside Mount Hope Medical Hospital for a few minutes in an attempt to get my composure together. As I stared at the orange-brick-and-white-cement trimmed building, I found it hard to believe that my brother had just been shot the night before and was inside lying on a hospital bed. My nerves started to tingle, but I forced myself to enter the building. At the information booth behind thick Plexiglas sat a gray-haired woman reviewing information on a computer screen. "Hello, I need to see my brother, Quincy Jenkins. He came in last night because he got shot and just had an operation," I stated somberly.

The woman adjusted the glasses on her nose, then clicked on a few keys on her computer. Her beige manicured nails tapped her screen. "Ah, yes, he's in room 705. Is anyone else here with you to see him?" she asked, and peered over my shoulder.

"No. My parents are already upstairs."

"Oh, I see. Well, just get a visitor's pass from the guard sitting right by the elevator bank and head right on up."

"Thanks," I said, and went to see the guard.

As I rode up in the elevator, the smell of alcohol seemed to engulf me, and the scent seemed to get stronger the higher up the elevator went. When the doors opened on the seventh floor, I startled to tremble. It almost felt as if I were going to a funeral, not going to see somebody who was still alive. I shook my head to clear those thoughts and looked for Quick's room.

Room 705 was right around the corner from the elevator, and the door was open. I slowly walked in and saw my brother lying in bed. The white sheets were pulled up to his chest, and there were tubes running from his arms to plastic bags hanging on poles.

Quick Digits must have sensed I was there, because he slowly opened his eyes and looked in my direction. "Angela, is that you?" he asked quietly. His voice was painfilled and he seemed to struggle to keep the agony from showing on his face.

"Yeah, it's me," I said, and wiped the tears from my eyes with the back of my hand. "I'm so sorry. This is all my fault. I put you here."

"Hey, hey. Stop all that crying. I'm still here. I'm not dead."

"I know, but you could have been." More hot tears poured down my cheeks. "I'm so stupid. This is all my fault. I was hanging with Shayla, that girl from the projects. She was helping me with the holiday fashion show contest, and she said I would win if I gave her money, so I did," I blurted out.

"Mom and Dad told me about that when they were here earlier."

Unable to stop the words spilling out of me, I continued. "Then Shayla got mad that I wouldn't give her more money, so she sent her people after us. Oh, Quick, I'm nothing but bad luck, always screwing up everything for you. I won't blame you if you never speak to me again."

"Okay, you were stupid for thinking that girl could be your friend. Real stupid," Quick said, and I started bawling out loud.

"Will you cut that out, or the whole hospital's gonna come in here and think somebody's dying," Quick said as an aggravated look settled on his face.

I managed to compose myself but was too choked up to speak.

"Angela, I always told you that you were hardheaded and that it would get you into trouble. This is what happens when you don't listen. Seems like I'm always paying the price for your mistakes."

I nodded and grabbed a few sheets of Kleenex off his nightstand to blow my nose and wipe my eyes. "I am so sorry. I really learned my lesson. Do you think you'll ever forgive me?" I asked timidly.

"Yeah, I do. But I want you to report everything you know to the police. If you chicken out and don't do it, I'm never speaking to you again. We can't let those people get away with what they did to me."

"No, I promise I'm reporting them. They're not my friends, and they deserve to get locked up."

"So, what are you going to do about that fashion election?" Quick asked, and looked me directly in the eye.

"I'm pulling out. Shayla's probably gonna report me for cheating, but I don't deserve to win. Not after everything that's happened." I thought back on the magnitude of the desire I'd had for winning. I'd been consumed by that contest, and my whole life had gotten sucked up in it. It was all for what? My friendship with Tia and Marcy was on the edge, I'd lost my parents' trust, and my brother had nearly gotten killed. I couldn't believe that contest had meant so much to me.

"It's not that you don't deserve to win. You had the talent all along. It's the way you went about it that's screwed up. If you have to cheat to win, you'll eventually get caught anyway. One way or another, the truth is gonna come out."

I nodded and looked at the floor.

Quick Digits stared at the ceiling. "Man, I can't believe I got shot. It all seems like a dream. A bad dream."

I brought my eyes to his face. "What about your record deal? Do you think you still have it?"

"Oh yeah. I've still got my fast hands, my voice and my mind," Quick Digits said, and crossed his eyes and twisted his lips to the side. "Besides, who could say no to a pretty face like this on a CD cover?"

I started laughing from relief. "Yeah, you're the same old Quick Digits."

"Hell yeah I am."

A nurse appeared in the doorway holding a tray covered by a white cloth. "I'm sorry, but I have to ask you to leave for a few minutes right now. We've got to change his dressing."

"Oh, okay," I said.

"Go on down to the cafeteria. I think that's where Mom and Dad went," Quick Digits said.

"Sure," I said, and took a few paces toward the door; then I walked back to the bed and grabbed my brother's hand. "Thanks for being my brother and not dying yesterday."

"I wouldn't have it any other way," Quick Digits said, and squeezed my hand. "Besides, somebody's got to stick around to keep an eye on you." I smiled at him and headed out the door.

As I waited for the elevator to take me downstairs to the cafeteria, I got a text message from JaRoli. "Heard about your bro. Hope he's OK. Talk 2 U soon." I read the message over and over and somehow felt as if it was a sign that things would get better soon.

For the next week, my parents wanted me to stay home from school. They were a bit worried for me because Big Bruce had been arrested by the police and there was a warrant out for Shayla and the second man, but they were on the run. For my own safety, everyone felt it was best if I stayed out school for that week because they were afraid of retaliation. My family had already received threatening phone calls both at home and at the restaurant. But we were determined to see justice served. My teachers e-mailed me my assignments. I visited with Quick Digits a lot, and it was actually kinda nice spending time with him. We hadn't spent a long stretch of time together in a while, so it was cool to play cards, watch television and just chill and talk. Four days after his operation, we were playing cards when my cell phone vibrated on my hip, and I picked it up and saw Adrian's number flashing. I clicked it on.

"You better not let the nurses see you using that cell phone," Quick Digits warned, and I held up my hand to quiet him. "That's against hospital policy."

"Hey, Adrian, I'm sitting here playing spades with Quick."

"Yeah, and she's cheating," Quick Digits yelled. "Come and get her." I balled my fist to quiet him.

"I just called to say congratulations," Adrian said.

"Congratulations? For what?" I asked.

"You won! You're the director of the holiday fashion show."

"Oh my gosh! The final presentations and vote-off were supposed to happen today," I said.

"That's right. Karen presented by herself and lost."

"I can't believe people voted for me after everything that went down."

"Why not? They loved your stuff. They picked you because they knew you were the best, and you didn't even have to give your second speech."

"Wow. Thanks for telling me," I said, stunned.

"Okay, bye."

"Whoa. That's great news," Quick Digits said as I clicked off the phone.

"Yeah, it is, but no way am I accepting it. I'm stepping down. It doesn't feel right, not after everything that's happened. Besides, they'll probably take it from me when they hear that Shayla was threatening people."

"I know how you feel, but just remember you won on your talent, otherwise, nobody would have voted for you."

I thought about how badly I'd wanted to win that contest and be number one. I couldn't lie to myself—deep down it hurt to walk away. My big goal was to show everybody how I could pull off an amazing show. But I realized I had the wrong attitude about everything from the start. If I had to cheat and steal to gain the title, I was never going to be happy about it. My guilt would have kept me from enjoying the victory.

My brother seemed to read my thoughts. "In the future, just depend on your own talent to win and you'll go far. You're unstoppable because your stuff is great, glamorous, gorgeous..."

I broke into a smile and said, "For once, big brother, I think you're right."

"For once? Oh hell, I'm always right," Quick Digits said, and crossed his eyes, and we broke into laughter.

Our closeness made me think about Omar. He had called the house last night and had a long conversation with my parents. I spoke to him for about fifteen minutes, and not once did he hurl an insult at me. He was actually nice. Omar was definitely changing, and I couldn't have been happier. I'd promised that I'd call him later today. At that moment

I was so grateful for everything, for my big brother surviving the shooting; my parents; my best friend, Adrian; my younger brother; my creative talent and most of all, for a second chance to get things right.

A READING GROUP GUIDE

ABOUT THIS GUIDE

The questions and discussion topics that follow are intended to enhance your group's reading of A MATTER OF ATTITUDE by Hayden. We hope this novel provided an enjoyable read for all your members.

FOR DISCUSSION

1. Do you think Angela is a strong person because she has a different fashion style and isn't afraid to stand out from the crowd?

2. Have you ever gone against the crowd and worn clothing or a hairstyle that you knew would cause a statement?

3. How did you feel about receiving a lot of attention? Did it make you want to never showcase that particular style again?

4. How important is it for you to have close friends? Do you feel Adrian is a loyal friend to Angela?

5. When Shayla speaks to Angela after the first fashion show meeting, do you believe Shayla wanted to start a friendship?

6. Should Angela's brother, Quick Digits, be angry with her after he is hospitalized?

7. Angela had doubts about her father getting back in the boxing ring. Should she have expressed her concerns to him and her family?

8. Angela's biggest desire is to become director of the holiday fashion show. When Karen becomes her opponent, her confidence is shaken. Have you ever been in a situation where your opponent was one of the most popular kids

in the school? Did it make you want to drop out of the competition? Or did it motivate you to prove your worth?

9. How important do you think it is to have a dream and pursue it, even though others doubt you?